WHEN YOUR HEART IS A BROKEN THING

THE CATS TURNED AND WALKED AWAY INTO THE FOREST
ARM IN ARM

WHEN YOUR HEART IS A BROKEN THING

STORIES & DRAWINGS

HELEN WHISTBERRY

Other Works by Helen Whistberry

Standalone Titles:

The Melody of Trees: 10 Tales from the Forest

The Tail of Nightshade

Once Upon a Wave of Witches (with Eli Belt)

The Jim Malhaven Mysteries series:

The Weird Sisters

The Avenging Angel

The Ghostly Groom

To Eli, Ian, Kait, and Jess, stalwart friends all
and to my sister who set my feet upon the path

Contents

Note from the Author

Thank you, dear reader, for giving this story collection a chance! I have long wanted to bring together some previously published favorites as well as stories that never found a home out in the world but that I think are worthy of an audience. I've roughly divided the collection by theme and you should feel free to dip in here and there as the mood strikes. Genres include ghost stories, sci fi/speculative, fantasy, retold and original fairy tales, animal fantasy, folk and general horror. A little something for everyone!

I enjoyed creating an original illustration for each story and hope they add to your experience. I decided to go with a slightly looser, sketchier style for this book and am pleased with the result.

As you might expect from ghost and horror tales, there are some potentially disturbing themes. Please check the content warning list for details.

CONTENT WARNINGS

STORIES MAY INCLUDE THEMES disturbing to some readers so please proceed with caution.

Content warnings as needed by story:

Vera: body and corpse horror, disinterment, violence, murder, spectral visitation

Knock Knock: spectral visitation, mention of mental health issues, violence, body horror

The Long Hallway: murder, claustrophobic theme, spectral visitation

From the Diary of...: animal and child endangerment and death, violence, murder

Forgotten: child endangerment and death, violence, murder, animate toys

Take My Hand...: violence, murder, spectral visitation, animal endangerment and death

Cotton: violence, murder, child death, body horror

Sisters: child endangerment and death, violence, body horror, cannibalism

The Price: child endangerment, animal cruelty, body horror, violence

Howl: death and grief

The Guard: anti-LGBTQIA+ government sanctions in a speculative future, imprisonment, starvation

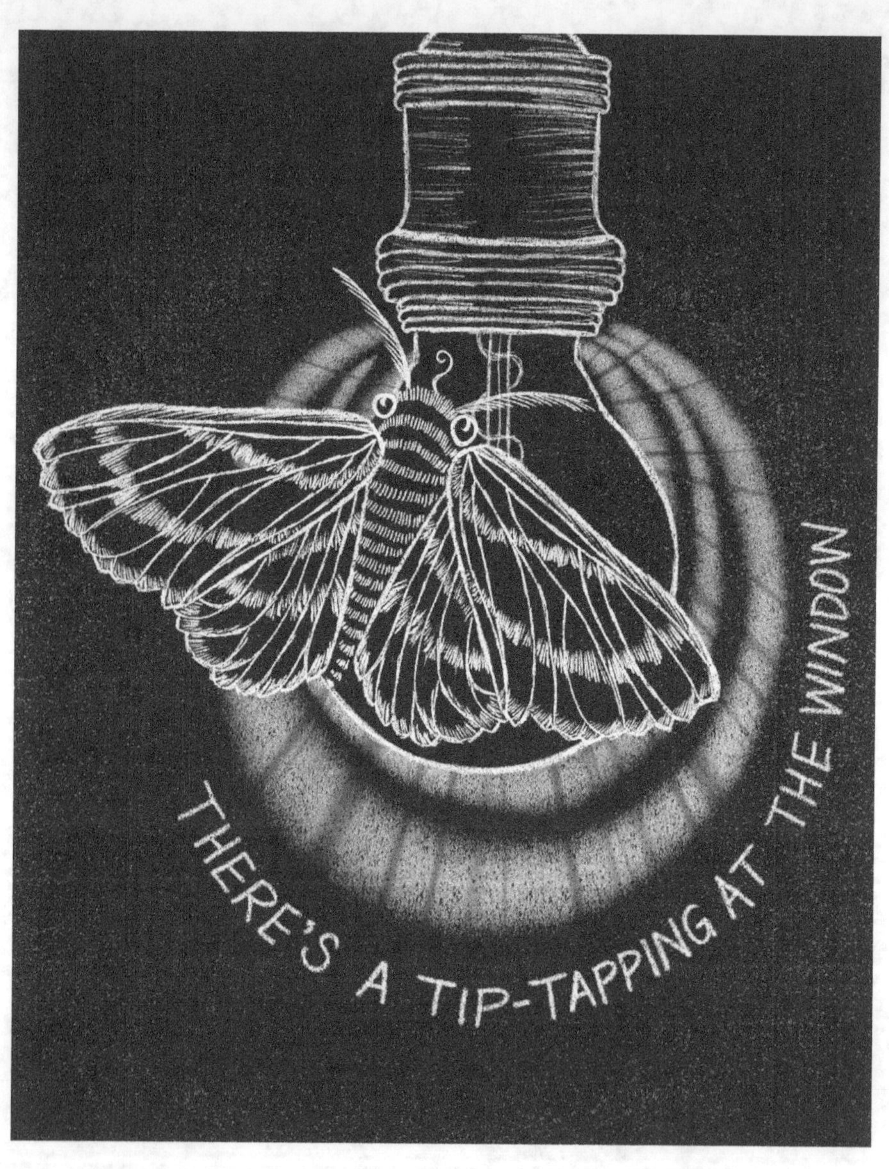

THERE'S A TIP-TAPPING AT THE WINDOW

Prologue: Loud

T̲he house is too loud.

The refrigerator moans. You're not sure what it's complaining about. You think maybe it's too full, so you empty it out, bin all the food, but it still isn't happy. It hisses at you. You take your revenge by unplugging it.

The heating vents howl and rattle when the air comes on. One squeaks. You try opening them, shutting them, tightening and loosening them. There's nothing to be done about it, so you shut off the heat.

The house is a little quieter now, but that just makes the other sounds more noticeable. The laptop whirs. You power it down. The router box hums. You cut the cord. The light overhead is blinking and buzzing. You flick the switch.

What is that dripping sound? The showerhead in the bathroom is leaking an infinitesimal amount of water. Enough to form a full drop every 53 seconds that explodes inside the tub like a bomb going off.

...51

...52

...53

...there it goes again. You go outside and shut off the main water valve.

There's a tip-tapping at the window. Moths attracted to the porch light, a shining beacon in the darkness. You turn it off, then go back inside and switch off the rest of the lights for good measure. The floors creak as you pace around the house, attending to your task. Better stop walking and sit very, very, very still.

There's enough moonlight streaming in to see by. You look around at the stillness of the house. You have shut down its vital components, but yet it seems to thrum with an energy just on the edge of hearing. You have an urge to burn it down to the ground to stop the noise, but the roaring and explosions of fire, the sirens, the barking of questions would be too much to take.

Uneasy in mind, you arise and stride to the front entrance to study the dark figures looking in at you through the peephole. Their eyes are black pits, dull and unreadable, but they themselves are so quiet—mind-blowingly, miraculously, marvelously silent. How restful.

You open the door and invite them in.

Part I: Otherworldly Visitations

HE SWIFTLY FOLLOWED
AND TURNED TO
READ THE
HEADSTONE

VERA

"**R**OUGH MANUAL LABOR. HARD *worker wanted. Discretion a must.*"

Most balked when they answered the newspaper advertisement and discovered the exact nature of the job, but Martin Breedlove was a towering figure of a man and laconic beyond measure, so the work and its peculiar requirements suited him fine.

In truth, he never felt so completely at home as when he walked through the cemetery gates under the cover of night. The dead welcomed him, never lied to him, didn't judge. Their bones and gristle droned with the sounds of decay, a quiet energy which hummed up through the soles of his hobnailed boots as he hunted for newly-dug graves. Corpses were simply vessels that had hosted a life from start to finish and were now at peace. Most of the time at least.

This night was different. As he stood chest-deep in muck, knocking the mud from his shovel against the coffin lid at midnight, the coffin knocked back. He uttered a loud curse in his deep baritone, then swore again silently at himself. Body snatching was a stealthy business. The authorities were well paid to look the other way, but only if he was discreet and didn't draw unnecessary attention to his activities.

Breedlove stood listening as long minutes ticked by, debating whether to abandon the grave and start anew, but that would mean hours wasted. It would be nearing dawn by the time he unearthed another body, and he didn't get paid if he came back empty-handed. He balled one filthy, rough hand into a fist and rapped his knuckles against the coffin.

A faint scratching came from within.

That decided him. He'd never seen any evidence of it himself, but he'd heard tales of tormented souls buried alive, found with fingernails torn off and splinters in their hands from a desperate struggle to free themselves from their under-ground prisons. He wasn't about to rebury someone who might have suffered such an unimaginable fate. He pulled a pry bar from one of the deep pockets in his greatcoat, methodically levered up the top of the coffin with practiced efficiency, then shoved the lid aside.

Abundant dark amber hair flowed loose and wild down to a sharply corseted waist. Breedlove swept his hands against his thighs to wipe away the worst of the grime before gently pushing strands of hair away from the face. Staring up at him, all soft brown skin and unblinking hazel eyes, was the most beautiful woman he'd ever seen.

Her skin radiated heat as though she burned with fever. He could feel it even through the heavy satin gown she wore. Cream and French lace and pearl buttons. Not a dress for burying. A wedding dress. He noted the thick band of gold on the ring finger of one of the hands arranged so carefully across her chest, a chest that never moved. No sign of breath or life.

Breedlove was not a superstitious man, nor an imaginative one, but rarely had he witnessed so uncanny a thing. He examined the inner lid of the coffin. There were thin scratches, though her hands were pristinely clean, her fingernails undamaged. He sensed movement from the corner of his eye. One white-booted foot flicked and shifted, but when he looked, all was still.

It is in some sort of stupor, he thought, *or else, I am overtired and out of sorts and seeing things*. Either way, he knew he would not leave her there beneath the cold and muddy ground, nor pass her on to his employers until he had unraveled the mystery.

She had a womanly figure, no fainting sack of bones here, but he had hefted much larger prizes from the earth and had no trouble lifting and setting her gently aboveground. He swiftly followed and turned to read the headstone. He rarely spared the markers a glance, uninterested in the person that once was, but he had to know her name:

Vera Masterson. Beloved wife and sister.

Vera. An unusual name, yet it suited her. It reminded him of verity, truth. There was a pureness to her expression that fascinated. Even her gown, though constructed of such fine materials, was simply cut and unadorned with the gaudy beading and excessive ornamentation which had lately come into fashion.

He glanced back into the grave and noticed a flash of white. Jumped down to investigate and found a filmy veil edged round with tatting in a simple looping pattern. Hair pins were scattered around the casket. Another puzzle. He assumed her hair had been carefully arranged, the veil attached when she was buried. How had it come undone?

Time was growing short. Dawn approached, and light was not an ally to such furtive work. He slid the lid back in place and returned to the surface, setting to work on pushing the mound of dirt into the grave to hide his handiwork. He couldn't help glancing over at the bride between nearly every shovelful as though he might catch some sign of life, some movement. But she remained inanimate, skin softly glowing in the moonlight, eyes glistening.

After patting down the last of the soil, he retrieved an old tarpaulin he'd used to hold the dirt so it wouldn't disturb the grass around the grave. Usually he would wrap the body in it, but he couldn't bear to sully her dress. He removed his greatcoat instead and wrapped it round her like a shroud, buttoning up the front until it swallowed her whole.

Breedlove folded the tarp and threw it and the bride over his shoulder, his long strides making short work of the walk back to his handcart. He lay her in reverently, setting the empty baskets he used as camouflage against prying eyes gently atop her swaddled form. Instead of heading north toward the medical college, he turned east to the grimier side of town where those deemed less deserving spun out their brutish and all too short lives.

An empty garret room awaited there. Its one saving grace was an old skylight with panes missing and stuffed with rags in a futile attempt to keep out the cold, but it was worth it for the light that seeped in even on gloomy days. On bright ones, he would drag his straw mattress into a sunspot and sleep away the daylight hours, basking like a cat until his next midnight mission.

Working men and women arose early by necessity, heeding the call of workshop and household service, but none gave him a second glance as he unloaded his cart. All had learned to keep curiosity and speculation to themselves while out on the streets if they wanted to survive.

Breedlove carried the woman up three long flights of stairs. Past rubbish and crying babes, arguments and lovers' rendezvous, the chaotic and muddled business of living crammed cheek and jowl like livestock into holding pens. They made way for him, his scowl and silence and size too intimidating to be worth the risk of asking him what burden he was bringing into their shared abode.

A mattress and a wreck of a wooden chair were his only furniture. He laid her on the mattress, removing his coat from around the body so he could see her face and form, and sat down on the chair to watch her.

Vera.

He turned the name over in his mind. It felt too intimate to think of her that way, but Mrs. Masterson seemed rather formal for a corpse. *The bride* felt too impersonal, *the woman* disrespectful.

Vera.

He whispered the name aloud, rolled it around on his tongue to get the taste of it. He swore her eyes flicked over at him as he spoke, but when he bent closer, they were staring straight ahead at the cracked and yellowed glass of the skylight above.

Now they were away from the earthy, moldy stench of the graveyard, he caught a whiff of something sweeter, like walking past the flower stalls at Hightown Market. He straightened her gown, smoothing out the folds before he arranged her hands. Then he took his old gap-toothed comb and ran it through her fine-stranded hair, gently loosening knots and tangles.

He was no lady's maid, but he'd watched his mother plait his sister's hair many a time when they were young. The pattern came back to him after a few false starts. He tied the end with a strip of cloth torn from the ragged hem of his shirt and lay the braid over her shoulder where it trailed down to her waist.

She looked peaceful enough, except for those staring eyes. He dug two heavy coins from out of his meager stash and attempted to weigh down her lids, but try as he might, they would not close. He gave up the fight and sat back down so he could gaze at her in what little comfort the rickety chair offered.

No sign of decay or corruption marred her smooth skin, but then her death date was only a few days ago. Give it time. Strange they had the grave marker already prepared and installed. As though they had anticipated her death and made ready. Perhaps a lingering illness, a slow decline. Her face was remarkably serene, if so. He'd seen enough of the ravages of disease to recognize its signs in the newly deceased.

The impulse to save her from her earthly imprisonment and the cruel implements of his employers' experiments had led them to the tiny piece of the city he called his own, but now what? He could hardly keep her forever, and his masters would be angry he had failed them. But the thought of a scalpel piercing that firm flesh, despoiling her perfect form was intolerable. Better to lose his job than deliver her up to such a fate.

His body rumbled with fatigue and hunger. It had been a long night. He took one of the coins that had failed to weigh down her eyes and bought a couple of hand pies from a street hawker. He wolfed them down in as few bites as possible, meaning to toss the scrap of old newspaper they came wrapped in before an irresistible compulsion overcame him. He returned to his loft, fished a small sliver of coal from the fireplace, smoothed out the greasy paper, and began to sketch.

He hadn't drawn since he was a boy. It had been an obsession then. He'd dreamed of being a famous artist, a painter, a sculptor. All daydreams too far out of reach for one of his humble birth, but an indulgent mother had sacrificed to buy him scant supplies, and a penniless artist come down in the world offered him lessons as a kindness after noticing some raw talent in the boy.

The skill he'd acquired from hours of practice came back to him now. He knelt by the chair, using it as a desk, while he stared at her face and drew. He'd created a pleasing likeness when he was done. Closer to the reality than he would have thought possible, but inspiration strikes that way sometimes. When creation flows through, rather than comes from, the creator.

Breedlove felt as if he were but a tool in some greater artist's hand. He stared in wonder from the drawing to his muse and back again. He had captured something melancholy, yet peaceful in the expression. What had her life been? She had lived long enough to be courted, to marry. *Beloved wife and sister* but not *mother*. Her time above the soil was cut short before reaching that milestone.

His fingers itched and danced. The sketch of black and grey was insufficient to portray her beauty. He longed for canvas and brush, paints and turpentine, but such items were expensive. He'd need more money, and more money meant more bodies. He lay the sketch beside her, a mirror image to keep her company while he was gone. Then he walked the long blocks to the medical college.

His masters were as displeased as he had expected. Much to their embarrassment and chagrin, they'd had to cancel their private exhibition. But he had never failed them before, as they grudgingly conceded. They were in a magnanimous mood; they would give him one more chance.

Breedlove listened, hat in hand, head bowed obsequiously in acknowledgment of their generosity, thinking cynically they would be hard pressed to find another so strong and silent and reliable, as they themselves well knew. If the public ever caught wind of where their specimens came from, these fine doctors might find themselves in a tricky situation indeed.

He left them with the reassurance he would redress his failure that very night. All the while they had scolded and rebuked, his thoughts had been with *her*. Had she awoken while he was gone? She would be frightened to find herself in a dirty, unfamiliar room. He never thought about it before, but now he was keenly aware of how unfitting his place was for such a gentlewoman—how unfitting he was.

There wasn't much he could do about himself, but the room was another story. He spent a penny he could ill-afford on a used and ragged straw broom from an odds and ends stall. It was with a strange mixture of relief and disappointment that he re-entered his home to find the scene exactly as he had left it. He removed his greatcoat and laid it over the body to protect her from dust as he swept vigorously.

It hardly seemed to make much difference, but he was satisfied he had done what he could, gently peeling back his coat and rearranging the amber braid it had disturbed. So tranquil in death, if death it was, and yet her skin glowed and she smelled as fresh as ever. He sat on the floor in a corner of the room across from her, watching for any sign of movement or life, eyes growing heavy until he fell into a restless slumber.

She called out to him, *Martin, Martin...*

Reached out a delicate hand, warm and real in his and laughed, a pretty, tinkling sound like a light drizzle of rain against the skylight glass. She placed his other hand around her waist and swayed and twirled, a dance he had never learned the steps to, yet in this dream world he was graceful and handsome, confident and bold. Her eyes danced with delight. With love. She reached up on tiptoe, her soft lips pressed to his. A kiss, never-ending, never-ending...

He woke with a start, breath hoarse and shallow, gasping for air, suffocating, and leapt to his feet, panting. A dream, a nightmare, nothing more. Perhaps to be expected in his line of work and with a corpse lying mere feet away, only he had never had one before. Not like that.

The light in the room had grown dim. Evening time. He hated to go out and leave her alone in the dark, but candles were too dear to leave burning. He lay a hand over hers and promised he'd be back before she missed him. He chuckled at himself. Talking to the dead now, was he? Yet he couldn't help one last backward glance as he left.

He was hungry and digging was tiring work, but he hated to spend money on food. The idea of painting her had taken hold in his mind. He would need every penny for art supplies. So instead, he found an apple, bruised and mealy, that had escaped notice along the street. Breedlove rubbed the worst of the grime off on his coat and ate it down, seeds and all. It was hardly sufficient, but it was something.

The city was rife with graveyards, but he knew better than to mine the same one twice in a row. It meant a longer walk, pulling the heavy handcart behind him, but he was used to it. He'd walked the length and breadth of the city countless times over. Death stalked its residents with such profligacy, he rarely had trouble finding a fresh grave but tonight, even greater fortune smiled upon him.

A dead drunkard, sprawled in the gutter, starved or frozen or both. He'd never stumbled upon such a fresh corpse before. From the looks of the man's clothes and long beard, he'd been living rough and was unlikely to be missed. If he took this offering, he could get back home all the sooner. Vera was calling to him. He missed her already. He would rather be gazing upon her stone beauty than wandering the streets and shoveling half the night away.

Breedlove glanced around. No one else about. The temptation was too great. He loaded up the body and headed to the college. The night watchman there accepted the package as usual and handed him his wages. When he subtracted his weekly rent and the bare minimum for food, there was far too little left to buy paints and brushes. Art was a rich man's game.

A rich man. He knew of one. A portrait painter, much sought after by the highest ranks of society. He knew where the man lived. The famous studio in the garden was often pointed out by guides to gawking tourists. Compulsion directed his feet there.

It took but a moment to vault the high wall, enter a door that had been carelessly left unlocked, and rifle about for what he needed amidst such a surplus, he doubted the artist would notice anything amiss. Still, as he stumbled home with his contraband, he was stunned at what he'd done. Life had been a hard slog, but he'd never stolen before. Except for the bodies, of course, but that was a job, paid for by respectable men even if the work itself was not strictly respectable.

Any guilt or regrets he had fled when he saw Vera lying in the pool of moonlight cast down through the skylight. There had never been anything so beautiful in all the world and never would be again. It was his duty to record it for posterity. He arranged his paints and prepared his canvas as he waited for the sun to rise. Debated poses. Decided on a three-quarter view, but those eyes... those eyes should be directed out at the viewer, at the creator, at him.

When there was enough light to see by, he began with the undercoating, washes of shape and color, building layer upon layer upon layer, too impatient to allow time for proper drying between application. Fumbling at first, unsure, until some long-ago muscle memory surfaced, guiding his efforts. He worked through the day with no thought of rest or hunger, the world narrowed down to brush, paint, and her. The work was far from finished by twilight, but the broad strokes were there. He lit his last two candles to better see as he worked as far into the night as he could before his strength gave out.

He awoke to daylight and a clearer view of what he'd accomplished and was amazed at the details he'd managed in the dress, her hair. There was only the face left to do, the most important part. It flowered on the canvas as naturally as a rose in bloom under his hand. Uncanny was the word that floated round his brain as he worked. Uncanny was the effort he'd expended, the speed at which he'd worked, and the skill which was surely far beyond his own.

As night fell again, he added the finishing touches. A gleam in the eye, a slight smile about the elegant lips. He propped the finished canvas up in the seat of the chair with a guttering candle in front for illumination. He leaned back against the wall and gazed at his work, more than satisfied. Now he would have a memento when her body inevitably decayed. Her beauty immortalized, perhaps even displayed somewhere all might gaze upon it.

The idea disturbed him. No, no one should ever gaze upon her again. No one but her portraitist. He was afraid they wouldn't see, wouldn't understand the miracle that was this woman, this *Vera*, this unfortunate bride. And yet, how fortunate she had been found by one who did appreciate her, who hadn't dressed her in her wedding finery only to discard her in a muddy hole in the earth for eternity.

He chided himself. Foolish thoughts. Lack of sleep, lack of food. Vera Masterson had fled and left this container behind. That's all it was. She was no longer a woman, a personality, a soul. He was as familiar with death and decay as any man living and no sentimentalist. He would doze a little, regain his strength, then take her back—take *it* back—to that empty box built to embrace this forlorn object. He'd no right to keep it. What had he been thinking? A temporary madness. A nap, a decent meal, and everything would return to normal.

She came to him again in his dream. Brushed her hand along the rough planes of his face, a gentle swipe of her thumb across his lips. Then she kissed him ever so softly along the sharp bone of his jaw. She was dressed in black now. A figure of mourning. Much more appropriate.

Do not abandon me, she whispered. *I do not want to be alone.*

Smoke roused him. The candle had burned down and set the corner of the canvas aflame. He flung the picture down from the chair and himself on top of it, smothered the fire and ruined his waistcoat with the still-wet oils. Anxiously, he held the painting up to the dawning light. A minor black smudge marred a section no larger than his hand. He had done more damage with his attempt to put it out. The face was no longer pristine, the flawless skin wiped away, canvas white as bone visible underneath.

He would have wept in frustration if he was the type of man who wept. Having never shed a tear in his life, he went to work repairing the damage instead, afraid it would never look as good again but determined to try. The hours flew by as he restored her beauty. Finally, he held up the finished work to compare with his model. Perfection.

Breedlove lay a hand against the cadaver's cheek and rubbed his thumb across her lips as she had done to him in the dream. He stopped short at the kiss. His madness did not extend quite so far yet. She was warm still. Not with the fiery burning she had radiated at first, but the natural warmth of a living, breathing woman. The horror of consigning her back to the worm-infested earth came over him along with a great weariness.

With effort, he tore himself away, nearly tumbled down the stairs to the street, stopped the first pie seller he saw, and bought all she had left in her tray. Returning to his room, he crouched, feasting like a wild animal, crumbs and filling flying, and felt some semblance of sanity return.

A knock at the door brought alarm. Had someone found out? Tipped off the authorities? None of his neighbors would have aught to do with coppers, but perhaps the surgeons had grown tired of him and wished to punish him for his failure. His word against theirs would carry no weight and he would be left holding the bag.

Ridiculous fears—no one knew, not even his employers—yet he didn't answer the summons. A slip of paper was pushed under the door. Waiting until footsteps receded, he cautiously retrieved it. It was a note from the medical college. They had an offer for a prestigious lecture. Another body was needed without delay. A large bonus awaited if he was successful.

Fools, he thought. *Where do they think I'll get a body in broad daylight?*

His eye fell upon that very thing laying before him. His mind went to war. Here was an opportunity, an excuse to kill two birds with one stone, satisfy his masters and earn more coin than he might see in a week or a month, while at the same time, be rid of this relic and the weird hold it had established on his imagination.

It might even be for the woman's own good. If she was in some catatonic state, surely the first cut of the knife would wake her, possibly leading to her restoration to friends and family. What a joyful reunion it would be. A second Lazarus. A miracle. And if she were well and truly dead, then what harm did it do? Her soul was already fled. The woman who visited him in his dreams was no more than a figment of his tired brain.

No less than three separate times, he wrapped her in his coat and lifted her from the floor, on the verge of smuggling her downstairs, but always unable to take the fateful step. He decided finally to go out hunting instead in order to postpone the time of reckoning. If he found an opportunity, an out-of-the-way cemetery, he could weigh the risks and take a chance.

Convincing himself this was a more sensible plan than using a corpse ready to hand, he entered the bustling streets. It was no easy task to weave in and out of traffic with his cart, but he knew the city well, the backways and byways people avoided or ignored. Those alleys and narrow streets where only the desperate loitered.

It was in one such dark passage where he spotted a man. Another drunkard like the night before. A common sight, for who wouldn't drink in times such as these if they had the coin? But this one was very much alive still, weaving and singing a seaman's chanty. The sailor stumbled and fell, hitting his head on the rough cobblestones.

The victim beckoned him over, groaning and crying pitifully for help. Breedlove stared at the blood pooling on the ground. He approached cautiously and examined the man's head. The skull was crushed, grey matter showing.

A kindness, he thought.

A kindness to speed the man on the journey he had embarked upon without further pain and suffering. He laid his huge palm across the man's nose and mouth, stifling breath. The man jerked and danced under his hand like a marionette on a string, but Breedlove was relentless, fixated on this solution, this alternative to giving up Vera to be butchered like a sacrificial lamb.

In the end, killing proved easier work than hours of backbreaking digging and seemingly was no more hazardous. He expected shouts or questions, accusations to ring out at any moment, but nothing stirred other than a stray orange tabby, flicking its tail as it watched the scene with avid curiosity. He wrapped the sailor up in his tarp and loaded him onto the cart.

At the college, the surgeons came down to inspect the delivery. They looked from the broken skull to Breedlove and back again. May have had suspicions, but a very important personage was expected. Someone with an interest in the burgeoning science of autopsy and with influence at court. They held their tongues and paid him triple the usual price.

Reaction set in as he wandered home. First stealing, now... well, murder seemed a little strong, didn't it? Mercy killing more like, but lines had been muddied, crossed. It was *her*. He had always got by, kept out of trouble. Resurrection men were viewed as a necessary evil these days rather than the rank criminals they had once been. They were helping advance the cause of science, medicine, discover cures for the myriad of diseases humanity was prey to. A noble profession, if one thought of it that way.

Breedlove didn't feel noble. He felt sullied, depressed, and more determined than ever to return the woman to her grave, destroy the painting, and forget the whole thing had ever happened. Maybe he would even move away from the city. He'd heard they needed strong men for farm labor down south or in the smoky factories up north. Life might be easier away from this city which chewed up and spit out all but the well-to-do.

By the time he walked through his door again, he had made up his mind to have done with her. By the time he strode across the room and gazed upon her face, his resolve had crumbled away.

A witch, he thought.

She must be. No woman had ever had this effect on him. He had been a loner, only occasionally seeking relief where lonely men do. He turned to the portrait and peered closely. The face was not as perfect as he remembered. The white of the canvas was again showing through on the jaw and cheek facing the viewer.

He felt compelled to repair it but was too exhausted and downtrodden in mind, body, and spirit at that moment to tackle it. He lay down on the cold floor and fell asleep.

She was there again, but this time, she was not alone. The two drunkards were her escorts, one on either side. They were dressed in the finest evening togs, such as he'd seen toffs wearing out on the town, a sharp contrast to their shabby beards and straggling hair. Her delicate hands were curled into the crooks of their elbows as she laughed up at them. They smiled down at her in indulgent admiration.

When they saw him, their merriment ground to a halt. They looked him up and down with contempt, then stared and stared, as still as statues. They did not point or accuse him in so many words, but he knew it was in their thoughts: *There is the man who has done us a grave disservice.*

He awoke, both horrified yet morbidly amused at the curious turn of phrase his mind had conjured up. *A grave disservice.* How apt. How true. He had robbed them of their natural rest, their dignity, their rights. His head throbbed. He was a common thief, a grave robber, and yes, a murderer. What a long way fallen from the artistic dreams of his youth. Little better than an outcast, whose one artistic masterpiece was destined never to be seen by an admiring public.

He picked up the painting and examined it closely, sucking in his breath and whistling in astonishment between his clenched teeth. The white was not canvas. It was clearly paint. A miniature schematic of jaw and cheek bone, of teeth, of the skeleton beneath the skin. How was it possible? He swore it was an exact likeness of her when he painted it, a mirror image.

A sudden terror struck him, that the cadaver's face would also have decayed to reveal the structure within. He whipped around, expecting to see her beauty gone. But she lay still as ever. A perfect effigy, untouched, unchanged.

With shaking hands, he picked up a brush and painted out the bone, covering it over with blushing skin. When he was done, he curled up in a dark corner of the room, as far from corpse and painting as possible, and slept like one dead.

She did not come to him in his dreams, but when he awoke, the painting was worse than ever. Bone, tendons, nerves. Like illustrations he'd seen in the surgeons' medical books. Fury rose in him. Paint flew again. Perfection achieved. He sat against the wall, holding the canvas in his hands and stared as little by little, almost imperceptibly, the fresh layers melted away and the underpinnings that should not have even been there in the first place emerged again.

Numb at first, rage slowly rose in him at this insidious decay. He gathered the will to rise, to act, smashing the painting across the back of the chair and ripping the canvas. He tore the wood framing apart with his bare hands, breaking the longer pieces against his knee, and feeding all into the fireplace, setting it to burning merrily with a lit match and a shaking hand.

A choking smoke, a horrid miasma, filled the room. He climbed the chair, pulling down rags from the broken panes in the skylight, so the dreadful fumes had somewhere to go.

Night had fallen yet again. How many days since he brought her home? He no longer knew or cared. Tonight she would go. There was some black magic at work that he would have no further part of. Not even bothering to wrap or disguise her in any way, he swept the bride over his shoulder and barreled down the stairs past shocked faces, beyond caring about any speculation he might engender. All that mattered was returning her. He would face any consequences later.

Filled with an unnatural energy, his long strides in front of the heavy handcart made short work of the journey. There had been no rain since last he stood at her graveside, so the soil was still loose and shifted easily. He had never dug so quickly in his life and was soon lifting her down on top of the discarded veil in the empty coffin.

Where once he might have reverently placed her and arranged her just so, he now tossed her in and pulled the lid into place, driving down the nails with the flat edge of his pry bar, driven by an anger that increased with each strike.

Her fault, her fault, her fault, he repeated with each blow.

He vaulted himself out of the hole and scooped the soil back in, smacking it down flat with his shovel and smoothing it out so no sign of disturbance could be seen. He expected relief and yet, instantly he missed her, yearned for her. It took every molecule of strength of will he possessed to walk away as a misty drizzle began to fall.

She would be cold and wet. So alone. No one, nothing to appreciate her beauty but the burrowing insects who feasted. With every step he took, he felt as a man split into pieces, half of him striding the earth above, half of him nestled beside her below.

Not pausing to collect his handcart or tools, he stumbled home. The few pedestrians about in the early morning hours made way, hurried across the street pulling their black umbrellas low as though to hide from him. Some even made the sign of the cross, chilled by the expression on his face.

He paid no mind. His thoughts were with her. The smooth satin of her gown, the soft fineness of her hair as he had braided it, the staring eyes which never closed, not even in death. He cursed the ill fate that had taken him to her grave when he might have set out in a hundred other directions that night. Unearthed any other corpse but hers.

Whispers abounded as Breedlove climbed the stairs to his room. A bold hand reached out to grab his arm, but he brushed it away as though it was no more than a bothersome fly. He slammed his door, shutting out the mutterings and speculation. He meant to throw himself down on the mattress where *she* had lain, to sleep and sleep and sleep in hopes of escaping to a dream, any dream where she would appear to him in any form, loving or disdainful, spectral or real. He stopped in his tracks.

It was there. Propped up in the chair. The painting. Whole and neat like it had never been slashed and burned, her face a grinning skull with bare wisps of hair and flesh still attached. A bony hand lay outspread against the surface as though it reached out to him. He lay his own against it. It felt of warmth and flesh. The scent of spring flowers wafted gently.

The paint was dry and set, but even as he watched, faint cracks appeared in bone. Spidery webs spread out forming crazy patterns like the glazing of an old porcelain doll. Decay was not done with her image even now.

Pounding at the door barely registered. The rush of bodies. A melee. He vaguely recognized men, some his neighbors, some from up and down the street. A gang had gathered to demand answers about the gentlewoman he'd been seen with, *plunked over his shoulder like she weren't no better than a sack of potatoes*, as one old cat screamed in his ear.

Let me take the painting, he pleaded.

What painting? Are ye daft? they hooted, and indeed when he looked again, the portrait was nowhere to be seen.

They pushed and prodded him down the stairs. He was too stupefied to bother resisting, but when they reached the street, he heard her calling.

Martin, Martin...

No one had called him by his first name, his true name since his old ma passed. It was Vera, calling for him. She was lonely. Lonely and afraid.

Breedlove fought back then, throwing massive roundhouses that landed indiscriminately but did the trick. The crowd receded, no one willing to be first in line before this display of brute power. He sprinted away with a speed none would have suspected given his size and impassive demeanor. He shed his coat as he ran, feeling that its great weight and the heavy cloth blowing in the wind were holding him back.

Pursuit was quickly abandoned. Not worth the trouble. *They'd given him a right good scare, hadn't they?* The mob all agreed, patting each other on the back in celebration. He wouldn't return to their neighborhood. They'd be safe from whatever evil lingered round him. Let others worry about it now.

Breedlove slowed. Running through the city streets coatless and sweating would only attract more unwanted attention, and he had a mission to fulfill. He slithered and slunk through back alleys and byways until he reached the gates of the cemetery, standing wide open in the morning light. He sauntered in casually, found a quiet out-of-the-way spot under a massively spreading oak tree, and curled up there, dozing amongst its mighty roots until nightfall.

She came to him, her dress shining and bright. The simple veil covering her face was crowned with white roses which pricked her scalp and made blood drip dark and black. He caught a drop on one finger and tasted. It was sweet.

Vera unwound her veil as though it was a shroud, until her face was revealed in its rotten glory, all fine bone china, so smooth to the touch. He kissed her lipless teeth; they tasted as sweet as her blood. He thought—no, he knew he had never felt such happiness before and never would again.

He awoke at moonrise, filled with the serenity known only to those who have seen a path illuminated clearly before them and mean to follow it to its end without wavering. He was in luck for a change. The shovel was where he had left it in the handcart abandoned earlier. The soil was heavy, rain-soaked, and the effort needed great as he piled shovelful after shovelful on the tarp spread out for the purpose. Long work, hard work for any other man, but his heart was light, his soul sang: *for her, for her, for her.*

He dug straight down to the coffin, leaving as much dirt along the sides as he could without risking a cave-in. The rain had helped, turning all to mud and clay more stable than loose, dry soil. Iron nails he had so angrily pounded into place were now gently pried up, the lid propped open once again.

She lay as he had left her, limbs askew, arms open as though welcoming him back. He cupped one hand along a soft cheek. Her skin no longer burned, was cold as ice, but intact and serene. Her eyes watched him closely, and he thought her lips curled slightly into the whisper of a smile.

Now for the difficult part, an inhuman feat for anyone without his strength and determination. His obsession lent him unnatural power as he grabbed the tarp where it hung over the edge of the grave and tugged with all his might. An impossible task seemingly. He groaned in effort and pain, felt muscle and sinew tear in back, arm, groin and thigh, but still he pulled.

Of a sudden, it shifted. So sudden, he fell back into her waiting arms as dirt and mud tumbled down upon them. A poor job, an incomplete job. Insufficient to fill the entire grave neatly and not give rise to speculation and investigation the next time someone happened by. No matter. He would have suffocated long before then, his soul fled to join hers in whatever lay beyond. What happened to the vessels left behind them was unimportant.

He clutched her arms tight around his chest as breath was squeezed out of his laboring lungs. He felt her both above and below him, becoming painfully aware of his own flesh and bone, and understanding how fragile a thing a man was after all.

Panic set in. A natural human instinct to breathe, to fight, to live. The muddy earth was slimy and cold, it filled his mouth and chilled his skin. Had he been tricked? Enchanted by some devil in disguise? It might still be possible to save himself. Scream and claw, kick and dig, leave the madness behind with this temptress of the earth.

He strained half-heartedly against the weight pressing down upon him, all the while knowing it was a lost cause and his fate was already sealed.

Don't worry, Martin, Vera's teeth chattered into his ear as darkness descended. *I'll keep you safe. You're home.*

THOSE EYES
SHINING LIKE
AMETHYST CRYSTALS
IN THE NIGHT

Knock Knock

THE KNOCKING AT THE drawing room window started again last night, but I didn't go look out this time. I knew what I would see if I pushed aside the heavy velvet curtains. Those eyes, shining like amethyst crystals in the night. Sometimes just one pair, sometimes more. Their light so blinding, it was always hard to make out the rest of the creatures other than a vague outline in the dark.

I say creatures, but they are human in form. On nights when my courage has allowed, I've stood and stared until my eyes adjusted enough to make out their figures, dressed in a fashion from another time. The women in long gowns with cinched-in waists and curious bonnets perched on their heads. The men in formal suits with swallowtails and high-collared shirts. I cannot decide if their clothing is black or if it only appears so in the shallow light that the great alder trees occasionally allow through from the faithless moon as it waxes and wanes.

I once looked forward to autumn and the falling leaves. The bare branches would let more moonlight through, and I thought I would be able to finally make out those details I had wondered about so often. Even see their faces and know whether they are happy or sad or something much worse. But as time passed and the trees turned colors and began to shed their coats for winter, I became less sure. Better not to find out, I thought. What I have seen is enough.

It was the children that bothered me most. There were always one or two, and so very, very still. While the adults—their parents, perhaps?—knocked at the glass and beckoned to me with gloved hands, the children only stood and stared with those brilliant purple eyes unblinking. On nights when only one pair of eyes appeared, it was always her: the girl with the long curls hanging over her shoulders, the hair a slightly paler shade of dark than the rest of her. There was an intensity about her and her quietness, like one of those portraits where the eyes seem to follow you around the room.

Those amethyst eyes. What makes them glow such a strange hue? Purple was once my favorite color, but no longer. I went through my clothes last week and got rid of all the lavender and lilac, grape and heliotrope, violet and periwinkle. Francis walked in on me while I was sorting, amazed at the mess I had made of my dressing room. I think I convinced him I was just winnowing down my extensive wardrobe, but I saw him eyeing the pile of purple clothes with curiosity and concern.

He's a decent brother though and didn't push the issue. Only helped me bag up the discards and drove me to the charity shop so I could donate them. I don't drive these days. Too nervous and fidgety. My mind is full of the screech of brakes, shattered glass, the stench of oil whenever I think about getting behind the wheel, so Francis kindly takes me out on the rare occasions I feel like going.

I am mostly content to stay at home. At least I was, until the visitors started rapping on the windows at night. It started shortly after we moved here when I was released from hospital. Francis and I were sitting in the drawing room after dinner, each enjoying a favorite book, when I heard the knocking for the first time.

Startled, I cried out, "What's that!?"

Francis looked up at me in surprise. "What's what, Lucy?" he said. A chill ran down my spine.

"Don't you hear anything?" I asked as the knocking continued, a slow but sharp rat-a-tat.

He got the look on his face I've grown to abhor. A mixture of pity and impatience. "It's as quiet as a tomb around here. Not even any traffic out on the road. Maybe you should make an early night of it. That was a long walk you took today and in such nasty weather. You may have overtired yourself."

"Of course," I agreed. I'd learned not to argue or protest. You see, I was recovering from what once upon a time they called a nervous breakdown. It now goes by a string of much fancier terms which I didn't bother to listen to as the doctor explained them to my brother. Things had gotten very bad before I went into hospital. The voices in my head, the vicious impulses, the public scenes. I knew now the hallucinations were just that. It wasn't real, any of it. Now that my meds were properly balanced, I accepted I had been quite mad, or rather, had mental health challenges as my brother always put it when explaining me away to acquaintances.

I preferred the word 'mad'. It made me feel important and distinguished to think that I had been a madwoman, like those characters in novels kept locked up in the attic so as not to bring shame upon the family. And there was no question Francis had been embarrassed by me. A well-known and celebrated solicitor doesn't want to be compromised by a sister with erratic and dangerous tendencies. Although I couldn't complain. He had been a stalwart champion for me even after our parents cut ties, fed up with the unpredictable and messy life I led.

It was he who found the best doctors for me after I drove my car into the gates of our ancestral family estate, enraged that my parents wouldn't open them to me. He was the one who paid for my private care, smoothed things over with the police, even arranged to have my parents' gates replaced, although by rights they should have done so. God knows they have more than enough money to replace a thousand gates, while I should have been irreplaceable in their eyes, a treasure, their only daughter—

But wait, I'm not supposed to get upset or dwell on things past. Look to the future is what those annoyingly cheerful doctors were always telling me. I could never remember their names. One I thought of as "tall, crinkly nose" and the other was "red-face, glasses." Time was a blur in that place. Each day so much like the one before it and the one to come, it seemed as though I was reliving the same day over and over again. At length, though, I did enough to make them happy with me so they could pat themselves on the back for a job well done and send me out into the big, wide world again.

Only, the world held nothing for me. No place, no job, no friends, no ambition, no skills. Again, it was Francis who rode to the rescue, purchasing a modest home far enough from town to allow for an extensive garden and easy access to endless walking paths for me, yet close enough for him to commute each day without too much strain. Some nights, if he was working late on an important case, he would stay at his bachelor's flat in the city. It was on one of those nights I first got up the courage to look out of the window beside the French doors leading out into the garden.

I had been hearing the knocking for several weeks at that point. I never mentioned it to Francis again since he so obviously did not hear it, and I learned not to flinch whenever the sharp noise started up. But my curiosity had been building. I thought more than once of getting up and pulling aside the curtains but was afraid Francis would be suspicious of my peering out into the garden in the dark and I didn't want to worry him. I'd had no strange visions or even many troubled thoughts since Francis had taken over doling out my meds to me and making sure I took them. None other than this knocking.

A side effect of the medication was what I had settled on. Something like tinnitus, only instead of ringing in the ears, it was this sharper noise. Curious that I only experienced it in the drawing room and only after dark, but it was the best—no, the safest explanation I could come up with. I had no friends. No one I could discuss such a thing with certainly. My brother's cronies treated me with a wary respect, as though I were a bomb that might explode at any moment if they said the wrong thing or made a sudden movement. I had no wish to speak of anything to anyone that might make Francis think his investment in my improved state of mind was all for naught.

But, as I said, a curiosity remained. I felt compelled by the sound to get up and investigate. Only Francis's presence held me back, so I was strangely relieved and excited the night he texted me to let me know he was staying over in town if I thought I'd be alright by myself. It would be my first night without him in our new home, but I had never been afraid of being alone. I liked my own company best, and as considerate a housemate as Francis was, I was giddy at the idea of an evening by myself, doing exactly as I pleased with no judgmental audience examining my every mood and movement for signs of relapse.

I ate a simple meal in the kitchen rather than in the formal dining room as Francis preferred, he being a traditionalist at heart. Then, with no little anticipation, I went to the drawing room and waited. I held a book on my lap, but I could no more have concentrated on the words on the page than I could have shot up into space and orbited the August moon. The ticking of the clock on the mantelpiece was unnaturally loud in the quiet. One of those noises that retreated to the background normally, but once you become aware of it, feels like it will drive you—

And there it was. The knocking. I jumped from my perch on the armchair nearest the doors and turned off the floor lamp so I was in darkness. I didn't want whoever was out there to be able to see me more clearly than I could see them. That would hardly be fair. I had no set idea what I thought I would see. The only vague theory I had—if there was really to be something out there—was it was a wild animal of some kind, digging or hunting close to the house. So convinced of this had I become that when I pulled aside the forest green curtains, I actually looked down toward the ground, thinking I might see a badger or fox playing tricks outside the window.

Instead, the unnatural purple glow drew my eyes up quickly. I froze as I took in two figures the first night. A woman and the girl, the girl with the long curls. The woman, dark-clothed, was reaching out a gloved hand to rap again and again. She would stop only long enough to beckon to me, inviting me out through the French doors into the garden. I don't know how long I stood staring, but finally, I dropped the curtains and backed slowly away to sink down into the chair I had abandoned earlier.

I was both amazed at what I had seen and horrified. Horrified it was a hallucination; horrified that it might not be. I couldn't decide which would be worse. In the first instance, it would mean the balance of my mind was becoming disturbed, and I had no wish to go down such a treacherous road again after finding some measure of peace. But what if it was real? How to explain these weird, otherworldly creatures in the garden? And what did they want of me? For it was only me who heard them, not Francis. Why did they want me to join them? Did they need assistance, or did they only want to swell their ranks by harming me if I opened the doors?

Such were the thoughts that kept me awake long into the night after my first sighting. The next morning, it seemed so incredible, I wondered if I had fallen asleep after dinner and dreamt it. I ventured out the French doors in the light of day and examined the earth around that part of the garden, but there was no sign of any footsteps or disturbance. I had half-convinced myself it was a dream by the time Francis called to see how I had done alone and whether I would mind another night of him staying in town.

I reassured him, and in the process myself, that I was perfectly fine. Sitting out in the morning sun which streamed through the sides of the gazebo at the end of the garden, enjoying the crisp fall air while watching the insects buzzily carrying on their business and listening to the incessant gossip of the birds, it was easy to believe it had been a dream brought on by the novelty of a night in the house alone. I wondered from what part of my subconscious I had unearthed such alien beings. They were nothing like the conventional ghosts I'd read of in many of the Gothic tales I enjoyed. They were the furthest thing possible from those pale, floating, flimsy figures, unable to interact with the living from beyond the veil.

The creatures in my vision had been earthy and substantial. I had no doubt if I had gone through the doors—in my dream, of course—I would have been met with solid flesh, would have felt the rich materials I imagined their clothes were made of and could have fingered those long, soft curls of the little girl. If nothing else, the sharp knocking indicated an ability to affect the physical world. But, Lucy, you're saying, you'd been hearing the knocking all along—that was no dream. True, but perhaps my sleeping mind had sought to answer the riddle with some amalgamation of fears brought on by an underlying anxiety of being alone in the house I was not even aware of.

It was the detail of the eyes I dwelt on the most. I supposed ghouls with glowing eyes were a not uncommon theme in horror tales, but such an unusual color! And then it struck me they looked very like those insufferable headlights some people install on their cars. I remembered how it used to exasperate me to have one of those following behind me in traffic, flashing and blinding me in the rearview mirror. I almost laughed out loud at the simple explanation. How like my poor jumbled brain to pick up on a forgotten annoyance to toss into my nightmare stew. My heart lightened at this most logical reasoning. If the amethyst eyes were easily explained, then I could accept the other features of the vision had their origins in memories tucked away in the deep recesses of my mind.

I decided to take a long walk across the countryside to clear my head and tire myself out. I'd found I often had the most restful, dreamless sleeps when I was physically exhausted. The farmlands and forests around our house were open for public trekking, and I had my favorite paths and haunts, so to speak. I stopped by the garden shed that sat at the end of our lot next to the gate I used for easy access to the open parkland bordering our property. I remembered a large sunbonnet I had noticed there when we first moved into the house and thought to adopt it for my own use to protect my fair skin, which had gone red rather than tan from my weeks of walking.

Francis had hired a professional gardening crew to maintain our grounds, which was just as well as I had no green thumb and was as likely to pull up a prize bloom as a weed, but it meant I'd had little reason to explore the shed which was full of old tools and implements that past owners hadn't bothered to pack up and take with them. Stepping into the dark interior out of the warm sun, I was surprised at how chilly the air was in the small space, although as it was made of the same stone as the house, it made sense it retained the coolness of our autumn nights.

I looked around, imagining clearing out the junk, cleaning the small, dust-encrusted window to let in some light, installing a desk and a comfortable chair. I had a vague thought of buying a typewriter and trying my hand at writing, but who used typewriters these days? More practical to run electricity from the house and make sure the wi-fi reached this far so I could use my laptop. I had to laugh at my ambitions. What had I to write about but my own jigsaw of a mind? Even I couldn't explain how its puzzle pieces fit together. Maybe I would write of my strange visitors. Would it be a horror tale or a ghost story, or perhaps a little of both? I determined to let my imagination run wild while I walked and see if I couldn't think up a plot to fit my characters.

Seeing the hat I wanted, I picked it up gingerly, unsure of its age and whether it would disintegrate in my hands or reveal a nest of spiders lurking under the brim. The straw it was made of was surprisingly soft and in good shape although the wide silk ribbon meant for tying under one's chin shredded into pieces when I pulled on it. It had faded to grey over time but the part that had been protected next to the hat showed its original mauve color still. I pulled out the ribbon and found a long piece of twine to take its place. I could only imagine I looked a sight in the huge hat with its rough fastening, but I rarely met anyone else on my walks and didn't mind if others thought me eccentric—I had been called much worse in my life.

As I turned to leave the shed, I heard a rapid rustling noise. Mice or other wild rodents? I looked about at my feet, more curious than afraid. I loved all animals of the field, one of the reasons Francis had brought me out to the country. He really was a most thoughtful and generous brother. I vowed once more to be kinder to him and make sure I did nothing to cause him additional trouble. The noise continued as I stood listening. An image came to my mind of stiff taffeta skirts rubbing and abrading against each other like Victorian ladies at a crowded dance. It was probably the old-fashioned hat which made me think of that of all things. And the dream, of course—the antiquated dress the woman had been wearing with the wide skirt. Far from being amused, I grew annoyed at my senses which seemed to be working overtime to provide my brain with stimuli it could well do without.

I went to step over the threshold of the door, anxious to get on with my walk to soothe myself, but a sudden reluctance came over me to leave the safety of the shed, which was a funny thought. Why safety? I couldn't explain it, but it was like I belonged there in that small, dark, damp place. As if I was welcome there and accepted in a way I had never felt before. I stood in indecision for quite some time. I would occasionally make a move forward but had the strongest sensation hands were grasping at my clothes, pulling me back into the shadows. It was only the buzzing of my phone which ended the stalemate. The discordant noise seemed to break a spell and I stepped out firmly and freely into the sunlight.

I didn't recognize the number displayed on the phone, so didn't bother answering, but I was shocked to see the time. It was well into late afternoon though it had been on the earlier side of mid-morning when I had first determined to take a walk. I felt a sense of dread. Losing track of hours, days, even weeks was one of the earliest signs of my illness. Adrenaline rushed through me and I suddenly emptied the contents of my stomach onto the lawn, sweat streaming from every pore. Shaking, I walked the path back to the house, concentrating on putting one foot in front of the other, afraid of tripping as my eyes were full of tears.

My main thought was for Francis. After all he had done for me. The care he had taken. I felt I was letting him down if my mania was returning. I tried to think.

Had I taken my medication? Francis was in the habit of doling it out to me when he was home, but he had left me several days' worth in a pill organizer. First thing on entering the house, I checked the pillbox and found to my relief, and then dismay, that I had taken the pills—relief I hadn't fallen down on my medication routine and dismay they hadn't prevented the loss of time in the garden.

Unable to face the idea my meds might be losing effectiveness and we might have to go through the ordeal of experimenting and finding new drugs, adjusting the dosages, dealing with side effects yet again, I lay down on the sofa in the drawing room, impatient to escape into the oblivion of sleep. I fell into a slumber so heavy that I dreamt over and over I had awoken, only to find I was still trapped in a dream. With a cry of despair, I finally wrenched myself awake, sitting up, befuddled and frightened. The room was dark. Night had come on while I slept.

The knocking, I thought. It's time for the knocking. And even then, the sharp raps started up. I sat and listened, half-intoxicated still from the depth of my torpor. I wondered how long it would go on. Always before, I had retreated from the room before the noise stopped. Would it go on all night, whether I was here or not? Or was it in my mind, ceasing when I left? I decided to wait it out and see. And so I sat, on and on. I amused myself by trying to find a pattern to the tapping, but truly, there was no discernible rhythm to the sound, only a remarkable consistency to the volume and sharpness of the raps.

It was mesmerizing in its way, so I was not surprised to find I must have fallen back asleep because next thing I knew, Francis was standing over me, shaking me awake.

"What are you doing here? What time is it?" I asked, bleary-eyed and confused.

"It's noon. I've been calling and texting you since yesterday evening. Why didn't you answer? You must have known it would make me worry. I had to reschedule meetings to come down and check on you. Really, Lucy, the only thing I've asked is that you always answer me when I contact you, so I know you're okay. It doesn't seem so much to expect..."

"...given all you've done for me," I finished for him. "I know, Francis. I'm sorry. I was unusually tired yesterday. I must have slept through your calls and texts," I added, checking my phone and seeing it lit up with notifications.

He eyed me critically. "You look like hell. Are you sure you've gotten enough sleep? Maybe you need a doctor. Are you coming down with something?" He lay the back of one of his thin, cool hands against my forehead. "You feel hot. Let's take your temperature," he suggested, sprinting away to the bathroom to fetch the thermometer before I could protest.

"It's normal," he reported a few minutes later, sounding almost disappointed. Perhaps he hoped for a physical reason for my dishevelment rather than a mental one.

"I'm fine. I took too long of a walk yesterday is all," I lied, determined not to start spouting off about lost time, ghostly rappings, and purple-eyed monsters. "I just need to eat a little something and take it easy today."

Pleased to have something practical to do, Francis retreated to the kitchen where he whipped up an omelet and some crusty French bread with fresh butter for the two of us to share. He left to head back to town after I assured him I was fine. I could tell he was torn between annoyance at having his day interrupted and concern at my flimsy excuses. I had never been a skilled liar and Francis knew me better than anyone else in the world, but I hoped I had allayed his worries.

Catching sight of the straw bonnet, I perched it on my head, tying the twine beneath my chin, and ventured back outside. The bright sun hurt my eyes and I instinctively moved down to the far end of the garden where it was shadier. The door to the shed was standing open and the sick I had left the day before was attracting flies. I fetched a shovel and turned over the grass and earth to bury the disgusting mess. Returning the shovel to the shed, I reveled in the darkness within, moving things around in a desultory way, attempting to bring some order to the chaos. I unearthed a short stool and sat down upon it to rest.

Closing my eyes, I listened to the air. There was a humming, a rustling, a murmuring. *I must get my hearing checked, or my brain,* I thought with a bitter snort of laughter. The noises were both soothing and provoking. The universe was singing to me and I wanted to answer, but what could I say to match this sublime, subliminal purring of sound?

I leapt from my seat at a sudden clanging. It was the reminder on my phone. Once a week, in a concession to my peacemaking brother, I called my mother. She had condescended to this gesture out of her regard for her successful child, the one she proudly claimed as her own. My father still ignored my existence, but Mother and I spoke every Thursday at 2 pm, a time arranged for her convenience, not mine naturally. Our conversations were stilted as I had little to report from my humdrum existence and she barely deigned to share anything of hers.

Usually, I dreaded the ordeal, but today I was thankful for the alarm. I had a sinking feeling I might have whiled away untold hours again if it had not sounded. I left the shed, closing the door firmly behind me as a visual reminder that it would be best not to enter it again. I didn't understand the pull the chilly space had on me, but I couldn't risk falling under its spell sometime when Francis was around, in case he discovered me dazed and out of joint with time.

I kept to my resolution in the following weeks, determinedly snubbing the small building whenever I was in the garden, though I was always keenly aware of its presence. The knocking continued unabated at the house. Francis spent no more nights away from home, convinced I had been up to some mischief while he was gone. However, he was busy with a terribly important case, so he took to spending his evenings in his office preparing briefs for upcoming court dates and engaging in conference calls with the barrister he was partnered with.

This suited me as it left me alone in the drawing room with my friends. Yes, I had started thinking of them as my friends, though in a kind of joking terror at first. Every night that Francis was closed up with his work was an opportunity for me to go to the curtains and slip behind them, standing close to the French doors, the better to see out. I counted as many as ten some nights, mostly adults with a few children. They crowded close together, their amethyst eyes staring straight ahead as one of them, usually a woman, would knock and knock at the glass. I experimented with moving from side to side and even crouching to see if their eyes would follow me, but they never did.

I couldn't be sure if they registered my presence and still had no idea whether the knocking occurred regardless if anyone was in the room or not. I had looked up cheap security cameras online, thinking to install one as an experiment, but I had no credit cards or money to call my own. Francis controlled my spending, which was fair given that I'd gone through a fortune and heavily into debt during my halcyon mania days. And besides, there was a part of me that considered it more fun not to know the answers. My life was a pretty dull routine. This mystery of the nightly visitors was the only interesting thing that had happened since I left hospital, and so far, they had never tried to harm me or demonstrated they could even if they wanted to.

I looked forward to their visits, and even started a game where I would try and guess how many would be waiting for me when I stole behind the curtains. A few times a week, there would only be the girl with the curls waiting for me. I always knew before I looked on those nights because the knocks when she had to rap for herself were lighter and less confident. I'd taken to calling her Serafina in my head because there was something angelic about her even with those glowing eyes.

One night when we were alone, just the two of us, I knelt on the carpet, the curtain splayed behind me like a cloak, and spoke to her. "What do you want, my Serafina angel? What can I do to help you and your kind?"

I expected no answer but to my amazement, she blinked. I thought I had imagined it, but then she did it again. There was no question that the violent purple light had dimmed as she shut her eyes. I felt elated that I had seemingly provoked a reaction, but it turned to terror in a moment as she opened her mouth wide in a silent scream. I heard no sound, but a hairline crack formed from corner to corner in one of the panes which separated us from each other. Other tiny cracks followed, and I put my hand up to the glass in awe and no small degree of fear. I'm not sure what I hoped to do—signal to the girl to stop or brace the window—but all I accomplished was sticking my hand straight through the damaged glass, raking long scratches in my wrist.

With the pane open to the night air, Serafina's unearthly screech poured in at me, scraping the surface of the bones beneath my skin in a cold shiver. There was no question now. Those violet eyes were staring at me in accusation or pleading or something in between. I was half-blinded and in a panic. I tried to pull my hand back through the glass but only succeeded in cutting myself deeper. The last thing I remember was the girl's mouth descending toward my imprisoned hand, teeth gnashing and snapping as they came ever closer.

I awoke in hospital. I knew before I even opened my eyes. There is a combination of smell and sound and even a sour taste on the tongue which is found nowhere else. I saw Francis sitting uncomfortably in a stiff wooden chair. He looked older and sloppier than his usual dapper self, with dark circles under his eyes. I felt a twinge of guilt. This was my fault. Always a burden to him. Never a help. I felt the tug of despair. All he had asked of me was that I stay out of trouble, and I couldn't even give him that one gift.

I shifted in bed to ease my aching back and woke him. He scooted his chair closer and gave me a wan smile.

"You're awake."

"And you," I said. "I'm sorry, Francis."

"What happened? I heard a scream from you like nothing I'd ever heard and rushed to the drawing room to find you'd put your hand through the glass. I thought you were feeling so much better. What possessed you, Lucy?"

It was on the tip of my tongue to tell him exactly what had possessed me, his word choice more appropriate than he knew, but he would never have believed me. It would only convince him my brain was playing tricks on me again.

"It was terribly silly, really," I said, throwing in some light laughter which sounded unconvincing to my own ears. "I wanted to look and see if the moon was full and managed to tangle myself up in the curtains and trip. I put my hands out to try to save myself from falling and you see the result." I held up my bandaged hand.

He examined my face skeptically but only commented, "You always have been a bit clumsy."

"The worst!" I agreed. "So, how bad is it?"

"It's not good, Lucy. Your hand was torn to shreds. You must have made it worse by trying to free yourself. The surgeon did her best, but they aren't sure how much use of it you'll have."

I thought of my last sight of Serafina, her small teeth snapping in the night and shuddered.

"Don't worry," Francis said, grabbing my good hand. "You're tough. You'll get through this."

"At least it was my right hand," I said with an attempt at a smile. "Good thing I'm left-handed."

My poor joke was rewarded with an answering smile that didn't reach my brother's worried eyes. I knew what he was thinking. Had I tried to harm myself? It wouldn't have been the first time. I wished I could explain it to him, for I was convinced now these beings were real. Had to believe that. The alternative was too hard to accept.

Well, I'd learned my lesson. My attempt to communicate had been a disaster. These creatures were not my friends. They could harm me if I let them get too close. I vowed to myself I would never answer the knocking again now that I knew the danger. If I granted them power by engaging with them, I would simply ignore them. Things cannot harm you if you refuse to acknowledge them, can they?

Francis drove me back home, my hand well-bandaged but with no pain meds. My brother and I were agreed it might be a slippery slope to start down, so I would make do with over-the-counter pills. The alder trees that surrounded the house welcomed us with a blaze of brilliant yellow and orange as we pulled up in the driveway. They would let their leaves fall and the moonlight through their heavy branches soon, but I remembered my determination not to investigate our visitors any further. I would leave them be and hope they would return the favor. And as for the knocking? What's a little noise in the night? Hardly worth worrying about.

Today marked the third day since I hurt my hand. The nurse who comes to change the bandages clucked her tongue at the state of it and looked at me with pity. It is swollen and throbs with every beat of my heart. I fear she thinks it can't be saved and they will have to chop it off before infection sets in and spreads. I have sat many a long hour and thought of what it would be like to lose it. I feel fortunate it was not my writing hand, for how then would I have written down my tale?

I hadn't planned to do any such thing, but I wandered out to the garden today and felt the shed beckoning to me. Weak and weary, I opened the door and sat down on the stool, looking around the dark damp. I noticed an old legal pad of yellow paper and rooted around in a toolbox until I found a sharp pencil. The blank page was daunting at first, but then the words started forming in my mind and spilled out through the lead onto the paper. I felt as if I was transcribing events and thoughts that had happened to someone other than me. I've never felt so inspired or so alive.

My pencil went dull from my scritching and scratching, but one of the dark gentlemen kindly stepped forward and took it from me, sharpening the point with a hatchet blade before handing it back to me with a nod. The others crowded around to read my story. I heard their murmurs and knew they approved. Serafina stood close to me and held my injured hand, landing little butterfly kisses on the bandages from time to time in apology at the damage she had wrought. I put down my pencil when I was finished and reached out my hand to capture one of her long curls. It was exactly as soft and silky as I had imagined.

I tore loose the pages of my tale from the pad and walked back to the house, escorted by my new family. They love me with an overwhelming passion I can feel deep into the most wounded parts of my innermost soul. Never have I known such acceptance. I know I must go and live with them, but I wanted to leave this record for my brother so he doesn't wonder what became of me.

Slipping the pages halfway under the French doors, I knocked with my good hand. I didn't know if he would answer or if he was even in the room but suddenly, he was there looking out at me. From the shock on his face, I knew he could see me. I put my bandaged hand up to the glass and he reached out his own to meet it on the other side. I wanted to draw his attention to the papers on the floor, but his face had gone a funny color. Empurpled, I thought, and laughed at having such a ridiculous word come to mind at a serious moment. But it was not him that had gone purple, it was my eyes. I could see them reflected in the glass like twinkling amethysts. Francis backed away from the window, shaking his head and mouthing, *no, no, no* at me.

I was disappointed he didn't notice the papers, but it was just as well because I gathered them up and brought them back to the shed with us and was able to add these final words. I will try sliding my story under the door again tomorrow night and every night if I must. And I will knock and knock until he answers.

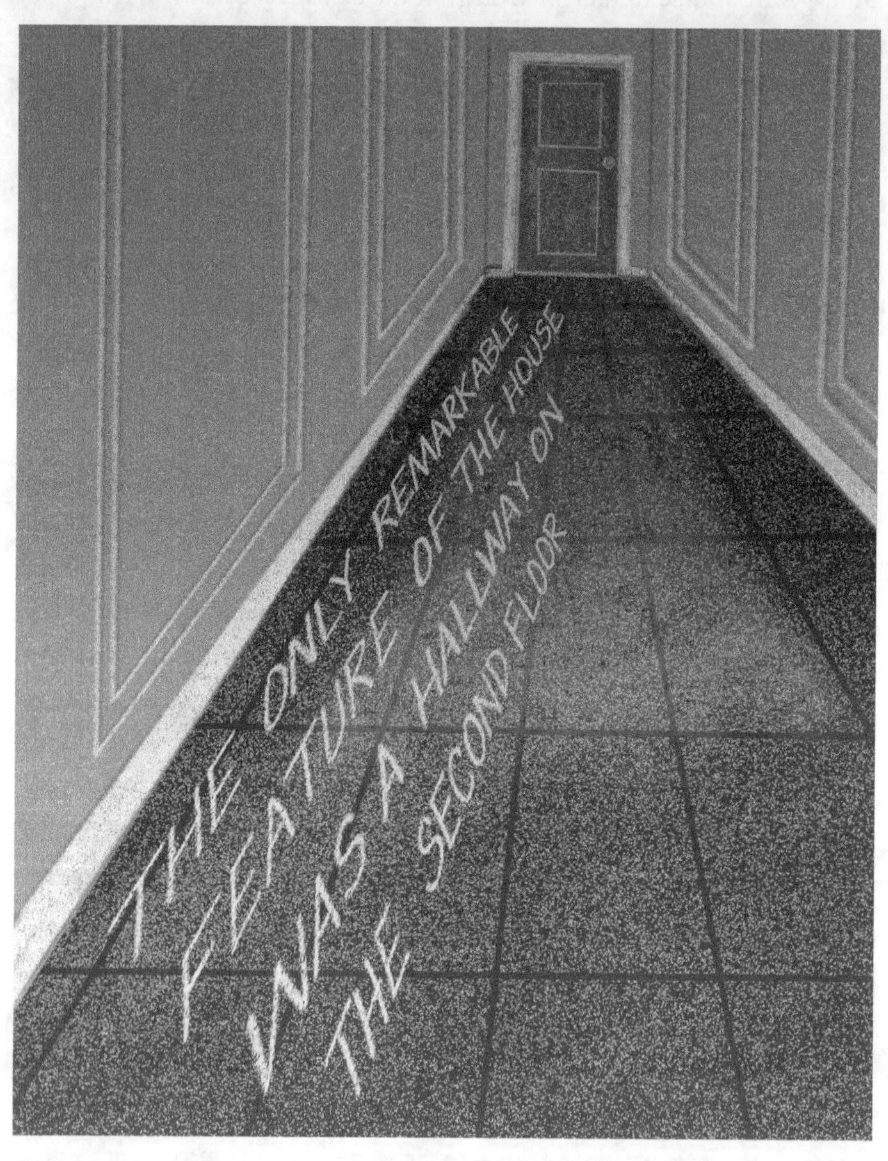

THE ONLY REMARKABLE
FEATURE OF THE HOUSE
WAS A HALLWAY ON
THE SECOND FLOOR

The Long Hallway

For sale: Quaint bungalow with gorgeous garden. Cozy rooms full of old-world charm and history. Full disclosure: Hallway upstairs has a faint iridescent shimmer from time to time and the previous owners disappeared under mysterious circumstances. Bring all offers!

I should have known it was too good to be true. In this market, nobody gets a cottage in the country for such an absurdly low price, but my heart overruled my head once I got a glimpse of Farrow's Hill. From the thatched roof which curved round the upper story windows just so, giving the house a whimsically wide-eyed façade, to the rabbit warren of rooms with two or three stairs up or down between each one, and such fabulous vintage wallpaper everywhere! A little stained and torn in places, but in remarkably good condition given its age.

On a whim, I sent in a bid, never expecting it to be accepted, but the agent was on the phone the very next day to make arrangements to sign the papers. They seemed remarkably glad to be rid of the responsibility of marketing the property. I suppose once a place has gotten a reputation, it can be a challenge, but you'd have to be a superstitious fool to believe such nonsense.

I wasn't completely reckless though. I did inquire at the local police station about the Beauregards. The no-nonsense inspector I spoke to chalked their disappearance up to a marital tiff. They were renowned in the village for their knockdown, drag out fights and threatened divorce frequently, but neither was willing to give up the cottage to the other. I expressed my hope that it didn't end in foul play, though I will admit, a tiny part of me, the part who had read far too many murder mysteries, hoped it did.

Perhaps I could play at amateur detecting, sticking my nose into village affairs and nearly getting done in myself before unmasking the villain to applause and admiration. The inspector tried to dampen my enthusiasm by declaring they had split up and gone their separate ways, each unwilling to give ground on ownership of the cottage. They'd left instructions with their lawyers to sell the property and donate the proceeds to a local animal charity.

This explanation was far from satisfactory to me. If anything, it sharpened my appetite for sleuthing. I entered my new home and spent my first days there thoroughly searching the place from top to bottom. To my immense disappointment, the furniture and belongings of the benighted couple had been cleared out. In fact, the cottage was immaculately clean. Even the attic was swept free of the dust and cobwebs you would expect to find.

All in all, everything seemed as ordinary and peaceful as could be. The only remarkable feature of the house was a hallway on the second floor, the site of the strange shimmer the advertisement (which was surely tongue-in-cheek) had warned of.

As you stood at the top of the stairs, there were short halls to the left and right leading to a couple of comfortably-sized bedrooms. But straight ahead, a hallway stretched out into the distance. It appeared unnaturally long for the size of the house. I felt I must squint and peer to see the door at the very end and that the walk to get there took more time than I would have expected.

The door opened to a room with no windows. I puzzled over it a long time, unable to picture in my mind the exact architecture of the second floor. And of what good was an empty room without windows or even an overhead light? Useful when I suffered from migraine and needed complete darkness. For the room would be very dark indeed with the door shut, I thought. I decided to test the theory.

How to describe the feeling of that lightless space? My brain spun with a dizzying array of images, and I collapsed to the ground. My understanding of what was real and what was unreal abandoned me. I pictured myself contending with angels in the garden and struggling to free a demon trapped in a cereal box on the top shelf of the kitchen. A banshee under my bed swallowed a goldfish as immense as an elephant and howled a lament which shattered every window. Chaos reigned in my fast-moving thoughts.

I was filled with a depth of despair I have never known. I crawled to the wall, disoriented, and scrabbled for the door but could feel nothing but the velvet-flocked wallpaper under my fingertips. I crept along the floor, first one wall, then the second and the third, but not until the fourth wall did I feel the door beneath my hand. I grasped the doorknob, but it wouldn't turn.

Imagine you are in an inky black room. The door is locked. You're trapped and alone. All is silent and still. Suppose a firefly were to sneak in through a crack under the door. Wouldn't that one feeble light, that tiny bit of company bring you unutterable joy? So it was with me when the ghost appeared. It wasn't your classic transparent apparition, alone and palely loitering. More of a shimmer of sparkles, a faint glow, but sufficient for me to know I was no longer alone.

It kept me company during those long days and nights and crooned to me gently in my final hours. But it was not until I was a wraith myself that I understood its laments. Mary Beauregard. Her spirit trapped in the house where her husband had bound her in death. The spell he had spoken over her kept her feeble and powerless, a literal shadow of her former self, but I am not so constrained. I have free will and a purpose I lacked in life.

Leonard Beauregard has bought back his cottage and moved in with a new wife and her two children. Goodness only knows what he told them or the estate agent, or the police for that matter, about a second disappearance. I've no family of my own to probe into the matter or raise a fuss. Besides, no one can see the long hallway. I suppose that is part of the spell he laid upon it, creating an invisible path into a trap of madness.

I shall never know why I could see it when others can't, but it's not something I dwell on. Contrary to expectations, I enjoy my new existence. Standing behind the woman as she does the dishes, I whisper in her ear. I tickle the kids and move their toys around, hiding them in unexpected places. And as for Mr. Leonard Beauregard, I know what he's planning. More disappearances. But this time, he won't get away with it.

THE OLD DOG WANDERS DOWN TO
THE CEMETERY ON NICE DAYS

FROM THE DIARY OF MRS. MADELINE SMYTHE

MONDAY, JUNE 2ND

Must do something about that dog. I don't like how it raises its dirty, shaggy head and sniffs the air whenever I enter a room. Stares at me with cataracted eyes as though it wasn't half-blind. Best speak to Maud about it. Or better yet, Molly. They may be twins and each as sly as can be, but Molly's the one who inherited the intelligence to carry out such schemes successfully.

Getting rid of the dog without being blamed for it is exactly the kind of prank they enjoy playing, for they have no love for animals. We won't dwell on the small graveyard at the edge of the woods where they discard their prey. At least they have the decency to give them all a proper burial and lovely crosses fashioned from twigs and pine needles. They are clever with their hands.

I've put up with the mongrel for Gerald's sake, but the other day, it actually growled at me. Me! The mistress of this house. The smelly old thing isn't long for this world anyway, why not hustle it along to the afterlife? We'd be doing it a favor. You can practically hear its bones creaking when it limps pathetically around the house. If Gerald wasn't such a sentimental fool, he'd have had the thing put down long since.

It's a pity my husband thinks more of a common cur than he does of his own children. The way he goes on and on about them, you'd think we'd raised a couple of hooligans instead of well-behaved young ladies. There are not many children these days who are so polite and quiet around adults. A bit of mischief here and there that causes no serious harm seems a small price to pay to appease their baser impulses, and I can't deny their proclivities come in handy. Yes, I most definitely will speak to the twins about that dog.

Tuesday, June 3rd

The girls got quite excited when I whispered into their delicate little ears my suggestion to do something about the mongrel. I assured them if they were terribly ingenious about it—which I had no doubt they would be—that their papa would never think to blame them.

I must admit that isn't true. He may suspect them given their peculiar predilections, but suspicion and proof are two very different things, aren't they? No matter how much he chooses to complain about their behavior, they are his only children after all, and I know from past experience the lengths he will go to protect them from gossip and scandal. I look forward to seeing what scheme they come up with, my clever darlings.

Wednesday, June 4th

The twins have wasted little time in drawing up a plan. Of course, it was Molly who took the lead. She is by far the dominant personality of the two. I worry about Maud. There is a way she looks at her sister sometimes when she thinks no one is watching. I can't put my finger on it, but it doesn't sit well with me. Call it the maternal instinct, I suppose.

But then I see how affectionate they are with one another—the constant embraces and sweet kisses they exchange—and it sets my mind at ease. No matter what life may bring, they will always have each other to rely on, even if there comes a time I can no longer be there with my guiding hand. All mothers must watch their children leave the nest sooner or later, but, oh, how I shall miss them!

Friday, June 6th

Yesterday was quite a day. I was so flustered and tired by the end of it, I forgot to make my usual diary entry, so today's will have to serve. In a nutshell, Molly's plan went far awry, through no fault of her own might I add. Maud stole the rat poison from the tool shed while Molly distracted that barmy old gardener who Gerald insists upon keeping.

Really, I don't believe I have ever met such a traditionalist stick-in-the-mud as my husband. Jenkins can barely walk anymore, much less tend the grounds as they deserve. The flowerbeds are a disgrace. But Jenkins has been the gardener since Gerald was a boy, and so he shall remain until he drops dead. Jenkins, that is, not Gerald. Although I suppose if Gerald were to drop dead, it might be easier to make some changes, but that is neither here nor there for our current predicament.

Maud has a talent for sneaking and easily retrieved the poison, and it was no trouble at all to pour it over the dog's dinner while Cook was distracted. What none of us could have foreseen was the tramp who happened by the open kitchen door. We've had such a problem with trespassers and these so-called ramblers, but no one minds me when I suggest building walls to keep them out. Now see the result!

I've also scolded Gerald over and over about what a foolish waste of money it is to serve up such choice cuts of meat to an animal, but he would insist upon feeding his dog only the best. Honestly, it is with no little amazement that I observe how often my advice goes unheeded to disastrous ends, for while the girls were away fetching the mongrel in for his final meal, this bold vagrant spies the plate of sliced prime rib left out on the counter and steals away with it!

Molly and Maud were perplexed when they returned to the kitchen. They unfortunately caused a bit of a hue and cry about the dog's missing meal. I scolded them about that. It would have been far better to say nothing rather than call attention to it or themselves. As it was, I could tell Gerald was disturbed by their reaction.

And then, disaster! The dirty beggar was found dead in the herb garden with an empty plate beside him! I should feel sorry for him, but it is no more than he deserved, the common thief. Cook is as soft-hearted as Gerald and would most certainly have offered him a warm meal if he had only inquired.

I am actually furious with the man. Not only did he thwart the girls' plan, but he put them in danger. Gerald is many things, but he is not a complete idiot. I watched the wheels turning in his mind as he put two and two together. The look he shot at our girls. A mixture of pity and disgust, as if he or anyone has a right to judge them.

He sent them upstairs to the nursery while he spoke with the police inspector. They are old school chums, so I have hopes Gerald convinced him that the tramp's heart simply gave out. If they should decide to do an autopsy or test for poisons, what on earth shall we do?

I now very much regret encouraging the girls in this plot. All was quiet today, but it felt like waiting for the proverbial other shoe to drop. I was nervous as a cat, expecting a knock at the door at any moment. The twins are too young for hanging, but what if they should be remanded to a mental asylum for life? I would prefer to see them dead then condemned to such a fate.

Saturday, June 7th

Reprieve! The inspector called this evening to let Gerald know they would be ruling it a death by natural causes. I can't help but speculate whether money exchanged hands under the table. It wouldn't be the first time, but Gerald has plenty of it to spare.

He spoke to the girls. Asked them if they had anything they wished to say to him, any secrets to share, but I have trained them well. They only shook their heads and went back to their play. They were more forthcoming when he left the room. Maud seemed inclined to blame me for the entire fiasco, although it was Molly who came up with the plan, so I'm not sure that's entirely fair.

Molly agreed with me and put Maud very much in her place. She has always been my favorite. They say you shouldn't show preference, and I've tried hard not to, but Molly and I have always been in sympathy with each other, often without saying a word. Maud is a dreamy child. Too much in her own thoughts. I predict she will end a spinster alone in this drafty house while Molly goes on to make an advantageous marriage.

I notice as they get older that the girls quarrel much more often. Though they look so alike most people cannot tell them apart, their personalities have diverged more and more. I believe they begin to look upon each other as rivals rather than friends and often compete against one another for attention.

Sibling jealousy is never easy. It is as well my brother died young.

Sunday, June 8th

Molly has a new plan. I had considered advising her to drop the idea of getting rid of Gerald's dog after their narrow escape, but she is headstrong and would only dig her heels in all the harder if I tried. She has never once failed at any plot she set her mind to and has no desire to start now.

Maud spent most of the day trying to convince her sister to give the whole thing up, but she was wasting her breath. At long last, she realized the futility and has been pouting all evening, playing with her best doll, Agatha, in the corner of the nursery. Molly's scheme does not require Maud's participation, but I do hate to see them quarreling. They will always be a stronger force together than apart. Maybe it is only a phase. I hope so.

Monday, June 9th

Another fiasco today. We do seem to be under a gloomy cloud where nothing is going right. Almost makes me think a dark angel is watching over us. Is there such a thing? The opposite of a guardian angel? If so, we may have attracted one's attention. How else to explain yet another complete catastrophe?

I thought Molly's plan sound. She would borrow one of the gamekeeper's shotguns, hide in the woods until Gerald and the dog came along the path on their daily perambulations, and then shoot the dog. Poachers are a constant nuisance in the forest. Any blame would be laid at their door as long as Molly made a quick getaway and returned the gun before anyone noticed.

Maud called us both mad to pursue such a vendetta against an animal who is so old, it will likely die at any time, and she has a point. Patience would have much more easily and safely achieved the same goal. But Molly is like one of those mechanical wind-up toys. Once you set her in motion, there is no stopping her. I will take this as a lesson to be more careful in future with my suggestions.

Maud refused to participate this time. I was pleased to see her standing up to her sister. I admire spunk and strength of will. Maud has been sadly lacking in both up to this point, so perhaps this exercise has not been without some positive result. Molly was undeterred and stole the gun herself.

When she returned without it, I assumed all had gone well, but quite the contrary. She had managed to shoot and return the gun without being seen, but through what sounds to me like some ill-judged timing or aim—though I would never tell Molly that as she was already downcast enough—she managed to shoot her father instead of the dog.

Since no one shall ever see this diary but myself, I will confess a part of me was thrilled at this news. It's not that Gerald is such a bad man or even a bad husband, but he has grown tiresome of late. I don't appreciate his attitude toward the girls one bit. My only concern was whether Molly would suffer any lasting guilt for her act, but I needn't have worried for two reasons: one being that, far from being contrite, Molly was only furious at again failing her assignment, and the second being that it turned out she had only winged Gerald with the buckshot. An annoyance for him to be sure, but not life-threatening.

He made it back to the house under his own power, that absurdly lucky hound trotting along at his heels. The doctor has been out and bandaged him up, sending him to bed early with a powder for the pain. Everyone seemed content with the theory a stray shot from a poacher was to blame. Molly and Maud were both quiet at supper. I suggested putting an end to the whole idea there and then. They neither agreed nor disagreed. Just stared at me. I sometimes think they like to keep secrets even from their own mother.

Tuesday, June 10th

I shouldn't be surprised at this point by anything Molly does. She is a preter-naturally intelligent child, always able to run circles around any adult, even myself as it turned out on one memorable occasion. But I am beginning to worry her successes prior to these most recent events have gone to her head. I spoiled her, spoiled both of the girls, I will admit. Maybe there is more truth than I once believed in the old chestnut that to spare the rod is to spoil the child. Looking back, I can see encouraging the children to think and act in ways beyond their tender years may have been a mistake.

And now—I hesitate to write the words, but I must—Molly is in danger of running right off the rails. I hoped against hope the disastrous consequences of her first two attempts on that mongrel would at least give her pause, but she is full steam ahead with yet another plan, the most elaborate one yet! Oh, my child, I have always taught you that you were special and destined for great things, but sometimes greatness and wisdom demand knowing when to quit. What a stubborn thing she is. I can see her now, her bottom lip stuck out, her arms folded. She peered up at me from under the angry furrows which marred her lovely brow as I tried to turn her from her path.

To my surprise, Maud supported this new idea wholeheartedly and even promised to help her sister. I'm not sure what brought about this change of heart as I thought she would be on my side, but I cannot fight them both. Such strong spirits they have. A testament to me as Gerald has none of their strength or resolve. His only desire is peace and quiet, to pass one day very much like the next, to not be bothered. The girls bother him. I suspect he wouldn't mind being rid of them. I wonder if he longs for the day when they will be old enough to leave home?

That will be a terrible day for me, the worst I can imagine. My children are everything to me. What will I do with myself when they are gone? Wander the grounds, talking to myself most likely. Gerald is useless. He never listens. I wonder if the girls will miss me at all. There are times I am sure they love me but then I catch them looking at me so strangely, it makes me doubt myself.

Wednesday, June 11th

The girls scouted out the location for their next attempt today. I tried to follow along to keep an eye on them and give them the benefit of my advice, but they were having none of it. They screamed and scolded me so, even threatening to throw rocks at me until I gave in and let them wander off alone. I felt indescribably melancholy, like the sun had ducked behind a cloud and left me shivering without the benefit of its warmth.

I can't help but think back to when they were younger. I was all in all to them then. When did the tide begin to turn? When did I become more of a nuisance than a help? A thing to be shooed away. It's not as though it is a shock they don't respect me as much as they used to—not after everything that has transpired between us—but I did think they might have retained a modicum of fondness for me. I am their mother after all. Shouldn't that count for something?

Thursday, June 12th

Tomorrow will be the third attempt. At least I think so. The girls have gone cagey when I am around. They never speak of their plan or give me any more details than the general outline I had already heard, so I have resorted to lurking to try and overhear their whispered conversations. I don't know why they are suddenly so secretive. Surely they know I would never interfere once their minds are made up?

Our relationship has changed more than I realized. The past year has not been easy for any of us. Mistakes were made on both sides, theirs and mine, though I will never concede mine were the greater sins. But I forgave them and thought they had returned the favor. Now I wonder. Has it all been a charade? Maybe this is a game to them and I've no real influence, not anymore. Maybe I never have.

No, I refuse to believe it. That would mean Gerald has been right about my girls all along. That they have no capacity to love. That they are monsters. Could it be true?

I think my heart is breaking.

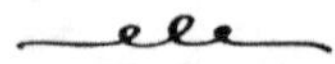

Friday, June 13th

Hours to go until dawn. The entire household is asleep. Such quiet should be peaceful, but I never feel so alone as when I am the only one awake. I decided to pass the time and try to relieve my feelings by writing. These days, it is the only outlet I have.

I am on pins and needles from the apprehension of worrying about how the girls' plans will turn out. Third time lucky is what they say, but I have just noted it is a Friday the 13th. I have never been the superstitious kind, but given how poorly the first two attempts went, I can't help but wish they had chosen a different day. I might be able to assist them if they would let me. I can only conclude they no longer trust me. A bitter thought. "How sharper than a serpent's tooth it is to have a thankless child," and I have two.

I saw the dog in the hall a little while ago. For a change, it did not growl at me but only sniffed the air as I passed. Maybe it recognized a kindred soul. Another wanderer in the night, unable to rest comfortably or enjoy the oblivion of sleep. I felt a pang of sympathy for the thing that I have never felt before. It may be its last night on earth. I wonder if it would mind if it knew? Perhaps the mongrel will welcome the change. It looks so old and tired.

I am tired too.

Saturday, June 14th

Too upset to write. Maybe tomorrow. Or the day after. Or the day after that. I don't know. My girls...

Friday, June 20th

A week has passed. I believe I have composed myself enough to record the events of last Friday. I remember the morning passed slowly. I kept track of the girls' whereabouts as best I could without letting on that I was, afraid they would slip from my grasp if they caught me spying. While I was resigned to being unable to put a stop to events I myself had set in motion, I wanted to be near enough to help them if I could.

It was early afternoon when I saw them slinking away from the house with the old dog in tow. It did not go willingly. They had slipped a piece of rope around its neck and were dragging it along behind them, hitting it in the rear with a sharp stick to keep it moving. Smart girls—they had waited until Gerald was taking his predictable nap after lunch to snatch the animal.

I kept my distance, following along discreetly but afraid of losing them. I had a good idea where they were headed, unless they had altered their original plan, but was reluctant to intervene unless I saw they were in need of assistance. I relaxed the nearer we got to our destination. They were indeed headed to the old ruins on the far side of the estate, a pile of stone rubble with an ancient tower being the only structure still standing.

The plan was to take the dog to the top and throw it off. The fall would most certainly kill it. Then some story about how it had followed the girls up while they were exploring and accidentally slipped off the edge. Gerald would see through it, I was sure, but he had always protected the girls and would again I had no doubt.

I have been too hard on Gerald. He is a good man trapped in an impossible circumstance. A moral man. His soul must ache for the lies he has told for his children and for me. I hope God will be kind to him when he goes at last to meet his Maker. How much better off he would be if we had never met.

But I must finish my tale. Empty my words onto the page. I am glad no one shall ever read them but me. I would not have even entertained the thought once, but now I know my girls and I would be judged harshly by an impartial observer.

Ah, Madeline, Madeline, you are procrastinating. Trying to put off the end to their story. Perhaps if I never write it down, you think, it never happened, but it did. It did. The girls at the top of the tower, the fight. I thought at first from where I observed that they were struggling with the dog, but then I realized to my horror it was the twins that were battling.

Molly was doubled back over the balcony grasping at her sister while Maud pushed with all her might, a look of frenzy on her face that I will never forget. I realized she had been planning all along to take advantage of this opportunity to rid herself of her doppelgänger, her shadow, her rival.

I was there in an instant, but an instant was too late. Even as I reached out my arms to them, they were gone. I rushed to the foot of the tower and found them, still locked in their fatal final embrace. I knelt beside them weeping. The dog came round and sat beside me. I thought to kill the beast myself but had no power to do so.

It was long, long waiting there for someone to notice the girls were missing and come for them. It was long waiting as they lay stretched out in their small white coffins in the back parlor which is never used. It was long waiting through the service, Gerald so stiff in his formal suit, the gossip and pitying looks behind him—*such an unfortunate man*, they whispered, *to lose his wife and then his children in little more than a year.*

And it was long waiting by my grave as my girls were lowered into theirs, one on either side of me. I thought it odd Gerald split them up, almost as though he had some intuition they had not been in sympathy with one another in their last moments, but at least they are close to me now. It is true they are a bit infuriated. They had gotten rid of me once, or so they thought. Their annoyance at finding out I had returned as a spirit to haunt them was nothing compared to their rage at finding themselves trapped on this spectral plane with me, but I hope in time they will come around.

Gerald never visits us, though we go up to the house for a change of scenery from time to time. He is not an imaginative man, so our presence does not disturb his quiet. I don't begrudge him this peace. I understand now that he has earned it.

The old dog wanders down to the cemetery on nice days and sprawls across our graves to bask in the glory of the sun's warmth. It is of some comfort, I suppose, to know we have not been completely forgotten. I have come to dread its death, for then we will be truly alone. Just me and my girls for eternity.

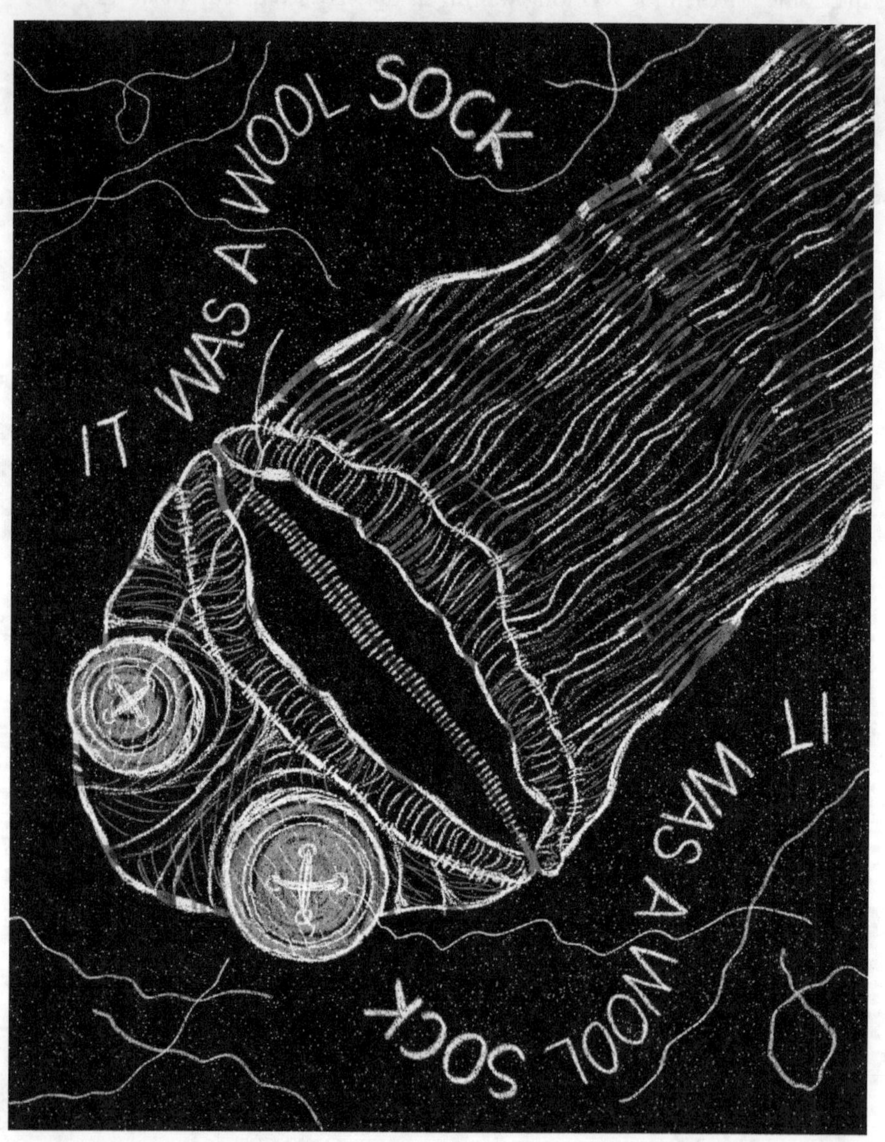

IT WAS A WOOL SOCK
IT WAS A WOOL SOCK

FORGOTTEN

W E WERE STARTLED BY the telephone ringing in the still, small hours of the night. It had not rung since The Incident. Lily's pale blue eyes got even wider than usual, and she blinked at me rapidly, her long black lashes clicking as they fanned her porcelain cheeks. I pushed myself off the shelf, landing on the carpet with a soft glumph, and sidled over to the nursery door.

"Don't leave me here, Teddy!" Lily cried. "I'm so frightened!"

Sighing, I pushed a chair over to the shelf and lifted the doll down carefully. She'd already lost one delicate arm, shattered to pieces. The left sleeve of her pink frilled dress hung empty, the lace embellishments torn and gray. The ebony curls she'd been so proud of shed a cloud of dust behind her as she toddled along in her patent leather shoes, dulled of their shine.

I wasn't in much better shape. My fur was worn thin in places from being so fiercely held and loved once upon a time. One horn-button eye dangled by a single thread. It was only a matter of time before it let go entirely. Rough cotton stuffing leaked out of the broken seam along my spine—another of the many indignities we'd learned to accept during these endless years of neglect.

The eyes of the other toys shone in the moonlight filtering through the over-sized windows. Most of them were indifferent, lost in their own dream worlds, past caring about events in this one. But the white kitten jumped to her feet to follow us, the rusty key in her back whirling, her internal wind-up mechanisms whining as she pranced along behind.

"Hsst," I spat at her, but Sasha was always a willful thing and paid me no mind.

Not that it mattered. We were alone in the house, had been for such a very long time. Which made the shrill insistence of the phone all the more disturbing. We crept along the moldy hall carpet easily enough, but navigating the stairs was a challenge. My soft legs were flexible, but Lily's didn't bend. I picked her up and held her across my lap as I scooted down one step at a time on my rear end. Before we were even halfway down the first flight, the ringing stopped.

"Great," I huffed, annoyed at the wasted effort and dreading the struggle back up to the nursery.

"Wait," Lily replied.

I don't know how she knew, but sure enough, after a few minutes of silence, the phone began to ring again. I shuddered. "We should ignore it."

The doll in my lap shook her oversized head at me. "Teddy! This is the first thing out of the ordinary that's happened in ages. Aren't you the least bit curious?"

"It's been my experience no good ever comes from anything out of the ordinary. Don't you remember?"

"Of course I do. I've more reason than most," Lily replied, glancing down at her missing limb. "But aren't you bored? Are we just to go on and on like this forever? Alone in this house until it falls down around our ears. That corner leak in the ceiling of the nursery is only the start. It will spread. How miserable it will be to be wet and cold all the time."

I glanced around us at the faded and peeling wallpaper, the water stains. The staircase was disintegrating, weakened by wood rot and burrowing insects. What a terrible fate for both us and this grand house. We weren't alive, so we could never die—only crumble away slowly with the passage of time. A painful erasure of our existence with no one to witness our passing. Maybe Lily was right.

The ringing ceased again, but I restarted my descent, bumping from step to step. Sasha pranced ahead, leaping playfully down the stairs. Before we'd gone much farther, the telephone began to shriek once more. Our progress was slow, but I was stubborn once I'd made up my mind to go on. Lily cheered for me, and Sasha mewed encouragement, a funny, rusty little sound.

Two full flights of stairs down to the telephone that I knew sat on the table in the front hallway. I'd passed it so many times, first dragged along by the girl and then later by her brother. The children had never dared to answer the ringing themselves. Father did not allow it.

When I finally bounced us down to the cold black and white tiles of the entrance hall, I set Lily on her feet and clambered up the overstuffed armchair that sat next to the telephone table. Pushing the heavy black handset out of its cradle, I shouted "hello" into the mouthpiece then lay my ear against the receiver.

A horrible hissing erupted, barely audible through the harsh interference of static on the line. "It isss in the basement. Find it or elssse."

Before I had a chance to ask any questions, a sharp click announced the end of the call.

"What did they say?" Lily asked.

I jumped down to the floor and repeated the weird message to the doll while Sasha danced in a circle chasing her own tail.

"Well, I never!" exclaimed Lily. "What on earth can it mean? And they didn't tell you what 'it' is?"

"Nope. Waste of time coming down here. And now we've got to climb back up all those stairs." I added, irritable at the thought of the effort it would take.

"Not until we go down to the basement."

"Why? We wouldn't know what we were looking for."

"Maybe we'll recognize it when we see it. Don't you think we ought to try? What if they carry out their threat?"

I snorted through my scuffed-leather nose. "'Or else' is hardly much of a threat. What are they gonna do, whoever they are, to a bunch of abandoned toys? The worst has already happened. We've been forgotten."

Lily lay her pink-nailed hand on my paw. "But we aren't the only ones left in the house, dear."

She was right, of course. There were The Others. They paid no attention to us, intent on their own pursuits. I'd long ago given up any interest in them in return, but Lily was the sentimental sort. She had a big heart and had always cared more than I did.

"And what do you suppose could be done to them? They've been forgotten too," I objected.

"Like us, they're tied to this place. What if something were to happen to the house? Where would they go?"

"This is silly. A mysterious voice on a phone, which shouldn't even be ringing, makes a vague threat and demands something without even telling us what it is, and we're supposed to jump to its bidding? It's the daftest thing I ever heard. Somebody's idea of a joke. Prank calls like Peter used to make when his parents weren't around," I added smugly. I prided myself on my common sense, but Lily was all sensibility.

"Come with me," she said, tottering away on her stiff legs toward the open door of the library.

I followed reluctantly, knowing what she wanted me to see, to remind me of. We used to roam the house often when we were first left alone, and the scene in that room was always the same.

Mother was seated at the desk, writing out letters in her elegant, looped handwriting, her sweet face scrunched in thought. No scratching of the pen's nib against the paper could be heard. It was like watching the silent family movies they used to project onto the once pristine white walls of the dining room.

The man lounged by the fireplace, soundlessly rustling the newspaper in his hands and folding down one corner to glare at the children playing on the rug from time to time. They were occupied with a rowdy game of quoits, tossing red and blue rope rings toward a wooden spike to see how many they could land.

I thought I'd gotten over it long ago, but a pang in my innermost stuffing stung to see them smiling and laughing. Peter and Amanda. Our children.

Lily loved to speak of them, but I'd rather pretend they'd never existed. It hurt too much to step into this room. See the same nightmare unfold. The man's anger. The argument with his wife. The gun, pulled from the top right-hand drawer of the desk. The struggle. The children cowering, running, hiding. They were never skilled at hide-and-seek. Their father always found them.

In the early days of our grief, we'd never imagined the house would remain empty. Innocently, we believed another family would come, bring their own children for us to play with. It wasn't until the day a man and woman walked through the nursery, whispering of how the tragedy had forever marked the house, that we began to fear what became reality. The house and all those within were to be abandoned to the whims of time and decay.

From that day to this, no other human had set foot through the imposing front doors. Silence reigned, other than the chewing and scurrying of rats, a raven that flew through a broken window once and toured the rooms in a panic until it escaped up a chimney, and a long, black snake that poured itself through the gap under the kitchen door and made a cozy living scooping up any mice too unwary of its shadowy presence beneath the stove.

Insects too numerous to count, of course, including the moths that were slowly devouring anything within reach of their greedy mouths. We waved them away from each other in the nursery, but the rest of the house was fair game, including the stuffed dead animals that lined the paneled library walls.

Taxidermy was the word for it. Peter had taught me that when he took me on a tour once, holding me up to better see as he named off the creatures one by one. Badger, fox, hare, deer, and of all strange things, an enormous hammer-headed bat, or so the boy had called it.

Mounted over the fireplace mantel with giant wings outspread, it was an absurd-looking thing. Its enormous snout and squared-off head more closely resembled one of the whimsical stuffed toys in the nursery than a real animal. Captured on their father's trip to a faraway place called Africa, along with a warthog, zebra, and roaring lion. That man had such a passion for killing, we should have seen it could only end badly for those within his reach.

The bat's golden eyes were watching us now, glinting in the moonlight that streamed through the French doors from the garden and lit up the autumn leaves from the ancient oak tree, falling like rain tap-tapping as their curled edges brushed against the glass.

Lily sighed sadly as we watched the ghostly play begin again. "We could at least try to find whatever is in the basement for their sake. If something were to happen to the house after all this time, what would become of them?"

"Maybe it would be for the best," I said, weary of the reminder of the day that had stolen any contentment from us.

"Indeed!" a deeply resonant voice chimed in, startling us both and causing even bold Sasha to run and hide beneath a flowered footstool leaving only her tiny white tail visible.

"Who is that?" I demanded.

"Up here." It was the weird bat. Lily and I exchanged an astonished glance.

"You... you can... talk?" Lily asked.

"Is that so unexpected? You two are talking."

"But you've never talked before."

"I never had anything worth saying, but if you are suggesting this house is in danger of being destroyed, I must agree it would be a good thing. It is terrible to watch this pantomime over and over. I've tried many a time to escape but I am nailed to this foolish board." It tried to flex its wings to demonstrate its helplessness.

I did feel sorry for it. Though similarly abandoned, at least we were free to move around. I knew there was a silver letter opener that had been dropped on the floor near the desk during the final struggle. I retrieved it, biting it in my red-felt mouth, and climbed up the rough stonework of the fire surround.

Looking down from time to time to gauge my progress, I saw Lily staring up at me with starry-eyed hero worship, which only made me more determined to complete my mission. I nearly fell as I tried to pull myself out and over the wooden mantelpiece. Lily gasped as I hung in the balance, but with a last burst of determination, I succeeded in cresting the top.

"This may hurt," I warned the bat.

"As I am no longer alive, that seems most unlikely, but it would be worth it to be free."

Clutching the knife awkwardly between my two padded paws, I exerted what strength I had to pry up the nails from the bat's hands, for want of a better word. My sturdy steel skeleton held me in good stead, and I gradually made progress, grunting and swearing a bit (for Peter had delighted in using forbidden words when his parents were not around, and I'd picked up one or two).

The first nail popped out, leaving the unfortunate creature swinging awkwardly from the second. I made quick work prying that one up too, and the bat fell, bumping its enormous nose against the mantel before landing in a sprawl on the carpet at the man's feet. He paid no attention, of course. Ghosts can be remarkably oblivious to anything which doesn't concern them.

Lily rushed to the bat's assistance, using her remaining arm to right it into a position from which it could fold up its wings.

"Thank you very much!" it cried, as I threw myself from the mantel, my stuffing softening my landing. "How delightful! May I have the honor of learning the names of my saviors?"

"I'm Lily and this is Teddy. Oh, and that's Sasha," Lily exclaimed, pointing at the kitten who had emerged from hiding because of its incurably catty curiosity.

"Very pleased to meet you! I am Tamzu."

Lily spread her flounced skirt in a curtsy, fluttering her long lashes. I grunted.

A chorus of voices arose in protest. The other animals had woken from their stupors and clamored to be released as well. A riot promised. There was no way I could free them all and what good would it do a zebra or deer head to be freed from their mounting anyway? They could hardly gallop away in their sadly reduced state.

"C'mon," I growled, ushering my small group away from the commotion.

Sasha and Tamzu followed me willingly out the library door, the bat waddling along the ground like a drunken duck. Lily lingered behind longest, torn between a tender desire to help the trapped animals while knowing there wasn't much to be done for them. The protesting voices faded as we moved away out of their sight.

"How delightful!" the bat repeated, stretching its wings. It gave little hops, squeaking and fluttering until it suddenly took off with a whoosh. It soared around the grand hallway, poking its head into corners, flying up and down the staircase, even momentarily hanging upside down from the crystal chandelier.

I watched in envy. What must it be like to soar, free of earthly bonds? I soon found out as it reappeared over my head and grabbed ahold of my shoulders before I had a chance to protest. It flew me round and round until I grew dizzy with the motion. I'd not enjoyed myself so much in ages. Not since Peter had gone. And what are toys meant for if not joy and fun?

A crusty laugh escaped me. I could see Lily watching from below, a delighted grin on her painted face. I struggled to look as dignified as possible in the circumstances. I had a reputation for seriousness to maintain, but giggles escaped me again and again. Tamzu was laughing too, a low, booming noise that rolled like the echoes of a drum off the walls of the house. As though the old place was waking up, its heartbeat sounding, returning to life. My spirit felt light, unburdened.

But then the phone rang again.

"Take me down," I ordered.

Tamzu released me onto the table. I hadn't replaced the receiver and yet there was no question the phone was ringing. I shivered. I'd been adamant we'd nothing to fear, but this was somehow eerier than the long-ago horror we'd endured.

"Hello?"

"Time issss running sssshort." *Click*.

"What's it about?" asked the bat, crouching on the floor near Lily and Sasha.

"Bunch of nonsense," I insisted. "Told us to find something in the basement or terrible things will happen but won't tell us who it is or what we're supposed to be looking for. It's a joke."

"I don't think so," Lily disagreed. "At least, I don't think we should take the chance. There's no one but us left to care for this house and our family. They gave us a home. It's the least we can do."

"Hmph," Tamzu puffed. "I was torn from my home and family and even my life. I don't owe those that did it a thing, but you freed me. You, I will help. Where's the basement?"

"Through here." Lily led the way to the back of the hall and the door to the kitchen.

We'd not ventured so far in ages. Everything was just as it was left, even the pumpkin Mother and the children had carved so joyously that last day. The grinning gourd had long since shriveled into a horrid caricature of its former self. Everything else edible had been eaten by vermin who found their way past the guardian who lurked under the iron beast of a stove. A long, flickering tongue tasted the air as we walked by, decided we were neither a danger nor particularly tasty and retreated back into the shadows.

Pausing at the closed door to the basement, Lily looked to me with confident trust. Grumbling, I shoved a stool over and climbed up to the knob. Like many in the house, it was glass, smooth and slick in my padded paws. It took me several tries but eventually I got it to turn. Unfortunately, I was leaning forward when the door swung away from me. I tumbled legs over head down the steps, landing in a heap in the dark at the bottom.

A harsh light appeared, a single bulb. Tamzu was swinging upside down from the long cord that controlled it, like the pendulum on the grandfather clock at the top of the second-floor landing. Lily and Sasha stood at the top of the stairs peering down at us. Supposing I was going to have to mount the stairs to retrieve them, I was relieved to see the bat fly up and bring them each down one by one, gently setting them beside me. The kitten immediately squealed off, gears whirring as she explored.

Looking at the jumble of junk and litter surrounding us, I wondered how on earth our oddball trio (or quartet if you included the kitten, which I was inclined not to since they weren't serious enough to be of any real assistance) was supposed to do any kind of practical or thorough search, especially when we had no idea what we were looking for.

"This is hopeless," I complained.

Lily started poking at things with her hand. "We can try at least. It's not like we have anything better to do with our time, do we? Let's keep an eye out for anything unusual."

"I'll do air reconnaissance." Tamzu took off overhead, circling around the immense space, stirring the dust with its generous wingspan. Its comically blunt head flipped from side to side as its oversized golden eyes scanned below.

I half-heartedly wandered around the vast cavity. It ran under the entire foundation, with massive columns spaced evenly to support the weight of the house above. The children had been afraid of it, so I'd never been down there before. It looked to be the last resting place of any old thing that hadn't found a use upstairs.

Lopsided chairs, a broken table, boxes grown grotty and green with age and the persistent damp. Trunks with lids too heavy for the likes of us to lift. Stacks of clothing, outdated but set aside in case they could be altered to suit current fashions. This was one of the many projects Mother used to talk about, always ambitiously planned with the best of intentions but rarely carried out. Another excuse for the rigid disapproval her husband showered her with.

At the bottom of one such pile, a long sock, once cream-colored but now gray with age, poked out. If I didn't know better, I could have sworn it moved, a sinisterly serpentine swish. Was this the kind of thing we were looking for? It was certainly unusual. Figuring I didn't have much to lose, I grabbed it between my paws and with much grunting and another curse or two, managed to pull it free.

It was a woolen sock, with red toe and heel and, bizarrely, two oversized wooden buttons sewn onto the bottom of the foot. It rose up like a cobra and nipped me on the nose with its red "mouth," cackling all the while. I dropped it hastily, backing away.

"It's a sock puppet," said Lily. "Mother made them once for the children. Remember?"

I did now that she'd reminded me. The children thrusting their arms deep into the stockings and using their hands to animate the cursed objects. I hadn't liked them then and liked it even less now that one had taken on a life of its own.

"Yesss, children," it hissed. "So eager to do my biddingsss."

"It was you!" I cried. "On the telephone. How? Why? Who?" I stammered, barely coherent in my astonishment.

"I have come back for you, Peter, and my dearest Amanda." The thing rubbed itself against Lily's cheek like an owner stroking a favorite pet. "Your father has summoned you and you obeyed."

I grabbed Lily's hand and pulled her away. "It's the man. He thinks we're his children."

It slid slinkily after us faster than we could retreat, stumbling over the dust-covered piles of clutter. Sasha appeared as a white fury, spitting and catching her claws in the tightly-knit wool. The puppet undulated violently, sending the kitten sailing off in a high arc. She landed with a sickening crunch on the unforgivingly hard floor as her key flew out from the hole in her back. Her whirring mechanism softly sighed and stopped.

The sock returned its attention to us, pursuing us around the piles of junk that threatened to block our movement at every turn. I might have outrun it, but Lily's stiff-legged gait was no match for its sinuous speed. I thrust her behind me, deciding to stand my ground and fight. It was simply a sock when everything was said and done, only soft wool and stitches. What harm could it do us?

I soon found out as it opened up its tail and swallowed me whole in the same way a stocking envelops a foot, an ankle, a calf. I cannot describe the feeling. None of us were alive or drew breath, and yet I felt exactly as I imagined the woman had as her husband throttled her in their desperate battle over the gun. My ideas grew confused. I became so sleepy, the idea of lying down where I was, ceasing all resistance, letting myself drift away seemed perfectly natural.

Just as I was fading out, the sock was pulled from my head with a *pop*, taking my loose eye with it, but it was a small price to pay to be free of that awful smothering sensation. Tamzu had come to my rescue, grasping the puppet with its clawed feet and carrying it toward the ceiling. The sock writhed, screeching curses. It managed to wrap its long length around the bat's wings, binding them and sending Tamzu plummeting to the ground. The bat hit headfirst, splitting open its head to reveal the white bone of skull beneath its fragile skin. Shocked by the impact, it let the sock go.

Once again, the puppet, the father's spirit, whatever you want to name it, turned its attention to us. The man had controlled his children with an iron fist, giving them life and taking it away, and he was no less obsessed with them in death. Useless to try and explain to him that Lily and I were merely animated toys. It should have been comical, seeing this sock with the big button eyes and red-grin mouth snaking toward us. I'd claimed I wasn't afraid of anything anymore, but I was terrified of this ridiculous, evil thing.

Tamzu recovered itself enough to lift from the ground, but the bat seemed dazed still, flying crazily in circles, knocking into the overhead bulb and sending it smashing into the ceiling. Sparks flew in every direction. Some landed in the piles of old clothes, smoldering. The chaotic distraction diverted the man's attention from us long enough.

"Come on," I whispered to Lily, dragging her over to the coal pile that dominated one corner of the cellar. I lifted her up and over the filthy stuff, toward the coal chute and moonlight. It was a steep climb and the doll was a deadweight, though she tried her best to pull herself along with one hand. Somehow we made it to the opening only to find our way blocked with a heavy iron grate.

The sound of coal shifting and sliding behind us told me the puppet had not given up its pursuit. Bracing myself against the walls of the narrow passage, I kicked out with one leg as hard as I possibly could and raised the grille enough for Lily to pull herself free into the cool autumn air. I did my best to follow, but just as I thought I was clear, I felt the sock twisting itself around my one still-dangling foot.

I turned, striking at it wildly with the other foot but only succeeded in knocking the grate closed on my leg. Now I was well and truly trapped. Lily appeared beside me with a sharp stick, poking it through the slots of the grate at the determined puppet. It grabbed it in its mouth, chewing through the wood like it was softened butter, all without loosening its grip on me. Lily wept in frustration while I swore.

All seemed hopeless until I felt hot breath on my neck. My head was engulfed by a mouth, spit-filled, nasty, and toothy, with a tongue rough as sandpaper. It twisted and pulled me back from the grille. I felt the soft stuffing and fur of my trapped leg tear and shred until only the strong steel armature was left, but I was liberated.

Whatever had me ran like the wind far from my enemy. After a rocky journey, I was spit out upon the ground where I lay staring up at two enormous, panting heads.

"Francis? Florence?" I asked in bewildered recognition. They were the enormous black mastiffs who had been the man's pride and joy. More beloved than his own children because they were more obedient. Beaten into submission in life, their earthly spirits were tied to the grounds just as the family was, as we were.

I realized in that moment we were all his prisoners: the toys in the nursery, the family, the dead beasts in the library, the dogs still patrolling the ground in their hereafter. The very house itself was held hostage to the man's evil influence. What level of deviltry must someone have achieved to wreak such havoc even after death?

I was weary, I was damaged, I was old, and I was very, very angry. I rolled over to see Lily in a similar state to my own, soaked with the saliva of the haunted hounds who had rescued us, but she had suffered no further injury. We reached out, paw to hand, momentarily relieved until we heard the sibilant voice.

"Francis.... Florence... where have you taken them?"

It was uncomfortably close. I had a vision in my head of that silly children's plaything slithering through the underbrush, unrelenting in its terrible purpose. Hysterical laughter bubbled below the surface.

"Where are we?" Lily whispered.

I recognized the place. Peter had loved to play here and often brought me with him. We had toy soldier battles in the overgrown grass and ate sandwiches perched on the grave markers. "It's the family cemetery."

"Oh, Teddy dear, do look." Lily cleared away a pile of bright red and orange fallen leaves to reveal two small stones etched with the simple words "Amanda" and "Peter." They were wedged between two larger monuments, one engraved "Mother" and one "Father." Somebody had taken pity on the woman and not buried her beside her husband. It gave me an idea, a story that Amanda had relished terrifying her brother with of the restless undead and what you must do to silence them at last.

"Florence, Francis," I called as commandingly as I could, not at all confident they would obey me, but they good-naturedly came over to us. I crawled to the man's grave, dragging my damaged metal leg behind me, and started pawing at the weeds and dirt, moving them to the side. One thing I remembered of these dogs is they loved any excuse to dig and that had not changed. They enthusiastically took over when they caught on, flinging dirt into our faces until Lily and I removed ourselves to a safe distance.

We kept a sharp ear out for the thing we knew was hunting us. The dogs were hardly quiet in their excitement, and it seemed inevitable the sound would attract the evil spirit. I could only hope the mastiffs would win this odd race against their former master.

The huge dogs were powerful and motivated. Maybe they smelt the intoxicating scent of bone and decay beneath their feet and were drawn to it. Long before I would have thought possible, bits of rotten wood joined the piles of dirt beside the open grave. As Lily and I rose to investigate, she screamed, a sharp sound quickly cut short.

I wrenched around to see what had happened. Lily's head was enrobed by the vile puppet wound round and round it, the two button eyes positioned as though to take the place of her own. Its red mouth stretched wide in a malicious smirk I will never forget, as Lily's body jerked and jumped. Though every instinct prodded me to limp to Lily's rescue, I turned away and hopped-skipped as best I could to the yawning hole the dogs had exposed in the earth.

The casket looked to be thin wood. No extra expense had been wasted on such a villain. It was rotten and weakened to such a degree that the dogs had easily broken through, exposing the body within from neck to thigh. Without hesitation, I leapt. Landing with a thump, I kicked at the corpse again and again with my skeletal leg, plunging the sharp steel rods that made up the core of me as deep as I could.

A hiss from above. The face of the thing looking down at me. It launched itself upon me as I kicked the man's chest one final time. The filthy sock landed on my face. I cried aloud, an incoherent note of horror and rage, as I flung it to one side where it landed, limp and still. Clutching my own chest where my beating heart would be if I had one, I tried to calm down. Forced myself to pick up the vile thing. It was nothing more than a piece of knitting now. Button eyes empty, red mouth slack. The man's vexed spirit was no more.

I was far too exhausted to pull myself from the hole. I lay back and gazed up at the night sky. There was an unnatural light coming from somewhere, reds and oranges. Dawn arriving at last, I thought. A fluttering movement over my head announced the arrival of Tamzu to pull me from the grave. The preserved skin on his forehead curled away from his wound, but he seemed otherwise unharmed.

We could not say the same for Lily. Her head was crushed into a thousand pieces. Not even her beautiful blue eyes had survived. How I mourned inconsolably over her I will leave to your imagination. The black mastiffs came and sat sphinx-like beside us, laying their giant heads on the ground in benediction at my suffering.

When some time had passed, my attention was drawn by a roaring noise. "What is it?" I asked, hardly expecting an answer or even wanting one, but the bat perched respectfully beside me answered.

"It's the house. It's being consumed by flames. My fault, I'm afraid. I am a clumsy fool."

"Don't be sorry. It's a good thing," I reassured it, struck by a thought, a possibility, an idea of my own. "Take us there. Please?"

I gathered up what was left of Lily in my arms. The bat grabbed my shoulders and flew high into the air as the dogs raced below us. And what a lovely flight it was through the cool night air that only turned to ash and flame as we neared the howling inferno.

"What now?" Tamzu asked.

"Throw us in."

"What? Oh... do you think? I see." The bat turned one quizzical, golden eye down to my own button one and winked as it flew swiftly into the heart of the flames.

The pain was brief but intense. Though we could not die, our physical selves could be destroyed just like the house and its inhabitants. The toys in the nursery. The glassy-eyed creatures from the library. The black hounds and the wind-up kitten. Tamzu and Lily and me. All perished and cleansed and restored again by fire.

We are each of us phantoms, our spectral shapes made whole. Together for eternity with Mother and the children without the evil that once haunted us and held us prisoner against our wills. Now we stay for the love which binds us here where even the house-that-was is but a ghost.

And we are no longer forgotten.

THE HILT WAS AN ELABORATE SWIRL OF A DRAGON
TOOLED WITH GOLD
AND THE BLADE WAS ETCHED
WITH FLAMES

Take My Hand at Midnight

I WAS MISSING POOR Tilda more than ever that morning. Her soft brown eyes which looked up at me so lovingly, her floppy leathery ears which flew like a bat's wings as she ran barking mad around the garden chasing the cat, the sharp tip-tap of her nails on the polished parquet floors of the Grand Hall. I missed stooping over to scoop her up in my arms and lug her up the stairs, her stumpy little legs too short to make easy work of the long climb. Scolding her when she was fussy with the food scraps Cook set aside for her. I even missed giving her a bath though she would wiggle and squirm so, I ended up nearly as wet as she did.

It felt like losing a part of my soul when Tilda went missing. I woke up one morning to find her absent from the wicker basket beside the fireplace in my bedroom. My door was closed, but I thought maybe the maid had accidentally let Tilda out when she came to lay and light a new fire for me as I slept. Thinking nothing of it, I dressed and went down to the breakfast room expecting to find my pet waiting in her favorite spot, under the table near my chair where she could snatch the treats I passed down to her from my plate, but she wasn't there.

Growing alarmed, I began to search the house. I'm not too modest to admit I was quite the favorite among the servants, so they quickly joined in the hunt. The head groundskeeper even organized his men into a search party of the gardens and park, though he always used to grumble at my little dog. I will admit she was often naughty and once dug up all the freshly planted tulip bulbs in the west garden. Father was still alive then and was furious, but Mother soon calmed him.

As penance, I helped to replant the bulbs, although the pattern of colors that year ended up being a jumble. Mother said she loved it. Looked like one of those modern paintings which were all the rage. Mother was like that. Always knowing what to say to smooth over troubled waters. Father adored her as did we all, and she adored him. Never a more suited couple as so many remarked.

His death two years previous had left a gaping hole in our lives, and then to lose Tilda only a few short months ago, although it seemed forever since I had last stroked her velvety brow, had been another crushing blow to me. I was almost a woman grown though, as Cook liked to remind me much too often, since I was then nearing my eighteenth year, so I kept my grief to myself so as not to burden Mother with any more sorrow.

Trying to shake off my melancholy thoughts, I went in search of Mother and found her as I expected in the library. It was Father's favorite room in the house, and since his death, Mother spent much of her spare time there going over the accounts and paging through the books they used to read aloud to one another, stopping often to discuss together this point or that, speculating where the plot might lead and whether the characters were acting wisely or quite, quite foolishly.

She was standing at the French doors that led out to the rose garden, watching the gentle drizzle falling steadily on the grey December morning. We would normally have had a thick blanket of snow upon the ground by this time, but that year, the weather played tricks on us, unseasonably warm and bright days followed by chilly, gloomy, rainy ones.

Her Irish wolfhounds, Connor and Tara, sat one on either side of her like over-sized bookends. Her favorite pair, they were allowed inside the house while the rest of the pack was confined to the kennels. Grandfather had bred wolfhounds all his life and had gifted his daughter a pair upon her wedding day. I couldn't remember a time when I didn't love the gentle giants, although when the day came for me to choose a companion of my own, I begged Mother to let me have a dachshund, a breed which had only recently come into fashion due to the Queen's love of them.

Ever indulgent, Mother gave in readily like the living angel she was. I wished I was more like her, but I took after Father, much to my chagrin. Tall and rangy, too tall and skinny for the current fashions, and my carroty hair did me no favors either. The other girls in the neighborhood teased me mercilessly about it, but Mother refused to let me try to dye it black again after one miserably failed attempt which turned it as purple as Cook's special mulberry jam.

Unlike me, Mother was tiny and tidy, with warm mahogany-colored hair which was her pride and joy and reached down almost to the floor on the rare occasions I saw it unpinned. She looked like a perfect porcelain doll posed quietly at the windows between her majestic canine companions, who could so easily have overpowered her were they not so well-trained.

She turned as she heard me enter and beckoned me come and join her, wrapping an arm around my waist companionably.

"Good morning, Katherine, dear. Rather a gloomy Christmas eve for us all, I'm afraid, but we shall bank up the fires brightly and light the candles on the tree to create our own good cheer, shan't we?"

"Of course, Mother. I can never be anything but cheerful as long as we two are together."

"And don't forget Mr. Horrock," she chided me. "We are three again now just as in the days when your dear father was still with us."

I stilled the protest that leapt to my tongue. In my opinion, my new stepfather should never even be mentioned within the same breath as my sainted father, but I knew better than to speak my thoughts aloud. Mother might be petite, but she ruled us all with a unique blend of gentleness and iron and did not take any disparagement of Mr. Horrock lightly.

"Don't forget Henry," I offered instead. "Though he must celebrate the holiday with his regiment, he is still as dear to us as if he were standing here beside us."

"Of course. My beautiful boy is never far from my thoughts. But what is this new sentiment? You and your brother have always butted heads like Paul and Matthew," she said with a smile, mentioning the two ornery rams who were always battling for supremacy over the ebon-faced flock of Suffolk sheep which roamed the gentle rolling hills on the east side of the estate.

"Absence makes the heart grow fonder." And in fact, I had never missed my dunderheaded brother more than I did then. He would never be mistaken for an intellectual and used to poke fun at my bluestocking ways, but he was tall and fit, solid as a rock and loyal to a fault. I wished with all my heart he was with us. I wouldn't be so afraid if such an ally was near at hand.

And I was afraid. I could no longer hide this awful fact from myself. I was terribly afraid and had been since the day Alfred Horrock proposed to my mother. Up until that time, I had paid him scant attention. Mother was a youngish and attractive widow left in charge of a considerable estate by the terms of my father's will. This made her a matchmaking target, and it was a common sight to see her at neighborhood parties seated on a sofa surrounded by gentlemen of all quality and ages vying for her attention.

I was so used to the sight, and so convinced Mother's devotion to her husband's memory would prevent her ever considering matrimony again, that I was shocked to my core when she informed me she had accepted a proposal. And nothing prepared me for the even greater shock of finding out Mr. Horrock was her intended.

How shall I describe him to you? A horrid little man, perhaps? That sounds impolite, I know. I try to give people the benefit of the doubt but from the time I first met him, I had never laid eyes on him again without feeling a shudder deep within my soul.

With his black hair slicked back tight with pomade to his whisper-thin waxed mustache, his fastidiously cared for hands waving fussily as he made some facile point or other in conversation, to his unceasing attention to every detail of his dress, he should have been the type that is easily dismissed. Just another of the drawing room fools which are found in plenty attending every polite society gathering.

And yet, there was a certain look in those icy-blue eyes when he thought nobody was watching, chilly and calculating. And the way his touch would linger a few moments too long when he helped me up the steps into the carriage or wrapped my shawl around my bare shoulders as we left the opera house. The little remarks, "All meant in fun, m'dear," that dripped from his pouty lips. I could not understand what Mother saw in him except he made her laugh, and she had not laughed much at all since Father passed over.

I'll admit he could be droll. He was an excellent mimic and often had company in stitches over his impersonations of various society figures. His political commentary was sharp and witty, and he was fond of making up limericks and cunning sayings that amused Mother. I think she missed the intellectual give and take she used to have with Father as most men did not take her views seriously.

Mr. Horrock paid her immense deference, and for a time I was appeased by that until I overheard him speaking of "his little woman" and her "dear sweet ditherings" to some of his cronies. To hear him speak so of a woman who was renowned among our circle for being better informed and better able to make cogent arguments for her positions on the issues of the day than many a man was galling beyond belief.

But while I seethed internally, Mother seemed content and her happiness was all in all to me. I determined to set aside my doubts and dislike and do what I could to welcome our new family member. But, oh, it was hard to watch as he attempted to take Father's place. Rearranging furniture in all the rooms to suit himself, aggravating our loyal staff with his petty complaints and constant requests, making plans for a ridiculous folly on the south lawn which would ruin the view. Mother humored him and made excuses for his behavior, considering none of it of as great a consequence as I did.

The only time she put her foot down was with Father's library. It remained exactly as it was on the day he died, and she asked Mr. Horrock to set up his own library in an unused parlor on the other side of the house instead. That was one of the times I saw his mask slip as he cajoled and teased her about her decree. Didn't she know the library was meant to be the headquarters of the Master of the house, he asked.

"Its master has left us, and I go there now only to remember and honor him," she replied, and for a moment, fury and loathing shone forth from her new husband's face as fiercely as the blaze in the fireplace where Mother sat gazing into the flames, a faraway look on her face. She may not have looked up in time to see the mask slip, but I did, and he saw that I did, and from that time, I was afraid.

He treated me as usual, but there was a tone to his voice that wasn't there before, harsh and warning. Warning me of what, I didn't know, but it frightened me. It was around the time of this argument about the library that Tilda went missing. My poor little dog had never taken to Mr. Horrock either and would bedevil him with barking and snarling whenever he entered a room. He would often snarl back at her, in jest, so he said.

I had no proof her disappearance was anything to do with him. She might have escaped the house and gotten lost or injured, but the falseness of his sympathy as I cried for her absence made me wonder. I could not decide if I disliked him so much because he was nothing compared to Father or if there was truly an evil hiding behind the smiling mask that was a danger to me and mine.

All in all, my heart was heavy and full of foreboding as I stood with Mother looking out at the dreary weather. She had not been well lately, which was unusual as her health had always been of the very best. I was worried and even wrote to Henry, imploring him to get leave to come home and visit us, but had heard nothing back from him. I felt very alone and impotent and at the mercy of whatever events might unfold without having any way to influence their outcome. Oh, to be a man, with a man's freedom and power. Then I might have found a way to thwart whatever plans the awful Horrock had in store for us.

Our reverie was interrupted by a sharp rap at the door, and Mr. Horrock himself poked his head in. "I thought I might find my two lovely ladies here."

Mother stiffened. She viewed Father's library as her special sanctuary, and only Henry and I were welcome there.

"I hesitate to intrude, naturally, but a large package has been delivered from France, and I did not want to deny you one moment of the delight such a present must incur."

"France!" I exclaimed. "It must be from Henry. Do let us go and see."

She smiled at my excitement and followed me gladly, her hounds trailing after.

In the Grand Hall, at the foot of our towering Christmas tree was a wooden crate with my name printed neatly on a large paper tag.

"Can I open it, Mother? Please?"

"I should make you wait for the morrow, but I can see the delay might make you ill. Woodrow," she called to our butler, "please have Jacob come in and see if he can open this for us."

The second footman came in and examined the package carefully then returned with some tools which made short work of prying off the top of the crate.

I darted forward to see a hessian-wrapped object resting in a sea of straw. My hand touched cold metal as I drew a sword out of a leather sheath. It was short, more of a dagger than a sword, and looked to be made for show rather than warfare. The hilt was an elaborate swirl of a dragon tooled with gold, and the blade was etched with flames.

There was a note in my brother's distinctive scrawl: *For K—thought you might enjoy something as sharp as your tongue. H.*

Mother laughed when I showed her the message. "Your brother understands you well."

And indeed, I was more thrilled than most girls I knew would have been to receive such a present. They would have expected perfume or fine lace from France, but I had always had a passion for the tale of St. George and the Dragon. Henry and I had often acted out the drama, me fencing with a stick from the garden while he growled and hissed at me fearsomely.

My eyes filled with tears at such a thoughtful gift, and my heart ached for him to be near to me once more. We had argued and fought all our lives, but I had never had a moment's doubt he would slay dragons for me as I would for him.

The sword was snatched from my hands by a well-manicured hand with a sniff of disdain.

"A highly inappropriate gift for a refined young lady. Your brother has a peculiar sense of humor. This is what comes from associating with whatever uncouth infantrymen he commands, I suppose. I've told your mother time and again the Army is no career for a gentleman and heir to an estate of this importance."

I clenched my fists to stop myself from striking his smug face. My brother had dreamed of being in the Army his entire life, and Father encouraged him, seeing it was his true passion. Henry had never been happier than he had since he received his commission. To endure that useless man belittling the dangers my brother faced for his country was intolerable.

Sensing my annoyance, Mother stepped in to prevent me disgracing myself.

"It is beautiful, Katherine. Would you like to take it up to your room where you can examine it in more detail?"

Still too angry to speak, I simply kissed her cheek and carried away my prize without a backward glance. I could feel *his* eyes on me as I climbed the stairs but refused to give him the satisfaction of acknowledging it.

Once safely in my room, I sank in the armchair by the fire and pulled the sword out of its sheath again to marvel at its beauty. I was no expert, but it looked finely tooled and detailed and must have cost Henry a tidy sum. As the estate was prosperous and Mother regularly sent him supplements to his Army pay, I was sure it caused no financial hardship for him, but I was moved, nonetheless.

It was by far the finest thing he had ever bought me, and touching something he had chosen especially for me and held in his own hands brought him closer. How I longed for those faraway days when we played together at slaying pretend dragons. I felt a real one had fallen in among us, and I did not know how best to defeat it alone.

Not wanting to allow myself to fall further into a funk, I decided to ride over to visit my best friend, Jessamyn. She and her family were our nearest neighbors since her father inherited Wilton Abbey from a distant cousin a few years past. We had bonded over our both being taller than average and having hair color that was out of favor, hers being as white blonde as mine was ginger. Though my mother never mentioned it, Mrs. Wilton spent a good bit of time lamenting to anyone who would listen about our unfashionable height and looks, speculating it would make it difficult if not impossible to land a worthy husband in spite of our private fortunes.

Jessamyn and I giggled over her mother's worries. We had long ago decided never to marry. We found we were sufficient just as we were and often daydreamed and schemed about growing old as two elegantly charming spinsters in a cottage near a quaint village where we could do good works and keep a menagerie of pets and maybe even some chickens in the garden.

I knew Jessamyn would be as interested in the sword as I was since she was a history and military enthusiast, so I changed into my warmest riding habit and saddled up Anna, the dainty chestnut mare Father had bought for me when I was learning to ride. The light rain had dwindled away leaving a clammy mist not pleasant to experience, but so glad was I to be away from the house and that man, I dawdled despite the inclement weather. We had ridden the path through the woods between the two houses so often, and Anna was so good natured a mount, I barely needed to guide her with the reins as we ambled along.

The hood of my woolen cloak protected me from the worst of the elements, but I was still damp and chilled by the time I rode up to the Abbey. A stable boy ran out to take Anna away to the stables as Jessamyn waved to me from her bedroom window on the second floor. She was flying down the stairs to greet me by the time the footman had relieved me of my dripping cloak.

"K! I was hoping you would come by today. Mama and Papa have gone visiting in the neighborhood, but I got out of it by pleading the headache."

"You look in the pink for one plagued by migraine, dear J," I teased her, well knowing her retiring nature which made it painful for her to visit with any but the closest of friends.

"It is much better," she agreed with that charming grin of hers which always disarmed me no matter how often I saw it. "But I'm more concerned about you. You look soaked through. Come up to my parlor. I've a fire lit, and you can change into a warm robe while Hester dries and presses your habit."

I still shared a lady's maid with my mother, but Jessamyn was thrilled to have been given one of her own on her eighteenth birthday a few weeks past. I knew she relished every opportunity of training her new servant. Indeed, Hester was such a fresh-faced, naïve country girl, still cheerfully learning the duties of her new station, that it was hard not to love her. She was around our own age and would have been living a very different life if the circumstances of her birth had been as ours, but she seemed to take it in good humor, being glad of the opportunity to earn extra wages for her family.

Hester fussed over me nearly as much as Jessamyn did. Between them, they got me out of my riding outfit and into one of Jessamyn's sensible woolen robes which she preferred to any other nighttime finery. We were soon settled into armchairs by the fire with cups of toasty hot cocoa and a plate of gooseberry jam biscuits. I pulled the dragon sword from its sheath and as I expected, Jessamyn's eyes kindled with excitement.

"How wonderful! Not suitable for combat, of course. Made for ceremonial occasions, I would think. Looks like a French design. And how fine the etching is on the blade, not to mention the elegant form of this dragon. It must have set Henry back quite a bit. The most my brothers ever give me is a new piece of ribbon or lace with which to redecorate my hats."

"Usually, that's what Henry sends me too. I have more French lace than I know what to do with. He must have been feeling guilty. I wrote to tell him of my troubles and ask him to come home, but perhaps he couldn't get leave and this is his way of making it up to me."

"Well, don't let Mama see it. She already thinks we are unnatural for our intellectual pursuits. She would find a weapon a terribly risqué thing for a young lady of station to own. How is your dear mother doing?"

"She seemed better this morning. More color in her cheeks. They were glowing quite pink and her eyes were bright."

"And Mr. Horrock?"

"As usual."

That was everything that needed to be said on that subject. Jessamyn had been the object of Mr. Horrock's attentions on more than one occasion herself and knew my own views well. She had often told me she feared for my virtue living under the same roof as such as my stepfather, but even I could not imagine he would attempt any assault on my person with my mother so close by.

I feared more the little acts of undermining I observed, countermanding my mother's orders to staff, slowly taking over as many of her tasks as she would allow. So far, she had maintained sole control of the estate's accounts, but I could foresee a day when he cajoled her into turning over management of those to him also.

Henry stood in line to inherit the estate upon my mother's death according to the terms set out in Father's will, but there was no reason to believe my mother would not live for thirty years or more and there was much Mr. Horrock might gain in that time by having a say in our affairs. And with Henry away following his career in the Army, and me with very little influence at all, I feared mother would fall more and more under his power.

Determined to shake off my megrims, I settled in to enjoy my visit with my friend. We shared neighborhood gossip and discussed the novel Jessamyn was reading. Though she was deeply versed in history, she could also never get enough of the latest sensational Gothic tales and loved nothing more than to regale me with the improbable plot twists and shocking developments therein.

I didn't mind. I enjoyed sitting and watching her, so animated, her deep blue eyes lit up with excitement, her rose lips forming the soft words in a low voice. These were the times I lived for, and I dragged my feet as much as possible to avoid returning home, even staying to partake of a light luncheon with the family when her parents and brothers returned from their visiting duties.

But knowing Mother would be expecting me for Christmas Eve dinner, I reluctantly took my farewell and mounted up for the ride home. The sun was already setting, and I barely made it home before darkness fell. I expected to find Mother waiting for me anxiously in Father's library and had prepared a sincere apology for worrying her, but the room was empty except for Connor and Tara, who ran to my side whining and barking.

I felt as though my heart dropped down into the soles of my riding boots at sight of them. Mother's dogs accompanied her everywhere. Even when she went out, they rode in the carriage and waited patiently with the grooms and horses for her. A dozen thoughts flew through my mind as I struggled to imagine what they were doing shut up in the library without her. Bidding the hounds to stay, I shut the door again and ran up the stairs to my mother's room.

I was met by old Dr. Payne and my fears multiplied.

"There you are, Katherine. You've been missed, naughty girl," he said, scolding me like I was still the infant he remembered holding on to my mother's skirt.

"What is it, Doctor? Is it Mother?"

"Come sit down a moment, my dear," he said, guiding me to the small chaise that sat upon the upstairs landing.

Numbly I sat, feeling unprepared for whatever news he had.

"I'm afraid your mother has taken ill. A dangerous fever. I've given her a tincture to try to draw it out, but I don't like the looks of it at all."

"But she'll be all right, won't she?"

"I wish I could say. These kinds of acute illness that appear so quickly can often have poor results. Maybe I shouldn't say so to you, but we have known each other all your life, haven't we? I suspect you wouldn't want me to sugarcoat the truth."

"No, I'd rather be...be prepared, I suppose. But surely you aren't saying she will die? It would be so unfair after losing Father, and she has always been the very picture of health."

"That was true until just lately. I have been concerned about how run down she looked the last few times I visited, and now this. She took your father's death hard. She may have suffered even more than we realized, and it has taken its toll on her. But let us not despair prematurely. I have some experience and skill, you know. I'm on my way out, but I'll send over a nurse to stay with your mother tonight. We should know by tomorrow whether the fever will break or not. Try to get some rest yourself. Your mother will need your strength and assistance to recover."

He gave me a fatherly pat on the shoulder and made his way down the stairs. I only vaguely registered him exchanging pleasantries with the butler as he left, my mind still reeling from the frightening news. My body shook so, it took me some time to collect myself and venture into Mother's room.

Walking in quietly so as not to disturb her, I saw her devoted maid, Eileen, leaning over her and bathing her face with cool water. I crept close to the other side of the bed and picked up one of Mother's hands in my own. Her skin was burning hot, and the pink flush I had noticed earlier in the day had become an ugly red stain upon her porcelain skin. Perspiration soaked her beautiful hair which had been braided and coiled up on her pillow to keep its warmth away from her. I prayed they wouldn't have to cut it off as often happened when patients suffered from fever. That would be a blow as it was her one true vanity.

"Where is Mr. Horrock?" I whispered to Eileen.

"No one knows, Miss Katherine. He ordered the carriage for the station and boarded the train for London. Didn't tell no one where or why he was going. And on Christmas Eve of all things. Mrs. Horrock was that put out and fretting so, I'm afraid we didn't realize she was really ill until she fainted dead away in the library and those hounds started in to howling like demons. I'm terrible sorry, Miss. I seen how flushed she was but thought she was just in a bother about the Master."

"It's not your fault, Eileen. I noticed it, too, but mistook it for a sign of renewed health after how pale she has been of late."

"Miss Katherine, whatever shall we do if…if…"

"Do not say it aloud. Even though it be in our thoughts, we must keep faith and pray it does not come to pass. Time enough to speak of it should such a calamity occur, but Mother is the strongest woman I know. I choose to believe she will rally, and we'll all ring in the New Year together."

I pulled up a chair and sat with Mother late into the evening. Eileen brought me tea and sandwiches, but I could eat little. A competent nurse arrived and encouraged me to get some rest, but I couldn't bear the thought of going to sleep and waking to the worst of news, so instead I lingered as we took turns exchanging the wet cloth on Mother's forehead with fresh ones and bathing her fevered body to try and bring down her temperature and soothe her restlessness.

Sometime during the evening, Eileen led Tara and Connor in. They had taken to howling in the library without end and none of the staff had the heart to banish them to the kennels. The dear ones seemed to understand something serious was afoot and lay down quietly one on either side of where I sat. And so, we three kept vigil.

The clock had just struck the half hour after eleven when Mother suddenly awoke and started speaking. Her voice was so hoarse and faint, I could barely make out the words though I leant in as close as I dared.

"The...will...the will..."

"The will, Mother? Whose? Father's? It is safe at Mr. Avery's office, isn't it?" I asked, mentioning the family lawyer.

"Brought home...he...wanted to...read it."

"He? Mr. Horrock? Why? What business is it of his?"

"Henry...He wanted to make sure...Henry was taken...care of."

"Why wouldn't he be? We all know the terms of the will. Mr. Avery explained it to us clearly after Father's death."

Mother shook her head and raised one hand weakly as though to halt my questioning.

"Don't...don't...make sure it's safe...library..."

And with that, her hand fell limp and I feared the worst. But the nurse came over and felt for her heartbeat and smiled at me reassuringly.

Relieved of that worry for the moment, an uneasiness came over me as I considered what I had learned. An insistence on seeing the will. Mother's declining health. Mr. Horrock's mysterious trip to London. None in and of itself sinister, but put together as a chain of events, they filled me with disquiet.

Telling the nurse I was going to my room to rest, I instead ran down the stairs with the hounds close at my heels. With Mother confined to bed, they seemed to have decided to turn their attention to me instead, and I must admit it was a comfort to have their reassuring presence near me to ease my fears.

We entered the library and I closed the door behind us. Gas lighting was common in the city but had not reached us yet out in the country, so I lit as many candles as I could so that I might see better what I was doing as I searched. I gathered from Mother's ramblings that the will had been brought to the house and was in the library somewhere. It was obviously disturbing her mind. If I could find and bring it to her, it might give her some ease.

I first checked the safe. Father had entrusted me with the combination years ago and Mother had never changed it. I looked through the papers within carefully but did not find the will. Next, I went through the desk and its drawers. It didn't take long. Mother always kept the accounts meticulously, and the estate documents were organized and tidy. I was soon satisfied the will was not among them. I proceeded around the room, searching methodically into as many nooks and crannies as I could with no success.

The mantel clock read a few minutes to midnight when I sat down in one of the worn leather chairs by the fire, at a loss as how best to proceed. Exhausted from the day's events, I rested my head against one wing of the chair. The next I knew was the sound of the French doors being blown wide open by a strong gust of wind as the clock chimed midnight. The door catch had never worked properly so I wasn't surprised, but I almost fainted when I heard a voice behind me as I shut and latched the doors.

"Hello, Kitty Kat."

Only one person ever called me by that silly name.

"Henry! Whatever are you doing here? I thought you couldn't get leave. And that beautiful sword you sent to me."

He was in shadow as the candles had all blown out from the wind. I fumbled around for the matches as he answered.

"Did you like it? I thought you might. I came because I wanted to see you and Mother. Where is she?"

I managed to light a candle and held it up so I could see him better although it was still too dark to see clearly. He wore his uniform, but it looked dirty and torn. I was surprised to see him so as he always prided himself on turning out smartly when not on the battlefield. Even more shocked was I to see his right leg bound up with bandages.

"You've been hurt!"

"It's nothing. 'Tis but a scratch," he added with a smile.

"Come closer, brother. May I not embrace you after so long apart?"

"Best not. This wound of mine is still tender. But you haven't answered me. Where is Mother?"

"She is terribly ill, a raging fever. Her skin burns so hotly, I do have such fears. Thank God you are come home."

"I am surprised you left her side."

"She is fretted about Father's will. She told me it was here in the library so I've been searching to try and ease her mind, but I can't find it anywhere."

"Have you tried the books?"

"Where would I start?" I said, waving the candle around at the bookshelves which lined every free bit of wall space in the room. "It would take ages to look through them all."

"Use your head, Kitty Kat. Which book would she have picked?"

I thought back to the hundreds of times I'd walked into the library to find Mother and Father, heads together over a book, reading snippets aloud to one another. They read widely and voraciously. There were few books on the shelves that one or the other of them had not read cover to cover. Of all the authors they read, they did have one favorite they returned to again and again. Sir Walter Scott and his romances. He was such a favorite, they had named Henry after a character in one of his novels.

"*Guy Mannering*!" I exclaimed, going to the exact spot where I knew it to be shelved. I pulled down the three volumes that made up the novel and saw immediately a thick wad of papers which had been folded and placed into the middle of the second volume. Unfolding them quickly, I confirmed it was indeed Father's will.

"Henry!" I called triumphantly. "You have proven your intelligence after all. Who would've known you would come to my assistance to help me puzzle out the answer?"

In my enthusiasm, I rushed toward where he was standing so still, holding the candle before me, only to stop short in shock. He was as pale as I'd ever seen him and his beautiful rich mahogany hair, so like Mother's, had turned pure white. I also noticed the dogs were still asleep by the fire. They had never woken in all this time, not even to welcome Henry home.

"I will return again when you are in need, dear sister," he whispered as the candle guttered and flamed and then went out. I came over faint and must have dropped down into the chair where I had been resting before, because when I came to, there I was.

"A dream. It was only a dream," I reassured myself. But then I felt a hard object in my hand and leaning over to the light of the fireplace, saw that I held the Scott volume with the will pressed between the pages. All confusion, half dead from exhaustion and shock, I roused the dogs and returned to Mother's room. The nurse informed me there had been no change.

Mother was sleeping and seemed very far away, but I whispered to her all the same. "Don't worry, dearest. I found the will. I'll keep it safe until you're better."

I did not think she could hear me, but then she reached out and took my hand lightly and a smile flickered across her face ever so briefly. I prayed she understood, and it would help bring her some peace.

The nurse encouraged me again to rest and this time, I followed her advice. Still shaken from the weird events in the library, I took the dogs with me to my room, their quiet loyalty comforting. I didn't think it possible I would sleep, but I must have dropped off because I was awoken by the grandfather clock in the hall striking the three o'clock hour. I pulled the covers closer against the night chill and was drifting back off when I heard the doorknob to my room turning. I quickly lit a candle just in time to see my stepfather's face peering into the room.

"Why, you're awake! I thought you would be sound asleep by now."

"As you can see, I am not," I said coldly. He had never entered my bedroom before and I wanted no new precedent set, but I was too curious not to engage him in conversation. "I am all amazement. The servants are under the impression you had journeyed to London today."

"A swift visit on business. I had planned to stay overnight, but dear Elizabeth," he said, referencing his wife and my mother, "was so upset to think I would miss any part of the Christmas festivities, I decided to hasten back and surprise her. Think what a shock it was to me to be informed she is so gravely ill. I looked in to see if you needed any comfort, my dear, and to assure you that come what may, you will always have a father in me."

"I presume you mean well, Sir, but my father is dead, while my mother still lives, and we must pray fervently for her return to full health."

"Of course, of course. Life without my love would be a poor thing indeed. But while she is recovering, there will be estate business to contend with. I must make sure that our affairs and documents are in order. The nurse was telling me Elizabeth was fretting about your father's will. You must help me search for it so we may ease her mind. Unless you have already discovered it?"

I refrained from glancing to my nightstand where I had secreted the will at the back of a drawer. "No. I did go down and search but could find nothing. I was planning to look further in the morning when there was more light to see by and I was better rested."

"Found nothing then. Are you sure?" he said, stepping farther into the room and closer to my bed than I liked.

I leapt from the other side of the bed, snatching up my robe and hugging it to me. Connor and Tara, who had been watching our conversation from under their twitching bushy brows as they lay by the fire, jumped to their feet and advanced upon him, growling in the low, scratchy sound that warned they meant business.

Mr. Horrock backed away as I answered. "Quite sure. Now if you don't mind, the dogs and I need our sleep so we may wait upon Mother refreshed."

Giving a last look of frustration toward the hounds, he turned a shallow smile on me. "Of course, my dear. A trying day for us all, I am sure. We'll talk on the morrow."

Once he departed, I ran over and locked the door then dropped to my knees, hugging Connor and Tara close to me. "Thank you, thank you, darling ones," I said, dropping kisses on their shaggy heads.

They returned to their cozy spot by the dying embers of the fire as I got into bed, but sleep eluded me as the upsets of the day played over and over in my mind. Finally, as dawn broke, I gave up the effort and rose, dressing in a plain woolen gown.

My eyes lingered a moment on the finely made dress my Mother had ordered for me for our Christmas festivities. With its deep forest green velvet skirts and white chinchilla trim, it was a special ensemble for what should have been a special day. And now, instead of joy and excitement, I was filled with grief and worry. A far cry from any other Christmas day I had yet spent in my life.

I unlocked my door and peered out cautiously. There being no one in sight, I ran the dogs down the stairs and for a short walk in the garden, stopping in the kitchen only long enough for them to wolf down their breakfast as Cook wept and wrung her hands and embraced me not a few times in her anxiety over Mother's health. Promising to send down a fresh report, I took Connor and Tara with me back upstairs, unwilling to part with their protection while I was so unsettled.

I entered Mother's room to find a new nurse in charge while Eileen looked on jealously, but no other changes. Mother's skin still burned to the touch, and she seemed farther away from me than ever. I longed to be able to talk to her. To discuss the strange dream I had in the library and to share my worries about Henry and about Mr. Horrock. I felt very young and alone in the world.

As though a genie had been listening to my thoughts, the door flew open, and Jessamyn rushed in followed more sedately by her mother. Overcome with joy to see my dearest friend, I burst into tears and collapsed in her arms.

"What nonsense!" Mrs. Wilton exclaimed, shooing us both out the door. "Such an uproar will do your mother no favors."

She escorted us down the stairs and to the breakfast room where a full breakfast was laid out in chafing dishes along the side table. To my surprise, Mr. Wilton and Jessamyn's brothers, Adam and Geoffrey, were there and already digging into the bountiful spread.

"I couldn't decide between spending Christmas morning with my family or coming over to visit you right away after we heard the news, so we decided to do both. I hope you don't mind, K?" asked Jessamyn.

I could only smile at the lively scene, relieved beyond measure that I didn't have to face Mr. Horrock alone. He strode into the room at that moment, looking taken aback at the unexpected company but shaking hands in a false "hail fellow, well met" fashion with Mr. Wilton. The two men engaged in a long-winded political debate which left the rest of us free to talk amongst ourselves.

Geoffrey and Adam gulped down their food, then took the dogs out to the garden for a romp, the weather having turned sunny and warmer again. Mrs. Wilton busied herself with perusing the pages of a fashion magazine as she planned Jessamyn's wardrobe for the London season. Jessamyn and I held hands under the table as we picked at our food. We soon excused ourselves and escaped to the library where I reported to her my dream of the night before.

"Oh, Katherine!" she exclaimed, stricken. "Poor Henry! It is just like the visitation of the ghost of Desdemona's fiancé in my latest novel. Do you think—"

"Do be quiet, Jessamyn!" I said, truly angry with her, something that rarely happened as we were so in sympathy as a rule. "This isn't one of your silly novels."

She withdrew so sharply and looked so hurt that I immediately regretted my reaction. I reached for her hand and gave it a kiss in apology. "I'm sorry, J. It's only I'm so worried about Mother that the thought anything might have happened to Henry is too much to bear."

"Of course, dearest. It's I who should apologize. You're right. This isn't something happening in a book. It was thoughtless of me. I'm sure it was just a dream, as you said. I dream the most absurd things all the time. Why the other night, I dreamt Papa turned into a pumpkin and launched himself from a cliff only to change into an eagle in flight. Isn't that droll?"

I squeezed her hand and smiled, all forgiven on both sides. It was always so with us. On the rare occasions we fell out, it never lasted long, our bond being too close to sever so easily.

"But you must admit this business about the will is sinister," she said. "What interest could Mr. Horrock have in it if the property is to pass to Henry anyway? And I have to ask if he would benefit from your mother's death since the timing seems suspect."

"My understanding is she is leaving him a reasonable inheritance from her own money that she brought into her marriage with Father, but of course, its value is nothing like what the estate will generate over time."

Jessamyn hesitated before plunging ahead. "I know you don't want to think about it, but if Henry should pass on before he has his own family and heir, what would happen then?"

"Mr. Avery explained it to us. If Henry dies without issue, the estate will pass to me. The same as if Henry were to...to die before Mother."

"So, if they were both out of the way, you would inherit a large estate, and you are still underage. That would mean a guardian would be appointed, and who better than your mother's husband?"

We looked at each other in horror.

I shook my head. "We are letting ourselves get carried away and as hysterical as one of those brainless heroines in your romances. People come down with the fever all the time and I have to believe Mother will weather this crisis. And we would surely have heard something from Henry's regiment if he had been injured. They send such news by wire these days."

"Unless the wire was intercepted!"

"What are you saying? That Mr. Horrock has a plan to ensure the death of all my remaining family in order to gain control of my fortune upon inheritance?"

"Maybe. Perhaps that's why he wanted to see the will for himself. To confirm the property would pass to you in those circumstances. What if he went to London on his flying visit to consult with a lawyer about gaining guardianship over you?"

"Maybe and perhaps and what if. We are conjuring up a fairytale out of a series of events that are most likely entirely unrelated. You're supposed to be comforting me, not filling my head with conspiracies and fear."

She wrapped her arms around my waist and pulled me close. "You're right. I have no place making such conjectures. Your mother will be well, and Henry will write you one of his indecipherable letters, and Mr. Horrock can go jump in a lake."

I smiled weakly at her attempt to divert my spirits.

"Come," she said, taking my hand, "the sun has decided to bless us today. We will take a walk around the gardens to clear our minds and blow the cobwebs of doubt away."

And so we did, reveling in the rare midwinter warmth and taking it in turn to recite our favorite poems and sing the slightly naughty songs that Jessamyn's brothers had taught us. We returned to the house as lunchtime neared, reluctant to leave the contentment of our own companionship but knowing Jessamyn's family would be anxious to return home to celebrate the rest of Christmas day.

Christmas Day, I thought as I watched their carriage disappear down the long drive. *And as an unhappy a one as I ever hope to celebrate.*

The wolfhounds and I returned to Mother's bedside where I fell into a doze, still tired from my interrupted night's sleep. I was awakened by Dr. Payne bustling in to fuss about with Mother, feeling her pulse and preparing more tinctures for the nurse to administer.

"How is she, Doctor?"

"Ah, you're awake. I disliked to disturb you. I believe I see some small improvement from last evening, but it is too soon to say whether this means the fever will break or not. The longer she is in this state, the more I fear for her. These brain fevers sometimes leave the body intact but not the mind. You must prepare yourself for all eventualities. I will speak to Mr. Horrock on my way out."

He took my hands in his.

"Take heart, my dear. In all truthfulness, I did not expect her to last the night. That she did should give us reason to hope."

I nodded, my heart too heavy to speak. The rest of the evening passed slowly. Mother was restless from time to time but mostly was so quiet that more than once I pressed close to her to reassure myself she still held breath.

Cook sent up a plate of food for the nurse and myself and bowls of meat for the dogs. We ate in a companionable silence, though I was yawning almost too often to chew. I finally acquiesced to the nurse's attempts to send me away to my bed. After a short turn around the garden with Tara and Connor, we trooped up to my room where I carefully locked my door before falling into bed.

My dreams were confused, full of Mother calling my name and Henry as I had seen him last, ghostly pale with that shock of white hair, and then a sharp tap-tap-tap sound I couldn't understand until I awoke and realized someone was throwing gravel from the drive against my window. I lit a candle and glanced at my watch on the bedside table. Not long until midnight. The witching hour again. I shivered as I climbed from my bed donning my robe and slippers.

Gathering my courage, I opened the casement window and leaned out to see Jessamyn standing in the drive in her riding habit and cloak. She waved at me and made short work of climbing the old elm tree that grew too close to the house providing the perfect stairway to my room.

This wasn't the first time she had visited me secretly on a lark, but never so late at night before and never by herself. It was usually her brothers who egged her on, and they would all come visit, us hoarsely whispering and muffling our laughter so as not to get caught. We thought it the height of naughtiness playing cards or telling bad jokes without the grownups knowing anything about it, though I sometimes wondered if Mother was aware but turned a blind eye to our innocent fun.

I couldn't help scolding Jessamyn this night as I helped her in through the window. "What on earth, J? Don't tell me you rode all this way by yourself? And where is Kimmie?" I asked, looking out the window for her bay mare.

"I took her round to the stables, of course. It is far too cold to leave her outside. One of your stable boys was most helpful."

"Jessamyn! If one of the stable boys knows, all of the servants will hear of it."

"What does it matter? Is it so strange I would visit my friend to comfort her when she has such trouble?"

"At this time of night? And alone? I can't believe you rode all that way by yourself in the dark."

"It's so clear tonight, and the moon is full. It was wonderful! I should ride at night more often. I felt free as a bird in flight." She started twirling around the room, her cloak billowing around her and knocking over half the trinkets on my vanity table.

"Hush! Do you want to wake the whole household?" I clutched at her to stop her wild dance. We stood thus listening, relieved when all remained quiet without.

She shed her cloak, pulling a small package from the pocket. "Besides, I forgot to bring you your Christmas present this morning, and Christmas Day is almost over."

I couldn't help but laugh at her childlike enthusiasm as she clapped her hands and bade me open the gift. Pulling off the gilded paper, I found a box, within which was nestled a darling gold bangle for my wrist. Putting it on, I held it up to the candlelight to admire its shine and shimmer before throwing my arms around her in thanks.

"We must retrieve yours from under the Christmas tree," I said. "If we are very quiet, we may get it without being caught."

As we turned to essay our secret mission, giggling softly, I saw her eyes widen as my own must have when we heard a rustling noise outside. We clasped hands as the doorknob rattled softly. Connor and Tara came to life, growling, and the rattling stopped.

"Stay here," I instructed Jessamyn. Before she could stop me, I stepped to the door and unlocked it as quietly as I could. I slowly cracked it open in time to see the door to my mother's room close. Worried Mother was worse and the doctor had been called, I rushed across the hallway and flung open the door impetuously, only to be met with an astonishing sight: Alfred Horrock standing at my mother's bedside and pushing a pillow down over her face.

Rage such as I had never before experienced boiled up inside of me at this villainy. How dare he, he who was not fit to even touch the hem of her skirt, think that he might wield the power of life and death over her. I ran at him screaming like a banshee, but his reflexes were quick and the blow he dealt to my cheek hard enough to crush me to the floor.

He bent over me with a fury in his eyes that left no doubt he would have struck me again and again had not Jessamyn appeared like an avenging goddess, wielding the dragon sword before her and chopping about her like a madwoman. As the dogs also joined in the fray with gnashing jaws, it was all Horrock could do to extricate himself from the onslaught without serious injury.

However, he was as determined and desperate as any cornered animal would be. He bullied his way through the chaos and reached the bedroom door with my band of vigilantes giving spirited chase. I leapt up to follow, scarcely believing the toffee-nosed little man could move so quickly. I was in despair of us catching him when suddenly Henry appeared from a shadow on the landing.

Caught off guard by the sudden apparition, Mr. Horrock tripped and fell, plummeting down the long staircase to land in a broken heap at the feet of a shocked nurse, who promptly dropped the tray of tea she was preparing to carry upstairs. She reached down to check for signs of life, but it was obvious from the way his limbs splayed out unnaturally, like a marionette with its strings cut, that he had breathed his last.

I looked around for Henry, but he was gone again. Another hallucination? But no, I looked into Jessamyn's eyes and knew she had seen him, too. I felt numb at the sudden turn of events and unable to truly take in the implications of this second unexpected appearance of my brother at a time and place where he should not be.

The nurse bustled up the steps as Eileen came out into the hallway to investigate the commotion. Between them, they ushered Jessamyn and I back to my room and plied us with hot tea and brandy as they wrapped us up in downy quilts to help quell our shivering. We held hands quietly, not speaking, and so the police inspector found us when he arrived to take charge.

We explained what we had seen. A murder thwarted. The attempted escape. An accident at the top of the stairs. But we withheld mention of Henry. Neither the nurse nor Eileen had talked of seeing him, so we felt safe to leave out that part of our tale. What more natural than a man in fear of prison, or worse, should stumble and fall in his mad rush to flee?

We could tell the inspector found our accusation of attempted murder difficult to swallow. *Two hysterical young girls* was what he so obviously thought that he might as well have shouted it aloud. Tired and shocked, we cared not whether we were believed. We stuck to our story and were vindicated when a sergeant brought in a diary they had found hidden in Mr. Horrock's room detailing his schemes.

After that, they let us go to sleep, tucked up with extra hot water bottles and blankets in my bed. Jessamyn wrapped her arms around me and we fell asleep thus, not waking until the thin morning sunshine streamed through the window.

The rest of that day was full of too many emotions to fully describe. Horror and anger at Mr. Horrock's treachery. Relief he was no longer able to hurt us. Sorrow at Henry's second visitation as I slowly came to accept it meant he had moved beyond the veil and I would not see his earthly self again. Joy when Mother revived enough to hold my hand and speak my name.

Jessamyn's family arrived, and Mrs. Wilton, after giving her daughter a tongue-lashing for scaring them all half to death by her disappearance, proved her worth by taking over many of the duties I was too numb or inexperienced to see to. I mostly sat with Mother as she slowly improved throughout the day. We kept the news of Mr. Horrock's villainy and death from her until she was stronger.

How I would ever inform her of Henry's passing, I knew not, but was glad to defer it to another day.

The Wiltons offered to stay the night or take me home with them, but I had a yearning to be alone after the turmoil of the last days and wanted to be near at hand to keep an eye on Mother. Even Jessamyn's tenderness felt too much to bear against the rawness of my feelings. Besides, I had a plan, one last task I felt I must perform.

I sat up in my room by the fire until a few minutes to midnight, then journeyed down the hall with the dogs padding along behind like silent witnesses. I didn't know if Henry would come to me no matter what room I was in, but I knew where I desired to see him if it was to be for the last time: his bedroom, kept exactly as he had left it by a doting mother and sister. It was an endearing mix of the childish and adult, bird's nests, animal bones, and school medals next to some of his favorite books and the numerous nature journals he had kept in that funny script of his.

I had no doubt he would appear. These things always happened in threes, and I felt in my heart he wouldn't leave me without a proper farewell. I caught a movement out of the corner of my eye as the hall clock chimed twelve times and turned to face him.

"Hello, Kitty Kat," he said with that crooked smile of his I knew so well.

Tears welled up in my eyes. Moonlight flooded the room through the windows and for the first time I could see him clearly. Or rather, see clearly that I could see through him as though he was only a faint echo of his former self.

"Henry, dear. Have you come to say goodbye?"

"I'm afraid so. How is Mother?"

"She's better. Dr. Payne has hopes of her. We won't tell her about Mr. Horrock or... or you until she is stronger."

"I understand. You will both be better off without that man."

"Yes. Thank you for that, Henry."

"I promised you I would return when you needed help, but now I must go."

"I hate to think of you being all alone."

"I won't be. Father and the grandparents, and oh so many of my friends and comrades in arms are there. And look who I found," he said, bending over to pick up something at his feet.

When he stood again, there was Tilda, my Tilda, squirming in his arms, barking joyously to see me. The wolfhounds who had been dozing lazily, unconcerned or unaware of a ghostly presence to this point, lifted their heads and sniffed the air, turning their heads to the side in puzzlement before deciding there was nothing there and closing their eyes again.

I had been brave up to this point and held back my tears, but seeing my little dog again, pressed close to my beloved brother's heart and knowing they were reunited beyond where I could reach, with Father and so many others, I couldn't help but sob, a wracking, painful sorrow searing through me.

"Don't cry, dear sister. One day we will be reunited, for we never grow older or know pain or sorrow here, and we wait most patiently for the next arrival. But you have many years to live before I shall see you again. For me, it will be but a moment, but for you, it may seem a long time. Fill the time with as much of joy and laughter as you can. Do you promise?"

"I promise," I barely choked out, but it seemed to satisfy him.

"And one last thing before I go."

"Yes?"

"It was me that poured itching powder all over your gown for the Greyson ball."

"Why you..." I said, half-laughing, eyes so water-filled that I didn't even see the moment when he and Tilda faded away into memory.

And so, dear reader, there ends my tale. It is not one I have ever shared in full before with anyone but my own dearest Jessamyn. Though pained by Henry's passing, she was thrilled to be part of a real-life ghost story, and our own story as it was written came closer to our daydreams than we ever dared hope.

Mother recovered from her fever, but the news of Horrock's betrayal on top of Henry's death proved too much for her. She died, I think, of a broken heart a few short years later and the estate passed to me. A large responsibility for one so young, but Mother spent her last months patiently teaching me what I needed to know. I have a sensible head on my shoulders and with our lawyer's guidance, I was soon running affairs as smoothly as my dear mother and father before me.

Being a wealthy young debutante drew men to me like flies to honey in spite of my carroty hair, and it took much tact and determination to fend them off. Jessamyn had a more difficult time managing her mother's matrimonial ambitions, and many stormy scenes ensued until the day she showed up at my door with a carriage full of her clothing and knick-knacks and never left again.

Her family pleaded with her and finally cut off most contact except for her youngest brother, who viewed our rebellion against societal expectations with the greatest amusement and pleasure. Our living arrangement was viewed as eccentric at best and kept the neighborhood gossips busy with speculation, but we didn't care. As long as we were two, with our own interests, charities, and menagerie of pets which grew exponentially year by year, we were content.

And so we come to today, when I thought to finally write down this tale because I sense my time in this world grows short. Soon, the midnight chimes will call my name and I must answer. My beloved J has gone on before to let the others know I am coming. I long to see their dear faces again: Mother, Father, Henry, and so many more. Even little Tilda, Connor and Tara, and all of the other animal companions recorded in my memory book.

And standing before them all, I will see her shining face, smiling that charming grin that is my favorite thing in all the world, holding open her arms to welcome me. I will take her hand in mine, and I will be home, at last.

Part 2: Fairy & Folk Tales

MISTRESS
HAS ALWAYS BEEN
and
ALWAYS WILL BE

A Tail

Don't none of us, nay not even the eldest of us all—that would be my very own self—remember a time before Mistress. Mistress has always been and always will be.

Eternal like the hungry fire in the hearth in front of which she kneels and scrapes the ashes, defying those flames that would nip out at us and singe our fur if we were to be so foolish as to get too close. But Mistress has no fear of such and only laughs if the fire gets fresh with her. Such a lovely soft noise her laughter, like the fairy bells we hear when we venture as far as the meadows on a rare summer day's adventure.

We love to hear her pretty, tinkling laugh above all other sounds in the world and willingly spend many an hour prancing around and playing the fool to tease her. We fetch and carry what we can for her, too weak to be of as much help as we would want. Still, Mistress loves us for trying to make her burdens lighter. She brings us crumbs, tends to our hurts if that ugly cat snags us by the tail for amusement, and cuddles us close when she weeps in the night.

She has much to weep of, treated cruel and made to do the humblest of chores from sunup to sundown every day. Her hands are raw and red from the washing. Her back pains her so, she groans when she rises from the rude bench where she sits to do her peeling and chopping. She squints and rubs her eyes made sore from the close needlework that is piled high always in a basket of mending by her side.

Who works her so hard as though she were no better than the oxen plowing up the fields? Those three, The Others. They come in, all a bustle and loud chatter, and we must scurry and hide quick as quick, peeking out fearfully to watch them abuse her and call her that hateful name that makes her cry. We never use the name, not even amongst ourselves. To us, she is Mistress, goddess and protector of all our kind.

I grow ever older, am ancient now. New generations will soon take my place, so I make sure to pass down the old, old tale so it will never be forgotten.

A tale of a dreadful night when all in a blinding light that did make our eyes smart and water, a mighty demon appeared where we were playing with Mistress by the hearth as she petted so sweet and gentle with us.

The demon laughed and danced and sang and poked at Mistress with an evil-looking stick. Weird words were spoken, and sparks flew about.

We didn't like it one bit and wanted so to help Mistress, but we are only very small, insignificant. What could such as we do to help her? We watched in horror as the ash-grey dress we loved so dear turned as blue as the sky on a bright summer's day. It twinkled with a thousand menacing stars, its skirts so wide we could not reach her and were swept away into the corners of the room when we tried.

Hateful thing. It made Mistress a stranger to us. And yet, how she laughed and twirled and primped, caught by the demon's spell. Her beautiful golden hair flew around her head like a whirlwind, caught up with flowers and jewels until it rose high above her sweet face. Her tiny feet sparkled as they were imprisoned in such unusual bindings as we had ever seen.

I was only a wee thing then. My mother pulled me close and hid my eyes so I wouldn't have to watch such devilry. Around me, I could hear the others gasp and moan to see our dear one transformed out of all recognition. They whispered worriedly, afraid of what new sorcery might appear every moment that passed.

Shaken and bewildered by what I had seen and wanting only to escape into blissful sleep, I slumbered pressed near to my mother's too-fast beating heart. We huddled together there by the hearth until we were awoken with a soft touch as Mistress knelt to sweep the ashes and lay the fire for a new day.

It was but a dream, we repeated one to the other, although it was odd we should all have had the very same nightmare. For it seemed nothing was changed. Here was our Mistress, unharmed, going about her never-ending list of tasks in her ash-grey dress like any other day.

True, she smiled more than usual and hummed a little tune over and over to herself. She danced with the broom, twirling and swirling, which we had never seen her do before, but otherwise she was much the same. We watched close to be sure, rattled by the nightmare of a demon's visit, but we could see no other difference in her.

The morning passed so. Right as we thought to let down our guard, The Others burst into the kitchen, sending us scurrying for cover. Mistress smiled a strange secret smile, so unlike her, as They chattered away, excited as magpies over the story they had to tell. At their words, she laughed and clapped her hands as though excited by some news they had shared.

They didn't like that she laughed and beat her worse than ever. When they were gone, Mistress was ours again. We crept out and climbed on her lap as her warm, wet tears fell heavily on us, her joy at their tidings lost in the punishment that followed. But Mistress is never sad for long. Jumping up, she set hollowed-out pumpkin shells around the fire for us. We had a jolly time playing hide and seek, feasting on the scraps of orange flesh within, and teasing the cat who came to watch us, the ugly brute.

We were not allowed beyond the kitchen on the orders of our Mistress, who wished to keep us safe, but every so often we broke her rule. We liked nothing better than to spy on The Others, talk over their curious ways among ourselves to try and make sense of their odd doings, and dream up things we might do to them to help our poor Mistress.

This day, when we were done with our playtime and Mistress was busy with her chores, a spy was sent to see if he could nose out the cause of the excitement of The Others. He ran back to fetch us with news there was some mischief underway. We crowded two-by-two into the narrow hole in the baseboard we had chewed carefully through the wall to use as our private passageway.

A crowd of Others, strangers to us, had gathered. More than we had ever seen before in one place. Packed into the room tightly, stretching their necks so far up and up to see that they never even noticed us scurrying forward amongst their long skirts and shifting feet for a better view.

Two of The Others, the young ones who liked to harry Mistress so, sat side by side, taking turns jamming their toes into one of those strange boxes they liked to wear on their feet. This box looked familiar to us, twinkling all over like the stars in the sky. So bright, it was impossible to look at directly without hurting our eyes.

One of our kind said it was like window glass glinting in the sun that breaks through a darkly cloudy sky on a stormy day. But Mother said don't be daft. Such things can't be made of glass, for they would shatter when they walked and slice their feet to ribbons.

A man taller than all the rest stood watching. Dark-haired, silent and still. Something about him made us nervous. A quiet power and purpose. What it was he sought was impossible for us to guess but had something to do with this sparkling box.

The Others tried everything they could think of to jam their horrid big feet into the dainty little thing. Even the old one joined in, plumping herself down between the two younger ones, shoving them aside to make room. What a sight it was to see them grunting and groaning, straining and crushing their monstrous feet 'til tears started from their eyes and they were as red in the face as the ripe raspberries Mistress gives us as a treat sometimes.

We giggled and snickered to each other and thought it great fun until we started hearing Her name. The Mistress. They were calling for her by that name they used that made her unhappy.

At first, we were unconcerned. They were always calling for her to bring them something or other, too lazy or proud to fetch it for themselves, and always Mistress brings it, so patient and sweet no matter how they scold her. It was fortunate beyond measure that the wisest of us saw the danger in good time: they meant to see if the sparkly thing was fit for her, our Mistress.

We murmured and whispered one to another, trembling as some instinct, old as time itself, warned of the gravest of dangers. We sprang to work, no time to confer further or plan, only to act and act quickly before disaster struck.

The Mistress entered the room in her soft and dignified manner, head held high. The huge crowd parted ways for her, opening a narrow path she trod as nimbly as the deer that picked their way through the garden during many a twilight hour. A chair being offered, she sat gracefully, pulling up her skirts slightly to display her dainty foot.

The grave man eyed her closely, then knelt and offered the pretty thing to her. We knew there was no time to waste. The bravest of us ran forward and up the arm of the dark one kneeling and offering that dread jeweled gift to Mistress. Startled, he dropped it and there was confusion and pushing and screaming and laughter among the crowd as Mistress chased after the brave one, finally picking him up and tucking him in her pocket for safekeeping.

He later told us he curled up there and went to sleep, so exhausted by his mighty deed, but others of us were not idle while the chase was on. They snatched a snowy white piece of cloth that was dropped amidst the madness, a cloth as soft as Mistress's warm cheek when we huddled against it while she slept. Working together with but a single purpose, they dragged it to the sparkly thing and stuffed it down in as tight as could be out of sight then scarpered away before being noticed.

The clamor died down and the Others turned their attention back to Mistress as she took her seat again, crowding forward for a better view. The man knelt and made offering anew as she pushed her delicate foot forward. The room seemed to hold its breath for endless moments that were all too long to us, as it was our future that lay in the balance, but finally, a collective sigh was heard.

It didn't fit.

Mistress pulled back her tiny foot and made as if to reach out for the dazzling, shiny thing, puzzled and grieved in some way we couldn't understand. However, the strange Others were already leaving, chattering and excited, on to somewhere we knew not and could not care as long as it was elsewhere. The man with dark hair, ever solemn and composed, lingered not a moment, swept away by the commotion of the crowd.

Escaping back through our humble tunnel to the warmth of the kitchen, we embraced and congratulated one and another, cavorting and prancing wildly in our relief. Our duty was done. Mistress was safe.

And from that time to this and forevermore, we tell the tale day after day so we will never forget how close we came to losing her. To serve as a warning to the next generation and the ones after to be ever vigilant. The Mistress is everything to us and must be guarded from any harm.

Some of us old ones notice she weeps even more now than she once did. We have never heard that soft tune from her lips nor seen her dance with the broom again, but we are fed and kept warm and guarded jealously from the horrid cat. For we are precious to Mistress. Her only true friends.

And so, all is well with us.

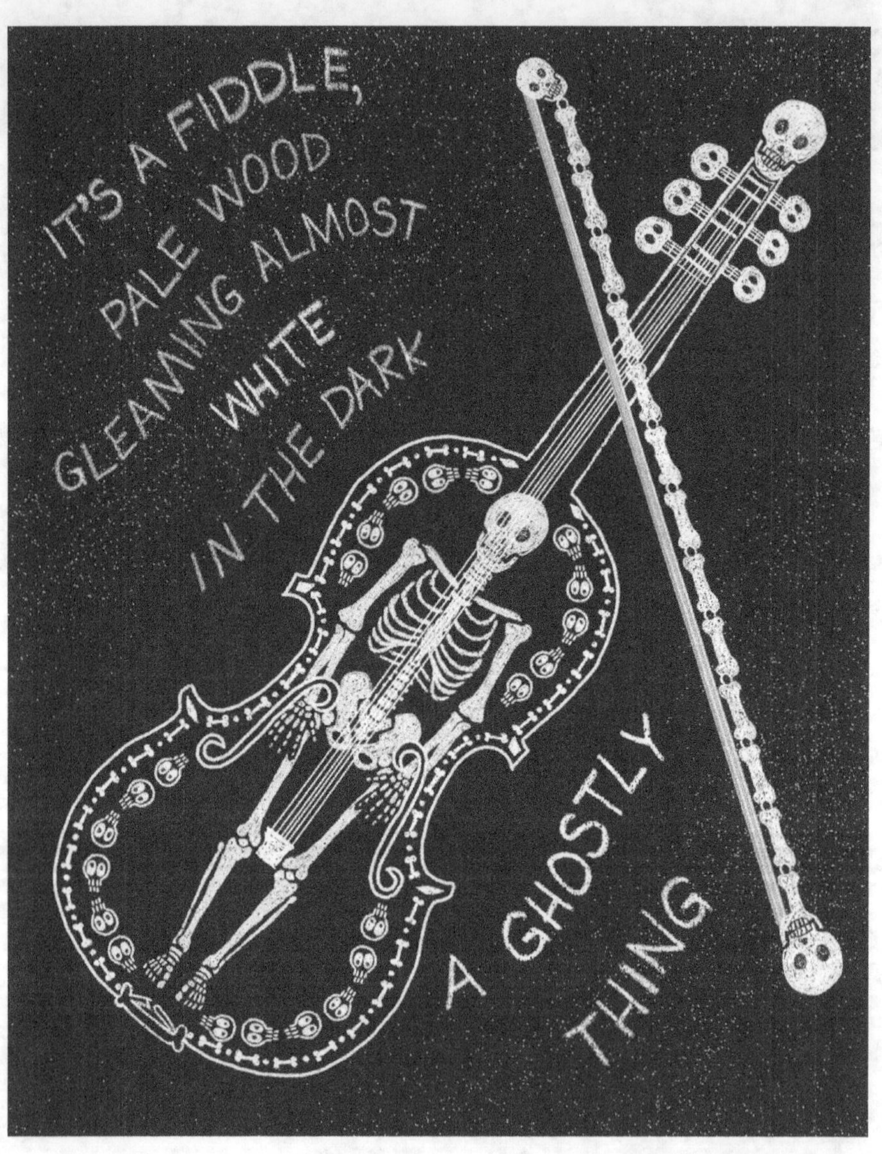

IT'S A FIDDLE,
PALE WOOD
GLEAMING ALMOST
WHITE
IN THE DARK
A GHOSTLY
THING

Cotton

I'm escorted out the main gates on a Tuesday afternoon in September with nothing but the clothes on my back, a ten-spot in my pocket, and the Warden's lecture about rejoining decent society ringing in my ears. The cheap shoes they gave me creak and chafe. Won't be long before my feet are a mess of blisters and the sun turns my prison-pale skin bright red, but I don't care. I've somewhere to be.

Don't have a timepiece, but I reckon by the rising of the moon and the pattern of stars it's 10 or 11 by the time I finally leave paved road for the gravel one that'll lead me home. A few folks passed me on the main highway, but I didn't bother to stick a thumb out for a ride. Nobody's gonna pick up a rough-looking fella this late at night.

As I walk, I keep my head down and my thoughts focused. I've had thirteen years to think about this. Thirteen years to grieve. Thirteen years to plan.

The crunch of gravel underfoot sounds loud in the night. Too loud. I move off onto the grassy edge. Don't want to be waking nobody. They might have questions I don't intend to answer.

I pass by Old Man Lowdry's house. Not changed much except the roof over the front stoop is sagging worse than ever. One day, it'll fall in completely. Hope his pack of blueticks are lazing out there when it does. He brings those hounds up to be as mean as he is, and the world wouldn't miss none of them.

Get a surprise when I see Ma Ranier's house. Burnt clear down to the foundation. Wonder when it happened, and if she and Lucille made it out alive. Once, I would've cared enough to find out, but those days are gone.

My place is at the end of the road, where the gravel peters out to dirt so dusty it chokes you in dry weather and so muddy it could suck the boots off your feet in wet. Not much more than a shack, but it was all mine. We were happy there, the three of us. Enough land to spread out, plant a garden, keep chickens and pigs out back. Not an easy life, but not so hard neither when you got someone to share it with.

No time to dwell on that. Got to get out to the cemetery by midnight. I rummage through the shed, glad to see my tools still there. Guess nobody thought there'd be anything of value to steal, or maybe they were too scared to go near a house of death and misfortune. Folks around here are a superstitious bunch.

I stuff an old canvas bag full of everything I need, grab a shovel and head west across the open fields of the Warner farm. Harvesting's done and the rustle of the dried corn stalks littering the ground keep me company. I steer clear of the Big House. I've business with those who live there, but it can wait 'til I'm ready.

The little white church where I've spent many a Sunday is as I remember except it looks like it's sporting a fresh coat of paint. The Reverend always was big on keeping up appearances.

But it's the graveyard I'm needing. We're a small congregation, so it ain't big and spread out, but even with several generations buried here, there's still plenty of open ground for others to join in.

It's a peaceful place. Three giant pin oaks, ancient and stately, keep guard over the dead. The pine forest circling the edge of the cemetery hums its own quiet hymns night and day. I hope they'll lay me somewhere here in the by and by when my labor is done.

By the light of the full moon, I search for my boy's grave. I was locked up by the time of burying, so I've no idea where he's at. I start just inside the graying wooden picket fence that marks off the realm of the dead from the living. Older stones here. Most you can barely read.

His'll be newer and likely small. The Reverend promised me the church would pay for a marker, but it's well-known he's a penny-pincher when there's no reflected glory to be had. There's rumors about where the collection money goes, and it ain't always to good works.

I find my son in a quiet corner. Small tombstone as expected, but nice enough. A lamb decorates the top, and his name and dates are carved in deep and clear. I run my fingers over the letters. Toby. Think on his dirty blond hair and flashing smile, full of mischief. He'd of been a heartbreaker if he'd lived.

It's weedy back here. Soil too sandy and fine to grow much else. Makes for easy digging though. Six feet down ain't much when you been breaking rocks for thirteen years. Not a big man, but I'm wiry strong and working to a purpose, so it's not long before my shovel hits the coffin.

I use my hands to clear the last bits of dirt, soil grinding in under my fingernails. Such a small box to hold an outsized spirit. Plain white ash, stained and soured from its years under the earth. The wood's brittle in places, eaten away by beetle and worm, but looks like there'll be enough.

Now for the hard part. I pry up the lid, heart pounding. Think I'm ready, but I'm not. No one's prepared to see the flesh of their flesh reduced to nothing but bone and bits of sinew too stubborn to rot.

How long a time passes as I stare at what remains, I can't say. A fox screaming in the woods breaks me out of my reverie. Reminds me to get a move on. I empty the tools from my canvas sack, and one by one, I replace them reverently with the sacred bones.

"This was Toby. And *this*. And *this*," I mutter as the dirty white pile grows and grows. Last of all, I arrange the skull and jawbone.

He grins up at me as he did in life. *"Look, Pop, look what I did! Look!"*

How many times did I brush him off, too impatient when he tried to tell me this, show me that? I had all the time in the world for him now.

I set the bag gently beside the open grave and heft the coffin and myself over the lip as well. The nails are rusted and weak. Easy to tear apart the box and lay the pieces out on the ground. I arrange my woodworking tools in a star pattern around the wood. Sit down cross-legged with my boy on my lap, wishing I'd a way to tell the time. Such doings are always best at midnight, but I'll have to take my chances.

Pulling back the sleeve on my right arm, I squint with one blue eye at the words tattooed roughly there by an untrained hand. I'm blind in the other eye. Born with it white as cotton. That's what gave me the name I've been called all my life. But I can make out the words right enough. The old man who'd taught them to me in the prison yard swore they'd work. Time to find out.

I rumble out the spell, low but clear. *Three times three* the old man said. I keep count on my fingers until the final round. The fox screams again, nearer this time. I turn to find it staring at me. Larger than average and redder than any I'd ever seen.

"Unwise," it says.

"How's that?" I ask, bold as can be, for I don't care enough about living to be afraid of anything, earthly or not.

The fox stalks around the tools laid out on the ground, tail twitching and long nose sniffing. "I see what is in your mind. It won't bring him back."

"No," I agree, "but they'll pay."

"As will you. Such things bear a heavy price."

I nod my head in acceptance. With Toby's bones settled on my lap, the slight weight and rattle of them a reminder I'd lost the only thing precious to me, I make a deal with a devil and have no regrets.

The fox laughs, a barking, harsh sound in the night. "So be it."

It runs in circles round me, faster and faster, until all I can see is a red blur with quick flashes of white. My tools and the wood from the coffin rise straight up in the air. A buzzing all around me, too close, too close. I fold myself over my son's bones to keep them safe, my face pressed to the dirt as a great stirring and uproar moves even my hardened heart to the edge of fear.

When I think I can't take one more minute, I do and do and do. Finally, when I can't stand no more, I hear a rooster crowing far off. The tools stop their frantic noise and drop to the ground.

The fox ceases its whirling and gives me an offering with a mocking flourish of a bow.

"Here, unwise one. Much good may it do you."

It's a fiddle, pale wood gleaming white in the dark. A ghostly thing. The strings are strange. Twangy tendons that remind me of the meaty sinew that clings to my son's bones. I accept the gift though it burns in my hands.

"I don't know how to play," I say.

The fox's eyes flash with anger and contempt. It draws a fiddler's bow out from behind its back and strikes me a fierce blow across the brow with it. My ears ring, dizzy and dazed as warm, slow drops of blood ooze down my face.

"Now you do." The devilish thing grins, nose to nose with me. Its hot breath smells of decay and blisters my skin. It slinks away and perches atop a monument to enjoy the show.

I pick up the bow and stand, slinging the strap of the bag of bones over my head and shifting them around to my back. Tuck the fiddle neath my chin. The talent for musicmaking comes into my fingertips as they slide over the bitter strings.

The bow sings out a peculiarly jaunty melody for such grim work. My fingers fly, strings cutting into skin. More blood flows.

The first to arrive is the Reverend's wife, dressed in an old cotton nightgown, her hair up in curlers. She's a sight to behold, dancing awkward through the graveyard, tripping over ground markers and nearly coming to grief more than once. Not a teaspoon of rhythm in her body, but she makes up for it with enthusiasm.

Mrs. Maisie Warner is next. A higher class of woman. Filmy robe like you see in pictures of those Hollywood starlets. She moves with grace and confidence even though her eyes are closed in bliss as she answers my siren call. Her feet patter in a pair of ridiculous mules done up with feathers, and the big diamond on her wedding ring flashes in the moonlight.

I play on. These two were just the closest. There's many more out there I mean to summon. My fingers protest their treatment, but I realize I can't stop, even if I wanted to. Luckily, I don't.

Others answer the tune, some on foot, some by horseback, by cart, even by automobile or truck for those blessed enough to afford such a thing in these hard times. They crowd into the graveyard, women made wanton and free by the never-ending melody that squeals out into the night.

Among the last to arrive are Lucille and Ma Ranier. Guess they survived that fire after all. Lucille looks so much older, tired and worn out and with a wide gray streak woven through her dark hair. She'd never visited me once in prison. I'd loved her, but that turned to hate as I'd seen her in the courtroom giving false witness against me, her own husband.

I watch the weird square dance unfold on that hallowed ground. The ladies circle round each other and the gravestones, trampling down the weeds and what little grass there is. Some of the older monuments topple in the chaos, stone shattering and cracking loud as gunshots. The women grow wilder, losing all control as my song rises and falls.

"Where did he come from? Where did he go?" They chant in time to the melody. Some of them venture close, brush their hands over my close-shaven head, feel the muscles straining in my neck and arms as I play. "Where did he come from? Where did he go?"

My fingers are shredded. Bone strikes string and blood flies as I play on and on. The women came all gradual-like, but the men show up sudden. A mob, angry and armed. A fearful sight to anyone who still cared about remaining among the living.

"You there!" one calls to me. It's Harold Warner. I'm not surprised he speaks up first. Everyone defers to the richest man in the county. "What in blazes do you think you're doing?"

"Just playing this here fiddle," I reply, shouting to be heard. "It's made from my boy's own coffin. The boy you sent to his grave."

He recognizes me then. Arrogance wars with caution on his face. He's not been held to account for any of the dark deeds of his long life and don't expect to be now. I look on him and the rest of the men without pity. They knew. They've always known the truth, but they'd closed ranks and protected the powerful. None of them had thought twice about sending a no-account away to prison as the sacrificial lamb.

Warner snorts. "Is that you, Joe Burton? Let you loose, did they? Well, it was a big mistake for you to come back here. You're not welcome in these parts."

"The ladies are pleased to see me." I nod my head at the frenzy of the dance. "They're helping me to celebrate. Did you know it's Toby's birthday? He would've been twenty-one today. A man full-grown. Instead, he's nothing but a sack of bones on my back. What do you think about that?"

"Stop this foolishness at once!" Warner dives into the crowd of women and tries to fish out his wife. She ain't pleased with the interruption and drags her sharp fingernails down his cheeks, ripping the skin wide open.

Other of the men leap in, but none are met with any warmer welcome. I shake my head. You don't mess with folks under a powerful spell. Even I know better than that.

The red fox and I look on with interest as the women tear their mates, their brothers, their uncles and fathers and sons into smaller and smaller pieces with an unnatural strength and determination, chanting all the while.

"Where did he come from? Where did he go?"

Poor things. They're wearied when they're done and collapse to the ground to sleep like the dead, draped over headstones and the remains of their men. The gore and guts and horror is a beautiful thing to see, but I wonder what the women will make of it when they come to and recollect what they've done.

Once, I would've cared. I was a good man before they killed my boy. Poor but a hard worker. Going along to get along. Took what slights came my way with a foolish grin and a tip of my hat. Turned the other cheek as the Reverend commanded. Caught and swallowed insults down deep into the bitter core of me.

But no more.

I'll leave this boneyard far behind. Travel the countryside playing my devilish tune. Drive other women to madness, teach their men a lesson. I'll wear myself away to skin and bone to keep my son company. He'll go with me everywhere, rattling and chattering on my back.

Maybe I'll turn into one of those ghost tales whispered round the fire. Celebrated in song. Why not? Even a cotton-eyed nobody can become a legend.

OWL SPIED
A SOFT SHAPE
IN THE MISTY FOREST

A FAWN,
COLD AND ALONE

Owl and Fawn

Owl spied a soft shape in the misty forest. A fawn, cold and alone. He wrapped one great wing around the small deer to still its shivers, hooting lowly of marvelous things he had seen in his flights. And so they stayed until the first light of dawn appeared in the east when the fawn arose, shaky but full of renewed hope in the sliver of warming sun that peeked through the thick canopy of trees.

"I believe you saved my life," she said to Owl.

"Piffle! Stuff and nonsense. I only did what anyone would do."

"But no one else did it. Only you."

Eager to change the subject, Owl asked "How came you to be alone in the forest?"

"I was grazing in the fields with Mother when a huge grey dog chased us. She ran one way and I another. Before I knew it I was lost."

"Sounds like Wolf. He's full of energy but has quaint manners when you meet him."

"I'd just as soon not take the risk of meeting this Wolf," said Fawn. "He looked very fierce!"

"Looks can be deceiving," said Owl.

A small toad landed on the fawn's head.

"Very, very true," it said. "I, for instance, am a faerie princess in disguise."

"Hmph," said Owl. "Likely story."

"It's true," said the small toad. "My name is Princess Serenity. My gift is to bring peace to all I draw near to. Don't you feel calm with me perched on your head?"

"I suppose so," Fawn replied doubtfully, rolling her eyes to try and catch a glimpse of her passenger.

"Princess Serenity. That's quite a title. Are you claiming to be royalty?" Owl asked.

"Oh, no," said the toad. "All of the Fae are named either Prince or Princess except for those who are neither one nor the other."

"And what are they called?" asked Fawn.

"Delightful."

"I'm afraid you'll have an uphill battle convincing me you are Faerie," said Owl to the small toad. "You'll have to change your form or do some other magic to prove it."

"Why should I? I've no need to prove myself to you or any creature. I know who I am. That is sufficient."

"I've no more time for this nonsense," scoffed Owl. "I must find Fawn's mother. The forest is a dangerous place for a child alone."

"How will you find her?" Fawn cried. "The world is an awfully big place."

"The veil between worlds is thin," the small toad said. "Tap any sparkle you see under a mushroom cap or in a tree hollow and you'll be transported."

"I have a much more practical idea. I will take flight," Owl said. "I've sharp eyes and a keen sense of smell."

"I suppose that's one way to do it."

"You have a better idea?"

"Might be faster to ask the wind."

"Ask the wind?" Owl scoffed. "Might as well ask the earth or the sky."

"Could do," said the small toad. "But the wind is capricious and moves more freely. It goes everywhere and will not yield to obstacles, only weave around them in a breathless embrace, ferreting out truth."

"Maybe it wouldn't hurt to try," Fawn said.

"Very well," said Owl. "Ask away, toad."

"My proper name is Serenity but you may call me Ren. First, we must adorn ourselves with drops of the morning dew then sing softly of stolen wishes and bitter dreams to call the wind to us. Are you willing to do this?"

Fawn nodded her head vigorously without thinking, sending her small passenger tumbling to the ground.

"Oh, dear!" she exclaimed. "Are you hurt, Ren?"

The small toad gazed up at them, a blank look on her face.

"Who is Ren?" she asked.

"You are Ren," Owl said.

"No, I am Toad."

"But you're also a Faerie princess in disguise," said Fawn.

"Am I? That doesn't seem likely."

"Just what I've been saying," Owl sighed.

"You hit your head," Fawn said. "Maybe you forgot."

"Things are a bit cloudy."

Owl scooped Toad up with the tip of a feathered wing and placed her gently on the bright yellow bloom of a dandelion.

"Thank you, my friend," Toad said.

"I would hardly call us friends," said Owl. "We've only just met."

"And yet you've already done me a service, friend. What is happening?"

"Did your fall erase your memories?" Owl asked.

"Not all, but I can't seem to remember how I came to be here with an owl and a fawn in the deep woods. Are we on an adventure?"

"We're going to look for my mother," said Fawn.

"A quest! Even better!"

A mole popped its head up from the rich soil of the forest floor. "A quest? May I join? I can travel swiftly underground and scout ahead."

A lean rabbit appeared from the forest ferns. "I am fleet of foot to cover far distances in the blink of an eye."

A raven landed. "I can search by air."

"That's my job," complained Owl.

"Now we have six for the quest, but we need seven," said Toad.

"Why?" asked Fawn.

"Seven is the lucky number. All quests need seven. We need a seventh."

"You sound like a broken gramophone," said Rabbit.

"What's that?"

"A creature humans keep. When it is angry, it repeats itself."

"I'm not angry."

A honeybee buzzed by. "I can be the seventh member of your quest!"

"You? What can you do?" asked Raven.

"I can lift morale. Here's a joke: What did the Queen say to the naughty drone? Bee-hive!"

Owl snorted. "I hardly see the humor in—"

Fawn giggled. "Bee-hive! I get it!"

"Now our band of adventurers is complete," said Toad.

"Which way shall we go first?" asked Mole.

"By Gaia's ichor on the blade of the mighty sword Xbilta, we shall journey south," proclaimed Raven.

"What on earth was that?" said Owl.

"A prophecy. It's my thing. I'm a raven."

"It doesn't seem very helpful in our current circumstance."

"Well, I never!" exclaimed the raven, but what it never was left unsaid.

"First things, first," said Toad. "What does your mother look like, Fawn?"

"She's just Mother. Beautiful and soft. She smells of fresh jasmine and holds the warmth of the summer sun in her eyes."

"Yes, but how will we know her?"

"She will be crying for her lost child."

"I saw a doe crying," said a tiny voice.

"Who said that?" the adventurers asked one another, craning their necks in every direction.

A fragile insect fluttered its lace wings to call their attention. "Tis I. I cannot join you but head south."

"As I prophesied!" cried Raven in triumph.

The insect flittered away before they could ask any more questions.

"I was right, wasn't I?" Raven bragged.

"Stop crowing, you silly bird," said Owl.

"But isn't it good to know which way to go? Otherwise, we'd have to meander around."

"I meander," said Bee. "You find more flowers that way."

"I think you were all sent to nettle me," said Owl. "I was rescuing Fawn before you crowd showed up and we have gotten nothing done since."

The others protested but Owl had had enough. "That's it, we're going!"

Owl set off at a brisk march. The others followed in his wake.

Owl strode far ahead, leaving the others behind. When they caught up, he was bogged down in a quagmire.

"You should've let me scout ahead," said Mole. "I'm an expert on all types of soils in the forest and I could have warned you."

"Never mind the lecture, help me out!"

"What a thing to happen," cried Toad.

"We're all doomed," said Bee, buzzing off.

With a howl of laughter, a great grey muzzle enveloped Owl's head, pulling him to safety.

"A wolf!" cried Fawn. "Are you going to eat us?"

"And miss the best entertainment I've had in ages?"

"It seems uncanny you were so close at hand," Raven said to Wolf, as Owl bathed his muddy feathers in a nearby stream after his timely rescue.

"Not at all," answered Wolf. "I've been following you. Hunters killed the rest of my pack and it's lonely now in the forest. Can I join your pack?"

"But then we would be eight," protested Toad.

"No," said Rabbit. "Bee ran away."

"At least my beautiful feathers are clean," said Owl.

"They're pretty but they aren't as vibrant as mine," said Raven.

"What? Yours are black."

"Not in the sun. Look!"

"Oooh," everyone exclaimed.

As they admired Raven's feathers flashing brilliant colors in the sunlight, Rabbit piped up. "First the prophecy and now this. Are you some kind of wizard?"

"A wizard? What's that?" asked Raven.

"A magical being."

"Aren't we all magical beings?"

"Enough of this yakking," said Owl. "Time's a-wasting."

"Agreed," said Toad. "I can't keep up with the rest of you as I'm only very small. You'd best go ahead without me."

"Nonsense," said Wolf, lowering his shaggy head to the ground. "Climb up here and hang on tight to one of my ears. We'll race the wind together."

"Oh, thank you!"

"Anchor yourself securely," said Wolf. "I wouldn't want you to fall off and have to find your own way."

"Me neither," said Toad. "I am already as far from home as I ever thought to be in my life."

"That's what adventure is all about."

"But am I brave enough?"

"Let's find out!" said Wolfe, bounding off with enthusiasm. "How are you doing up there?"

Toad giggled and laughed. "This is pure bliss! It feels like I'm flying!"

"You call that flying? This is flying," said Raven, dive-bombing the pair before soaring back up into the skies.

"Show-off. Best stop and wait for the rest to catch up," said Wolf.

Fawn arrived with a flustered Owl, who huffed and puffed in annoyance. "Give us a moment to collect ourselves!"

"Why don't you fly instead of walk?" asked Toad.

"Someone responsible must look after Fawn."

"I can do it," said Wolf.

"I said responsible."

"What a drab life you lead," Wolf scolded Owl. "Always fussing about responsibility and telling others what to do."

"Someone has to take charge or there would be complete chaos."

"Chaos can be fun!"

"For you, maybe, but spare a thought for those around you."

"I do! That's why I share the madness."

"It is the eternal question, isn't it?" piped up Mole. "Is our primary responsibility to our own idea of contentment or is it to concentrate on the well-being of others? Many a philosopher has pondered this very—"

"I'm hungry," said Fawn.

"Shush, child, I was speaking!"

"See," said Owl. "This is exactly what I mean. From the time Fawn and I saw the first orange flame of the sun this morning, there has been nothing but chaos and now she is starving and we are no closer to finding her mother than ever and none of you are helping!"

"I was in the human's garden when the sun came up," said Rabbit. "The light glinted off the glass of their windows."

"What are windows?" asked Toad.

"Holes they cut in their warren so they can look out into the world."

"Why don't they just go outside?"

"Humans are strange, unknowable creatures."

"Argh!" screamed Owl in frustration at the roundabout conversation.

"I'm sorry," said Rabbit. "I only brought it up because it occurs to me the human who lives there is very kind. She has hair as silver as the moon and many tame animals. Maybe she would help us."

"You can't trust humans," growled Wolf.

"That's true as a rule," said Rabbit. "But this one lets me steal all I want from her garden and only watches and croons a sweet tune to me."

"Anything would be better than this incessant talking," said Owl. "Is it far?"

"No. We've been going around in circles, you know."

"Here she is," said Rabbit after they had walked a little way, pointing out a human at a fence feeding a rowdy commotion of goats.

"How shall we judge if we can trust her?" asked Wolf.

"See how patient she is with those goats and everyone knows what abominable pests they are," Rabbit answered.

"Whatcha doing?" a small voice asked.

The others made way as an orange kitten pranced through the crowd.

"Who are you?" asked Owl.

"I'm Ruby."

"What's a ruby?" asked Mole.

"Me! It's my name. What's your name?"

"Mole."

"That's what you are but what's your name?"

"I guess I don't know."

"How sad not to know your own name," said Ruby to Mole. "I shall call you Beatrice."

"Why on earth?" asked Owl.

"She looks like one. A beautiful dark creature of mystery."

Mole's voice rang out in silver laughter. "Bee-a-triss. I love it!"

"Ooh, name me next," cried Toad.

"I'll name you Pearl," said Ruby. "For your shining skin."

"And me?" asked Rabbit.

"Velvet, for your luxurious fur. And the owl shall be Merlin, after a wise human."

Raven stepped up. "Only a macabre name will do for me, for I am the night."

"How about Rob?"

"Rob?" scoffed Raven.

"Yes," said Ruby. "Don't ravens steal shiny things?"

"Don't be insulting. That's magpies."

"I'm sorry. I wasn't looking down my nose at you. How about Sylvester? Nehemiah? or Quintilian? Quint for short."

"Squint," laughed Wolf. "For your one beady eye."

"Once again," complained Owl, "you've all lost the plot. We must find some food for Fawn, not to mention finding her mother."

Ruby exclaimed, "My human will help. She is the most powerful being in the world!"

"Have you seen the whole world?" asked Wolf.

"You mean there's more than this?"

"Much more."

"I'm hungry," cried Fawn, her head held low.

Ruby's tiny pink nose touched Fawn's. "Come with me. My human will feed you. You may all come if you like."

"We'll wait here," said Owl. "Some of us have good reason not to trust a human. We will wait and see."

"Suit yourselves!" The kitten led the fawn away.

The human smiled as she saw them approach and sat on the ground, holding out a hand for Fawn to sniff.

"She seems nice," said Toad. "The question is what do the rest of us do?"

"Some stay here to keep watch. The rest will pursue our search for her mother," said Owl.

"Who'll go and who'll stay?" asked Mole.

"Raven and I will take to the skies, one each side of the river. Wolf's a swift runner with a keen nose. He'll cover the ground. The rest of you are too small to travel quickly. Stay and keep an eye on Fawn."

Owl and Raven took to the skies in a hurricane of whispered feathers. Wolf bounded away into the forest on padded paws. Rabbit, Toad, and Mole stared at one another.

"Harrumph, rather a comedown for us," Toad complained.

"Stiffen your spine," said Rabbit. "They also serve who only stand and wait, or so I have heard."

Owl flew South, his keen eyes searching for Fawn's mother. He spied a mouse, dove and caught it in his talons, but was startled by a badger bumbling through the underbrush. Dropping the mouse, he winged away again.

"Business first, breakfast later," he said to himself.

Raven flew North but was diverted by a pink sock caught on a tree branch. He pulled at a loose thread, one keen eye watching it unravel bit by bit.

What a fun game! What a find! It only occurred to him later that he was supposed to be doing something else entirely.

Wolf returned to the field where he had chased Fawn and her mother. It had only been a bit of fun with no thought for the consequences. His conscience, usually silent as the world after a heavy winter snowfall, awoke.

"I will find her."

He snuffled the dirt. Many deer had passed this way. How was he to know which trail to follow? Despair settled on his heart until he caught the whiff of a perfume of terror with subtle notes of a mother's fear, not for herself, but for her child.

"Yes, this is the one."

Wolf followed his nose. His body crashed faster and faster through the trees and fallen leaves as the scent grew stronger. He breathed in the agony of a creature in such pain, their mourning stained the very air.

At last, he found his prey. A doe, head hung low. She never moved as he approached, saying only, "You've caught me. I am so tired of running. I have sacrificed my life for my child and am content."

Wolf's eyes overflowed with tears, staining his light grey coat black in mourning. "I meant no harm. Let me take you to her."

The doe's own eyes threatened a deluge of tears. "You want to help me?"

"Yes," said Wolf, "and it's not only me. There's an owl, raven, a mole, rabbit, even a very small toad."

"But why would you all help? You are not of our kind."

"It just seems like the right thing to do. Besides," said Wolf, "I am all for equality. There is nothing inherently better about being a wolf than a deer. No reason we can't be friends."

"Except you have teeth and eat my kind," said the doe in a voice pregnant with painful memory.

"Except maybe that." Wolf sighed. "There's a fog in my mind. Right, wrong. Friend, foe. I don't usually think so hard. Life should be fun."

"Easy to say if you've never known sorrow."

"Humans killed my pack," Wolf replied. He raised his muzzle to the sky and howled an eerie lament that caused the doe to shiver.

"I'm sorry for your loss," she said. "I feel the pain in your soul. Don't let the gravity of it pull you apart."

"Life goes on," said Wolf. "I try to always look ahead. Shall we go? I can lead you back to your child. A good thing to balance the bad."

"Oh, yes! Let's go!"

Wolf loped ahead, looking back to check on the doe from time to time.

"Am I going too fast?" he called.

"Never," she replied. "I'm going home and can't get there quickly enough."

"I thought deer roamed freely and had no settled place?"

"My home is wherever my child is," said the doe.

—ℓℓℓ—

Toad, Mole, and Rabbit were debating. The human had disappeared with Fawn and they needed to keep an eye on their friend.

"I should go," said Rabbit. "I can tie a carrot top to my tail and slick back my ears to impersonate a cat."

"That is a terrible disguise," said Mole.

"Do you have a better idea?" Toad asked.

"Yes, I'll tunnel under the garden and sneak up to the house and spy on the human. I will write my observations in my journal."

"What journal?"

"The one I keep back in my hole... oh... I suppose that's not a good plan either."

"This is silly," said Toad. "I'm going."

She hopped away toward the house, Rabbit and Mole following, reluctant to lose sight of yet another friend. They climbed aboard an overturned washtub to peer in the window. Toad, being only very small, scaled the side of the cottage to perch on the windowsill. A kettle was whistling.

"What a happy sound!" cried Mole.

They saw Fawn wrapped in a cozy blanket on the floor. The human knelt with a bottle and Fawn gobbled greedily.

"What if it's poison?" cried Mole.

"There are far easier ways for humans to kill us," Rabbit replied. "Besides, this one has an aura of light. She is a good human, I think."

Toad laughed. "Look, the milk went everywhere."

"What's the human doing?" asked Mole. "She is strangling a hideous creature!"

"That's a mop," said Rabbit. "They help humans."

"Why?"

"I don't know. Maybe the human feeds them well?"

"It's drinking the milk Fawn spilled."

"Fawn seems fine," said Toad. "And I'm hungry. YIKES!"

"Oh, dear," said Rabbit. "Are you ok?"

"What happened?"

"You fell. Are you alright?"

"My head aches. And what a weird form. Here!" Toad shook her skin away to reveal a small faerie creature with a necklace of tiny seeds.

"What... what are you?" asked Mole.

"I am Princess Serenity, but you may call me Ren."

"We thought you were a toad."

"So did I! I forgot my true self for a time, but I know who I am now."

"Why are you here?"

"I crossed the ocean to see the world but got entangled in a quest instead."

"This seems an unlikely turn of events," said Mole.

"I agree," said Ren, "but if anteaters can dance on the head of a pin, I suppose a toad can turn into a princess."

"Can they?"

"I think so. I heard a human say so once. Or maybe it was armadillos. I get those confused."

"Looks like I missed a lot!" said Bee, buzzing up to Mole.

"You again? You abandoned us when Wolf appeared."

"I had to go check on our Queen. It's the responsibility of every worker to make sure she's safe."

"You sure it wasn't your own safety you were worried about?"

"Bzz."

Raven tumbled down from the sky in a flurry of iridescent feathers. "I have returned as was foretold!"

"Was it?" asked Rabbit. "By who?"

"Me."

"Good for you, but where is Fawn's mother?"

"I got distracted by a pretty thing and forgot to search."

"I could have foretold that."

"I wonder how Owl and Wolf are doing," said Mole. "Wish they could send us a sign. What if they never find Fawn's mother?"

"I'll perform some faerie magic and fix everything," said Ren.

"Why didn't you do that before?"

"Forgot I could. I was too busy being a small toad."

"What a treasure you are," Raven said to the faerie. "To think that you can solve all our problems! What should we do first?"

"Check on Owl and Wolf!" cried Mole.

"Gather all the pollen in the garden," said Bee.

"Always thinking of yourself!"

"No, the hive. The hive is all."

"Oh, buzz off," said Mole.

"Very well. Good luck with the young spotted urchin. May you find her mother soon."

"What a useless creature!"

"To us perhaps," said Rabbit, "but not to its family."

"But you should care for others, too!"

"Not everyone sees it that way."

"Well, in any case," said the faerie, "we should see about finding Fawn's mother now that I have remembered my powers. Shall I turn myself into a vixen or a stoat or maybe a badger?"

"Why can't you go as yourself to find her?" said Raven.

"I could but where's the fun in that? I know! I'll turn into a wraith and fly howling through the forest, caring not for obstacles or danger until I find Fawn's mother."

"Or you could just turn around," said a deep voice.

Wolf and Doe stood panting from their run.

"Where is my child?" she asked.

"By yarrow and thistle, you startled us!" cried Raven. "Where did you come from, Wolf?"

"I completed our mission. Here's Fawn's mother. What have you been doing all this time?"

"Um, this and that, hither and yon, you know, mystical things."

"You got distracted, didn't you?"

"This will make a great story to set down in my journal when I get home," said Mole.

"Are you an author?" asked Raven.

"No, only a writer."

"Just as well. One of my ancestors used to hang out with an author. Nevermore, he always advised anyone who would listen ever after."

"Where's my child?" asked Doe impatiently.

"She's in there with the human," Rabbit explained.

"How shall I get her?"

"I could sail a boat made of dreams in through the window," said the faerie.

"I'll go," said Ruby the kitten, prancing up to them in orange delight. "The human listens to me."

The kitten marched over to the house and disappeared through a hole in the wall.

"I will hide," said Wolf. "I don't trust humans and they don't trust my kind."

"You can trust this one," said Rabbit. "She might have harmed me any time but instead lets me eat all the carrots I want."

"I will hide away just the same," said Wolf. "It was the destiny of my pack to meet their ends at the hands of humans. I must survive. I'm the only one left who remembers them. Their dear faces, their fierceness and kindness. The memory will live on only as long as I do."

Wolf wandered away, tail held low.

"How long must we wait for my child to appear?" asked the doe.

Raven answered:

"Eleven times eleven must the bell chime

And all the stars shall dance in rhyme

The tree roots themselves will climb—

No, wait, I'm wrong. Here they are."

Fawn ran to them most joyfully. "Mother! I lost you when we ran from the field and I wandered alone until an owl found me and then more and more friends and they took care of me until they found you and..."

The doe only repeated over and over, "My child, my child, my child..."

The human stood at her gate watching:

a raven puffing up its feathers

a mole weeping slow tears
a rabbit twitching its nose and ears
a mother and daughter reunited
a hulking grey shape at the forest's edge
and a twinkling light which was always moving just out of sight

The friends dispersed with many earnest promises to keep in touch. The day wore on to twilight. A swift flurry of heavy wings heralded the arrival of one very tired owl.

"Where is everybody?" he wondered. "Did they leave while I was on the hunt? I am alone again. Alone, alone."

"Not quite," a low voice rumbled in his ear.

"Wolf! Where are the rest?"

"I found the doe. The quest was complete, so all rejoiced and departed."

"They forgot about me."

"They didn't mean to. Happy creatures are sometimes careless."

"I suppose we might as well go about our business then," said Owl.

"How is a wolf like an owl?" asked Wolf.

"I don't know."

"They both need a friend."

"Is that supposed to be a joke? I don't get it."

"That's because it's not a joke, my friend."

And so our tale has ended, for now at least.

Is there a moral?

Perhaps just this: Keep as open a mind and heart as you can in this cruel world and maybe you too will find a friend in an unlikely place.

May peace be with you, my friends.

A NARROW HEAD
SOMEWHAT LIKE
A HORSE
THE LONG, TWISTING BODY
OF A SERPENT
ALL SHINING WHITE

Kelpie

When I came of age, Mama sat me down and told me the facts of life. At the end, she warned me fiercely to never tease a horse standing close to water. Might be a kelpie that'd steal me away to Faerie Land, and I'd never see her or Papa again. So, of course, I pulled the tail of the first horse I saw, but it only ran away. Disappointing, but I've never been easily discouraged.

The vast lake near our village had shores for miles and I scoured them all, clambering up rocks that towered over my head and scuffing my feet along beaches that filled my slippers with sand and bothersome pebbles. I pulled a lot of tails and even tweaked a donkey's ear one time, just in case, but nothing ever happened other than I came near to getting the devil kicked out of me more than once.

I'd about given up on the whole idea, when one day, I saw a woman standing on a rock looking out over the lake like the figurehead of a sailing ship. She wore a white flowing gown, and her long, unbound silver hair writhed about her body in mimicry of the murmuration of a flock of starlings in flight. Her waist was girdled round and round with a silver chain, the links shining and winking at me in the sunlight.

Curious to find out what such a fantastical person was doing, I loped along the water's edge. Spray flew from where the tide tickled at my feet like it was trying to catch me, slow me down, save me. But it was too late for such. Nothing would've stopped me from speaking to that vision, if only to hear her voice one time.

It was deep and low—so low, I had to listen close to catch the words.

"Pretty thing, what do you want of me?"

"Who are you? What's your name?" I asked.

"Oh, is that all? You only want my true name. So that you may master me? Tether me here to this realm?" Sparks flew from her hair, and a darkness formed around her like storm clouds gathering in the sky. "You dare to ask me for my name!"

"Well, not if you're going to get snippy about it," I retorted. "It's just that it's only polite to introduce oneself where I come from. My name is Rowan. See, that wasn't so hard, was it?"

The woman startled me with a thrilling roll of laughter, and her face softened. "You mean to teach me my manners, I see. It is long since anything so amusing has happened, young Rowan. Come here."

I would have gladly gone even before the strange compulsion that came over me when she spoke my name, but I stumbled and nearly fell as I tried to mount the high rock she stood upon. She reached out a hand and caught the belt at my waist, lifting me up and setting me on my feet beside her as though I weighed no more than a butterfly.

"And what brings you wandering along these shores all alone?" she asked.

"I've been looking for a kelpie. Mama told me about them. She said to be careful to never tease a horse near water because it might be one and would steal me away to Faerie Land but doesn't that sound like the most delightful thing ever?"

"Your mother is confused, I think. Kelpies turn into water horses when they're in the water. On shore, they look as human as you, only there are one or two things that might give them away."

"And what is that?" I asked, eager to learn everything I could and chagrined to think I had been pulling at horse's smelly rear ends for nothing.

"They have a certain, shall we say, otherworldly feel about them, as though they do not belong in this place or time."

"Kind of like you. I've never seen anyone like you before."

She laughed. "Indeed. And they will always wear a chain of silver."

"Like the one around your waist? Oh—" I could have kicked myself for being so slow. I should have known from the start that I was conversing with one from the Faerie realm. Magic seeped from her, causing the air around us to tingle and burn, but in the most pleasant way possible. "Are you... are you a kelpie then?"

"Why don't we find out?"

So saying, she grabbed my hand and leapt from the rock far out into the lake, dragging me with her. It felt like flying until we hit the water with a shock of cold which knocked the breath from my lungs. I'd never learned to swim and knew I was going to drown. How sad Mama and Papa would be when I never came home. How foolish I'd been to think a kelpie would be kind when they were renowned for their cruel sense of humor.

I'd barely had time to lament my premature demise when I was lifted from the water and set on top of the back of the weirdest creature I'd ever seen. A narrow head somewhat like a horse, but the long, twisting body of a serpent, all shining white. A kelpie, sure as sure.

Her head turned and the beast kissed me on the forehead, then we were diving and diving, but I found I no longer needed breath or air. An odd sensation, but one I soon got used to. I could see, too, as well as I could on land. What marvels of fish flashed around us and lush forests of plants invisible from above. The kelpie carried me farther and farther down until I saw a shining curtain of violet light.

We journeyed through it, broke the surface of the water, and climbed out onto a wide ledge inside of a cave. Glowing flowers lit the roughhewn stone room as I jumped down from the kelpie's back. She returned to her womanly form with a hiss and groan as though the effort of switching was painful.

"You've kidnapped me! What happens next?" I asked, both terrified and exhilarated as I awaited the answer.

"What a bold one you are!" she exclaimed. "Aren't you frightened of me?"

"I suppose, but this is the only truly interesting or unusual thing that's ever happened to me or is ever likely to around here. Besides, what good would it do for you to hurt me? Aren't you lonely down here? I could keep you company."

"You'd do that? Give up your family and home?"

"Why not? It isn't everyone who gets the chance to be friends with a kelpie."

"Friends?" The woman spit the word out awkwardly like she'd never had need of it before.

"Aren't you lonely? Or are there more of you?" I asked.

"No more exactly like me, and the other denizens of Faerie look down upon us shapeshifters anyway. They think it a shabby parlor trick, I'm afraid."

"But it's so wonderful! What I wouldn't give to be able to turn into such a creature." I sighed to think of one so humble as myself exalted so high.

"You shouldn't say such things. It is dangerously close to a wish, and when wishes are granted, one can never predict the consequences. I made a wish once and would dearly love to take it back if I could, but time moves only in one direction. Ever onward."

She looked suddenly ancient and so infinitely sad, I couldn't help blurting out, "I wish I might relieve you of whatever burden you carry."

Looking back, I'm surprised there wasn't a clap of thunder or flash of light or other portentous signs, but it happened very quietly. She lay one hand upon the silver chain round her waist and suddenly it was around mine instead.

"I have been released," she whispered, and dissolved into a pool of water around my feet.

I had no time to marvel or mourn her passing as my own body was changing form. What agony it was, I could never properly describe. Try to imagine that every bone in your spine, your limbs, your face were converted into another shape entirely. That your skin stretched and thinned. Sharp scales forced their way to the surface and a flowing mane sprouted down your neck.

All in a moment, you become a stranger to yourself, and yet, and yet, you fall into the water as into the arms of your mother. The cool liquid soothes your burning skin, and every muscle understands its job, propelling you through the darkness with effortless ease. Power surges, knowledge floods in. You know everything and nothing at all.

Those first days were delightful. Exploring the lake and the extent of my new abilities kept me occupied for quite some time. It was only gradually I awoke to the true awfulness of my plight. There were no others like me, at least not in this lake, and I knew of no means to break the tie that held me to it. I couldn't return home so transformed. As the kelpie had warned me, the few other Faeries I encountered scorned me, only stopping to ask what had happened to Amerdine. Thus, I found out the answer to my question—her true name—but far too late to save myself.

Now I stand on the rock where she stood. My hair, grown into a silvery waterfall, flails about in the breeze. I keep watch on the shore for another as foolish as me to come along and take my place. One will, I have no doubt, for humans are endlessly curious and endlessly unwise. I will bide my time with as much patience as I can muster.

A LOVELY BLUE BOTTLE

Sisters

TODAY WAS LONG AND tiring. I spent the morning baking off gingerbread bricks for repairs to the south wall. Making the batter left me exhausted, but I want to get the patchwork done before the winter snowfalls set in, so no rest for these weary bones. I enjoy the meditative work of building. Slathering on the icing just so with the trowel, fitting the bricks into their herringbone design. The pattern is more trouble than a simpler one would be, but I love the effect so much, it's worth the extra effort. Besides, I haven't much else to pass my time as I wait for my next visitor, so why not make the cottage as beautiful as possible?

Upkeep is a constant battle. Squirrel and deer, badger and fox, any bit of wildlife you can imagine munching away constantly. The birds are the most troublesome. So many varieties and all with a sweet tooth. I send Lucifer out to chase them, but he is the laziest cat I've ever met and can hardly be bothered. Perhaps a watch dog would be better. I must see if any puppies are for sale the next time I venture to market. A fierce breed to snap and snatch at these trespassers that harass me to the point of madness.

Last night a gang of rats caused mischief on the roof, chewing through the chimney and stopping it up. The smoke from the wood oven backed up through the whole house and now I smell like knackwurst. I'll have to do laundry tomorrow and air out the house if the weather is fine. These autumn days are fickle. Sunshine one moment, bitter cold thunderstorms the next. I've covered every inch of the cottage with water repelling tinctures, but the pelting rains wear away and wear away, another worry to add to my long list.

My sister never fails to remind me of the folly of my building a house of sugar to withstand this harsh forest life. Real bricks and mortar, even wood, she says, would have been so much more sensible. But she has to admit when the sunlight hits the gum drops and crystal rock candy just right, there is no more beautiful place in the world. The colors reflect and shine like miniature rainbows around the glen. Lucifer chases the twinkling lights as though he were but a kitten once more. Those are the best of times. The worst? The agony of hunger when my stomach roars angrily, ceaselessly nagging me of the time passing since our last meal.

My sister always bids me patience in that condescendingly serene way she has. We make a strange pair, she and I. Bitterest enemies and rivals since my youngest memories, yet either of us would die for the other. I have often pondered our weird fate, tied up as collaborators in this scheme, the result of a momentary lapse in judgment.

Life was simpler when we were girls. Fighting over clothes and toys. Scrambling for our parents' attention. Teasing the servants and racing for hours across the meadows on our fearless ponies. She always won, just as she now has the better end of the bargain imposed on us by a devil in disguise. I dwell here alone, waiting, always waiting, while she travels the countryside, flirting with any widower she meets. Well, not any. They must have children, of course, or she won't waste her time.

It was an easy decision when we had to divide our labor and pick our roles. She got the looks and charm in the family. I was the plain one, the wallflower destined to be an old maid. To impersonate a crone, the old witch of legend, fell naturally to my lot. Some gritty earth rubbed into my skin and a ratty wig of silver horsehair are all it takes to shift my looks to better fit my chosen profession.

I say chosen, but that word is hardly fitting. Who would choose this lonely, ghastly existence? Isolated until the children arrive, and they are hardly company with their terrified screaming and endless whimpers in the night. I feel sorry for them, naturally. I'm not a monster, but I've been forced to behave as one in order to survive. Don't judge me unless you were given the same choice and looked death in the face.

The will to live is as strong in me as it is in these infants I take in. Their life force is so vital, I can taste it well before our meal. It hums along my veins, intoxicating my mind. When I am drunk enough on their fumes, I do the deed and eat my meat. Enough to keep me alive until the next time and the next. And my sister, of course.

She shows up in time to enjoy the spoils of our latest plotting without having to participate in the nastier bits. So like her to swan around like a queen, picking daintily at the dish I've labored over, as though she'd no idea what she was consuming. But make no mistake, she is as much a murderer as I. More so in my view, for without her, no children would wander this way by accident. We are too deep in the woods here. By design, too far from a civilized world that would string us from the nearest tree if they discovered our lifestyle.

What a tangle it all is! So far from what I intended for my life. I never dreamt of snagging a titled and handsome husband like my sister might have, but I did think I might find a cheerful fellow in possession of a modest estate where I could live comfortably surrounded by an attentive and efficient staff. How I would have laughed in those days to see me now, covered in gingerbread dust and dried icing, performing the oddest sort of manual labor. Or perhaps, not even laughed. I would have just stared in shock, unable to comprehend what had brought me to this pass.

It started innocently enough. A traveling magician was in the neighborhood. Our friends were all mad about him. He was an intriguing fellow, swathed in exotic silk robes but with the palest skin and darkest eyes. Those eyes. I see them still in my nightmares.

Such a cliché, the silliest girlhood fantasy, but it did seem as though he could see into your soul and liked what he found there very much. Maybe he used some of his mystical powers to cast this spell, but we were each convinced he was in love with us and us only, when naturally he was simply playing our social group for the provincial fools we were.

First there was Lotte, who stole pieces of her mother's jewelry and pawned them for a fraction of their worth, to buy Arnulf love tokens which he casually tossed aside. Then Dagmar, who was left with a bundle which brought her no joy. And poor, despairing Sigrid, fished from the icy river waters. She looked quite beautiful with her long red hair draped around her like a shroud.

But it was my sister he paid most attention to and no wonder. I must jealously admit she has a startling beauty, and a charm, a charisma about her none can resist even to this day. So much the opposite of me in every way. Nature has a twisted sense of humor, doesn't it? To gift her with so much and me with so little though our parents were the same. It might have crushed a gentler soul than mine, but I have a spine of steel and determination to match.

I decided Arnulf was mine, and I didn't care what it took to snag him for my own. I'd heard talk of a woman who sold potions from a dank cellar room in the meanest corner of our modest town. I snuck out one night, walking the muddy lanes under the intense light of a full moon. I'll never forget the excitement, the downright wickedness I felt in parading the countryside alone. My soft boots were made for riding, not walking, and my toes were squeezed and aching by the time I reached the outskirts.

Then there was the mad thrill of evading the night watch as I skulked along unfamiliar streets. Knocking at the unmarked door, praying it was the right one, prepared to flee if it was not. The woman who answered was not what I expected. Plainly dressed and looking exhausted; her hands red and inflamed from hard labor and the cold. Physician, heal thyself, I couldn't help but think. If she hadn't the power to grant herself any better existence, what did I think she could do for me?

But I had come too far, taken too great a risk to simply turn around and walk away. (Don't think I haven't rued that decision a thousand times since.) Instead, I whispered low of my desire. A love potion to bind Arnulf to me for all time. She protested. Said it was too dangerous unless my devotion was true and pure. I know now it was nothing more than a passing infatuation with the mystery of the strange and new, but what girl of seventeen doesn't believe her first crush is the greatest romance the world has ever known? Besides, I had coin and she looked in desperate need of it. The battle was quickly won.

I ran home, a lovely blue bottle clutched in one hand. I have it still. It sits on a shelf in the kitchen to goad me with my heedless folly. Mistakes that cannot be undone, cannot be atoned for, eat away at the soul like I gnaw at the delicate bones of my victims. The victims of the decision of an immature and thoughtless girl. In idle moments, I wonder how many more will suffer from this one act of mine.

It was the work of a moment to pour the contents of the bottle into Arnulf's drink. The woman had warned me we must be the only ones in the room, for if he set his eyes on another before he saw me, they might be bonded instead. I'd laid my plans carefully. Made sure we were alone in the house. Sent my sister away on an errand, telling her if she fetched new trim from town, I would freshen up her favorite hat. But I did not take into account her insatiable curiosity and wasn't clever or subtle enough in my subterfuge. As Arnulf drained the cup, she appeared in her full blooming beauty. I suppose it is easy for you to guess the rest.

Or perhaps not? How did we go from a love potion gone awry to our current state of affairs? Well, as the woman had warned me, it only worked if one of the parties felt a true and pure love for the other. My sister had enjoyed the attention, the flirting, the little gifts she'd received from Arnulf, but felt no more for him than the statue of Poseidon that adorned the fountain in our garden. I should really have asked the woman what the result would be without true love's blessing.

Turns out, it was an implacable and bitter hatred on the part of the one who drank the potion. It also transpired Arnulf was no ordinary magician. He had learned the art of charm but also the harsh alchemy of curses. His retribution on us was swift and irreversible. From that day on, no food would sustain us but the flesh of young children. His intent, I think, that we should starve and die a lingering and horrible death rather than embrace such an unthinkable taboo, but he did not reckon with our will to live.

Of course, at first, we tried everything. Ate every food imaginable, always seeking out new and more exotic fare, but the result was always the same. Violent sickness and voiding within moments of anything we consumed. Our parents wrung their hands, doctors and specialists were called in. Hysteria was the diagnosis, so common in impressionable young minds. It is all in your heads, we were told over and over as they offered us every treat imaginable.

We endured for a week before we made our pact. Neither of us was resigned to lying abed dying and that is what we knew would happen unless we acted. Arnulf had left the neighborhood immediately upon cursing us. We knew the nature of the poison I'd fed him would not allow him to relent even if we followed and pleaded with him. Instead, we crept away from the house one night, too weak to take even the smallest bag with us. We and the clothes we wore on our backs were all we had, and we knew once we crossed that forbidden boundary of human behavior, we would be on our own forevermore.

The first one was the hardest. If we had not been driven so desperately by hunger, I don't believe we could have done it. The pattern followed one we employ even to this day. My sister lured in a slum child with her charm and I wielded the knife. We tore into it raw, too ravenous for the niceties of preparing a more appetizing dish. I will never forget the sensation, the rough rubbery feel in the mouth, despair of having the strength necessary to chew, then swallowing and feeling my very being revived, made new by this manna of the gods.

You recoil in disgust, but I will say once more, do not sit in judgment unless you too have felt how near you were to death, to complete and utter nothingness for the simple lack of nourishment. We are no worse than one of those jungle cats who must catch and kill to eat, whether the flesh be that of a beast or a man.

We quickly moved on, afraid the discovery of the remains of even a poor child, the dregs of our town in so many eyes, would remind those who knew us of what they considered to be our bizarre fancy and cause them to hunt us down. What strange days, to go from being the pampered daughters of modest wealth and comfort to outcasts, vampires, monsters. I thought we would go mad at first, and we quarreled endlessly with each other. My sister blamed me for our predicament, and I could not gainsay her, for it was my rash decision which had caused the disaster.

On the other hand, there seemed no remedy, so I encouraged her to be practical. We must embrace that this was our fate. Unless we were prepared to lay down and die, which we'd already demonstrated we were not, we must discover how best to manage, unless we wished to find ourselves dangling from the end of a swaying rope.

Our first dilemma was where to find shelter without attracting unwanted attention. Two refined young ladies such as ourselves, wandering the countryside unaccompanied, was bound to be noticed and remarked upon. Our families would track us down, and even if they did not connect us with the murder of that street urchin, we would be no better off than before we left home.

Driven by fear, we stumbled through the forest, following the paths left by huntsmen and woodcutters, surviving on the remnants of the meat wrapped up in a piece of one of my petticoats, until we found an open glade deep in the woods. A rough lean-to made from fallen branches served as a shelter. We were fortunate it was summer and the nights were mild, or we would surely have died of exposure.

Gradually, we built up our little encampment. Our poor dresses did not hold up well and it proved hard to bathe with any regularity, so we soon no longer looked like proper young ladies, but that was only to our advantage as it made it easier to blend into crowds in nearby towns and villages. No more than yet another servant out doing errands for their masters. My sister became adept at causing distractions while I crept around stealing tools, clothes, and other comforts to supplement our camp.

I was ransacking the backroom of a bakery when I first got the idea for the cottage. There was the sweetest gingerbread castle being built for some celebration feast, no doubt. I poked it with my finger, amazed at how rigid and strong the construction was. It was a crazy thought, but I was bored. We hadn't much to do to pass our time as outcasts since we kept our trips into more populated areas short so as not to attract attention.

It wasn't practical to build a cottage entirely of gingerbread, but then it wasn't practical to think of obtaining and transporting the heavy building materials we would need for a more permanent establishment. Bricks and mortar, wood beams and roof shingles. How were we two girls to wield such things?

But baking I knew well from all the time spent in our kitchen back home watching Cook. Our first obstacle was the oven. We painstakingly gathered stones, rocks, even the stray brick or cobblestone from town streets to create the very oven that stands in pride of place in the midst of our confectionary marvel today. To gather enough ingredients for an entire building was not the work of days, of course. It took a year of backbreaking labor to complete.

It was my sister who sped things along by attracting the attention of a local baker and wedding him. I thought it dangerous to take such a public position as a merchant's wife, but she delighted in the challenge. She convinced him to save money on a delivery driver by allowing her to take the horse and wagons to nearby towns. It was no trouble at all to stop by and offload bags of sugar and flour to aid my building efforts. It meant all the heavy work was up to me, but the bricks of gingerbread were light and easy to lift, yet dried hard enough to serve as a sturdy shelter.

Her tenure as baker's wife did not last too long as he became suspicious of the delivery tallies that did not add up. Along with the town's uproar over a spate of missing infants, she decided it was time to move along. She next snagged a prosperous farmer, but he expected her to get up at the crack of dawn and work until sunset, which was not to her liking one bit. We culled a few of the local offspring there before she gave it up, so it wasn't a total loss.

About this time, rumors and panic were arising around the countryside about the children who had been lost. Everything from faeries to goblins to a demonic wildcat roaming the wilderness were blamed. My sister wanted us to take to the roads again, fearful our hidey hole in the deep woods would be discovered, but I had just put the finishing touches on our sugar palace and was reluctant to abandon it and start over.

You will think me mad, but if you could see it with your own eyes, you would understand. Whatever fancies your imagination can conjure, it is ten, no, a hundred times that. My hands have laid every brick, the icing lovingly applied, every gum drop carefully placed. The beauty of my pulled-sugar windows with their depictions of wildflowers and creatures of the forest. The candy cane fence laboriously installed. How can I find the heart to simply walk away, leaving it to rot and be consumed by the forest?

But deep down, I know my sister is right. We make each meal last as long as we can. I dry and preserve the meat to keep us going during the lean times. Neither of us has an extra ounce of body fat. You can see we are not profligate in our hunting. The bare minimum to survive has always been our motto, but even so, even as careful as we try to be, the number of children adds up and must cause a stir and a reaction. There are murmurings of hunting parties to search the woods for a wild animal on the loose or an escaped lunatic. If they should stumble upon such an unusual dwelling as ours in this forest, we would be undone.

We bury the bones deep, deep beneath the earth but there will be questions. Why are we living out here alone? How did we build such a structure? How do we survive? Such scrutiny would be the death of us, for any such anomaly must excite suspicion among such superstitious folk as are our brethren.

And so, as I labored today, patching the wall, it is with the greatest sadness. All too soon, we will have no choice but to walk away from this, my masterpiece. You could begin anew somewhere else you say, but I don't know that I would have the heart to start over. It pains me to even think of it.

I have a few more days at least to enjoy my putterings around the place. My sister has conjured up a simple woodcutter on the edge of the forest, a widower with two children. He lives an isolated life there and has not heard the rumors yet. She laughs at how amazed and flattered he was to think she would live with him and take care of his offspring.

Poor man. How distraught he was to come home and find them gone. *Lost in the forest*, she tells him through her crocodile tears. *I've looked and looked for them, but I think they've run away, the naughty things.*

How gullible men are to a pretty face. If I had ever had children, I would have been more fiercely loyal to them, but of course, I never shall. The sweet scent of their innocent flesh would drive me wild with hunger. I would see the terror in their eyes. Children are so intuitive. Even addled by sugar, they always cower back when I open the door and invite them in.

These two were woefully underfed. The boy is particularly skinny. I popped him into a cage at once and have been stuffing him with every variety of cookie and cake. If we are to move house, it may be a while before we can hunt again, so it is important to plan ahead and store up as much meat as we can carry with us. Between moaning and yelling, he is a non-stop chatterbox, asking me a million questions from morning to night. It gets exhausting, frankly.

The girl is quiet. She has a kind of charm about her that reminds me of my sister, but she is nothing like as bold. I kept her chained at first, but she is such a meek and mild little thing that I let her run free as long as I am around to keep an eye on her. Besides, she is overly attached to her brother and will not leave him behind even should the opportunity to flee arise. And as long as I have the key to his cage safe in my pocket, he will remain my prisoner.

I don't like having to keep them like this. It only prolongs their suffering and makes it harder to do the deed in the end, but they were so starved when they arrived, it would hardly have been worth the trouble of killing them. At least in their final days, they no longer endure those terrible pangs of hunger that I am all too familiar with. They may finally eat their fill and sleep with full stomachs.

There, that is the last brick in place. A foolish waste of time since our departure seems imminent, but it is satisfying to think I will leave the cottage in good order when we go. I step back to take it in. A true work of art. A pity no one will ever see it to appreciate it.

I had pretensions to becoming an artist when I was a girl, producing some fine sketches and watercolors, but this achievement proves to me my well of creativity has no bounds. I have built this sweet palace in the wilderness, conjured it up out of my imagination, poured my own sweat into the foundations. Whatever else may become of us, I will always remember it most fondly and proudly.

I stow away my tools and go back inside. Pass the mirror in the hall and neaten my wig and am surprised to discover my sister has arrived without my noticing.

"Sister, dear, whatever are you doing here?"

"We must hurry. Their father grows restless. Talks of raising a search party from town. Let us be done with these children and this place before they discover us."

"Shush, you're frightening them," I say, noticing the girl watching wide-eyed. "Go outside and fetch me a pail of water, little one. We'll be having stew for dinner tonight."

She exchanges a glance with her brother, trapped in his cage, but I have no fear. Even if she were brave enough to run through the forest for help, she would get hopelessly lost. Besides, I know she would not abandon her sibling any more than I would ever abandon mine. Some bonds cannot be broken however much it would be to our own benefit.

As she closes the door, I turn back to my sister. "The time has come, I agree. The girl tonight, the boy tomorrow. And we'll need time to prepare our food for the road. We do not want to be caught out in the open with no sustenance at hand. But the day after, first light, we will leave."

"You are always so confident. It will be your undoing. You think you can outsmart the world, but one day you will meet your match."

"Perhaps, but look at how far we've come. When first struck down by this curse, did you think we would last this long? You do not give us enough credit, me enough credit. The architect of this confectionary marvel you stand in is not one to be easily discouraged or fooled. I was blessed with higher-than-average intellect."

She laughs at me. "You and this gingerbread folly. You were always a silly one with your head in the clouds. Don't forget it was your brain, your 'intellect' that got us into this mess."

"As if you ever let me forget it. I was only a girl, a girl who made a mistake. If I could take it back, I would a thousand times over, but it's not possible. We must look to the future and not the past."

The child returns with the water, interrupting my tête-à-tête with my sister by dumping the pail all over my skirt. An accident, I presume, though I wouldn't put it past her to have contrived to do it on purpose. You must never underestimate the sly intelligence of children. They have an almost animal instinct for survival.

By the time I've changed my clothes, my sister has vanished. Typical. She never wants to sully her hands with the fatal deed. I look at my own, starting to gnarl with age and hard manual labor. The nails are permanently encrusted with a residue of sugar and blood, a sweet and salty grime that no amount of scrubbing will remove.

A rare feeling of disgust comes over me. I thought I had come to accept our outlaw way of life, but suddenly, I'm weary to the bone at the thought of another slaughter. The hard work of butchering and drying the meat for the road.

The road, the road. That's what's bothering me, I decide. The idea of leaving my cozy, comfortable gingerbread dwelling and wandering again, far, far away from where our deeds have caused such suspicion and fear. I think of the children of that yet unknown land, innocently going about their business, unaware of the darkness that will descend upon them soon.

I am not a religious person, but we dutifully attended church every Sunday as girls and suffered through many a sermon on the wages of sin. Will my sister and I be called to account one day for our deeds in the fiery pits of Hell? I imagine them to be gigantic versions of my own beloved oven, baking souls instead of cookies and pies and think that might be a fitting punishment though I can think of worse.

What if the spirits of the children we've consumed gathered together to haunt us, pointing their tiny fingers in blame? What if they wailed and screamed as they did in life when they felt the first cut of the blade? I can't pretend I've grown completely immune to the horror of what we do to survive, but the hunger, the hunger spurs us on. A very human imperative that is impossible to resist.

"Shall I fetch some more water, Mother?"

An affectation the girl has adopted, calling me Mother. A tribute to my—in her eyes, at least—advanced age, no doubt, but I don't like it. I want no latent maternal feelings called forth to make my path any harder. The sooner I am rid of her, the better.

"Leave it, child. Come and help me with this oven. The rats have gotten into the chimney. Step in and have a look and tell me if you can see the blue of the sky."

She is an obedient child and quickly complies. "It is all black and looks stopped up."

"Take this soup ladle and poke around as far up as you can. See if you can clear the way from here. Otherwise, we'll have to go up on the roof and see what can be done."

"I'm not sure how to do it, Mother."

Wretched child. No use at all, but I am used to doing everything myself from these many years of isolation.

"Step aside then and let me see."

I crawl in and peer up the chimney to see the brilliant azure sky clearly above. She lied to me, I realize, as the oven door slams shut with a dull whomp and I hear the locking bar fall into place.

A feeling of admiration floods in. I, who pride myself on my wisdom and cunning, have been outmaneuvered by a slip of a girl. What a woman she might have become if she had not crossed our path.

"Now, Gretel, what is the meaning of this? How am I to make supper for you and your brother if I'm trapped in here?"

No response. I didn't really expect one. She is no doubt figuring out some method of freeing her brother from his cage so they can flee back into the forest. It's annoying to be sure, but all I need do is wait for my sister to return and let me out and we can hunt them down together.

I finger the ladle in my hand, tapping it idly against the door from time to time to get her attention the moment she arrives. When I hear a rustling sound, I call out to her but there's no answer.

More noise. It seems familiar. Takes me a moment, but then I recognize it. The sound of logs being loaded into the firebox under the oven. Is it the children? Are they bloodthirsty enough to plot this revenge? Or maybe they view it as a necessary evil to protect others of their kind, for they have no way of knowing whether they will find their way out of the forest or could lead anyone back here to bring us to justice if they did.

Panic arises. To be cooked alive! Such an unthinkable fate and one we never once subjected any of the children to. It was always a quick, clean death for them, but I may not be so lucky. I feel the warmth now. I've always been so proud of this oven. It heats up quickly and holds the fire in well. I start to sweat as smoke seeps in through some cracks I hadn't noticed before.

Coughing, my thoughts turn to my sister. Will she return in time to save me from this fate? If not, what will she think, what will she do when she finds my remains? I've always been the leader, she the follower. Two sides of the same coin, yet so different. So very different.

My lungs start to burn, my eyes sting. Feet blister from the heat radiating through the stones and the thin leather of my slippers. A slow, agonizing death and nothing to be done about it.

But wait, I remember putting my mortar knife into my pocket earlier when I was working on the gingerbread repairs. The metal feels blissfully cool as I fish it out, clutching it in my hand. The edge is dulled from rough use but will be sharp enough if wielded by a determined hand.

Half delirious from the heat and lack of air, I raise the soup ladle with my other hand so I can see my reflection. I want to aim the knife accurately on the first try as I may not have another chance. I'm surprised to see my sister staring back from the reflection. How was it she came to be in the oven with me?

"Do it," she whispers.

I pull the blade across my throat as I watch her do the same. A ragged slice but sufficient if we are patient.

The heat, the blood fade away from my consciousness as I stare at my sister. I am her and she is me and how....

very...

very...

strange...

I never noticed...

before...

THICK
GNARLED VINES
CORRUPT WITH
MOURNING

Beanstalk

Simon Mankiller was lonely in his cloud palace. He had a menagerie of scolding geese that lay emerald eggs, fainting goats that enjoyed butting their heads playfully against his hands, and a few dozen cats he wore draped over every limb throughout the day for warmth. Still, he couldn't help but feel something was missing.

He was the last of his kind so far as he knew, but there were other creatures in the down below. He spent many an hour watching them scurrying around like ants. How often they met and doffed a hat to one another or spread their skirts wide in graceful curtsies. What was it like to be acknowledged so, reassured that one existed?

He grew to love them and gave them names: Red Hat, Honking Cough, Golden Curls. Smirk and Wink and Scowl. Fergus and Aloysius, Adelaide and Theodosia. Me, he christened Claribel, with a voice so light and high, it carried up to the heavens and made him smile. I was but a child then, but I can't help feeling responsible, for it was me who tempted him down from his cloud.

It was my birthday, and I was playing in the meadow near my village with my present, a tiny terrier named Tosh. I've never laughed so hard and long as I did that day watching Tosh make a fool of himself chasing after a wily old hare, too fast and experienced to be caught but enjoying the game as much as we.

Simon saw us, saw our joy and merriment, and wanted a share in it, however small. He dropped a seed no bigger or heavier than a thistledown. It landed and took root, bristling with magic. Tosh and I visited it day by day, astonished to see it doubling and tripling in height. I told Ma and she came, and Pa, and then more and more, until all the village was gathered staring up to where the green stalk touched the heavens so far above our heads.

What did it mean? we wondered. Some thought it a miracle, others the end of the world. It was, of course, a bit of both.

How impatient was the giant as he watched and waited until the vine was tall and sturdy enough to hold his weight. He put on his best shirt—the crisp, white one with red and blue embroidery his mother had made for him so many years ago. It had lain in her old hope chest and now he donned it with hope in his heart. He shined up his leather boots and tucked his cleanest trousers in. Braided his long beard and slicked back his auburn hair.

He stood in front of the mirror practicing, bowing and baring his teeth.

"How do ye do?"

"Pleased to make your acquaintance, I'm sure."

"Fine weather we're having, ain't it?"

Crows wrestled in his stomach and twisted his bowels as he dithered up top. Was today the day? No, better wait until tomorrow. But there, the little girl was playing with her puppy again, and the other villagers were picnicking. A celebration of sorts in veneration and awe at this new plant, unique in all the world.

The urge to join them, join a community overwhelmed him. The beanstalk was immeasurably long to those below, but for a giant, with his long limbs and immense strength, it was the work of a moment to scramble down. Too quick for those below to register the looming danger and flee.

As he stepped off, his right foot wiped out Mr. Perry's herd of cows, grazing in a nearby field. His left foot crushed half our village. I stood and stared, too shocked to move as Tosh leapt forward and attacked the giant's shoelaces. My shock was no greater than Simon's own, mortified and grieved over his disastrous debut into our society.

From that day to this, he has never moved another step, but weeps bitterly over our fate and his. His salty tears killed the beanstalk, ending any hope he had of retreating home to escape from his inadvertently tragic faux pas. So he stands, still as a rock. Thick, gnarled vines, corrupt with mourning, sprouted from the scorched earth, wind round his feet and legs, rooting him still further.

Many were the calls to put him to death at first but, laying aside the practical- ities of killing such an immense being and the damage he would do if he fell to slaughter like a tree in the forest, most felt sorry for Simon. Mankiller by name but not by nature. A gentler soul you will never meet.

We've trained a flock of mourning doves to deliver packages of food and water to his hands. The more adventurous villagers climb the vines that surround him to enjoy the unparalleled views. Those of us who understand him best, perch up high and tell him our secrets. His fame has grown wide, and the village reaps the rewards through a brisk tourist trade. Every year on the anniversary, bouquets are laid at the giant's feet in memory of those entombed below them.

Tosh is grey now and no longer runs after hares, but lazes in the sun. I catch Simon staring at him and at me and wonder if he regrets his decision. I would never dare ask—the guilt I carry is already heavy. But as I sit in the warm curve of his ear and watch the people milling about below, I hear the thrum-thrum-thrum of his heart. He will never be short of company again as long as I live.

HE BALANCED GRACEFULLY ON A ... SPHERE OF PURE ORANGE FIRE ...

THE PRICE

"NEVER VENTURE INTO THE forest without us."

Their parents had warned them so many a time, but children would not be children if they were not occasionally naughty. Even the best may be tempted from the path. Marta, Jakob, and Henrik were well-brought-up children, but one evening as they played in the meadow behind their family's cottage under the fading twilight, they were lured into doing what they had never dreamt of doing before.

It was the far-off song of a calliope that first enticed them. A high eerie noise, like a chorus of agitated songbirds piping an alert when a raptor was hunting overhead. Henrik was the youngest and least cautious of them all. He ran to the edge of the woods, clapping his hands in time to the distant melody. Jakob joined his brother, and they chattered together in delight and wonder at the extraordinary sound.

"Come back from there," cried Marta, as her brothers joined hands and dashed away through the trees. She sighed in vexation. At thirteen, she was four years older than Jakob and six years older than Henrik but felt it might have been a hundred years instead, so much more mature and sensible was she. However, she loved them all the same, so, as any good big sister would, she followed.

She quickly caught them up and grabbed onto the backs of their woolen jackets to stop their flight. They twisted and bucked in her grasp, but she had plenty of practice at bridling them and would not be shaken off.

"Listen, Marta," said Jakob. "Isn't it a lovely sound?"

"Lovely? It sounds like a chorus of dying canaries to me," snorted Marta, but even as she said it, she felt the spell of the tune, just as her brothers had done. Almost without thought, she let them go and grabbed Henrik's other hand. The three moved forward as one, drawn deeper and deeper into the forest with an overwhelming desire to know what was creating this music so far from any town or neighbor.

It was dark under the trees, the fading rays of an autumn sun insufficient to light their way. They might have turned back then, daunted by the gloom and the eldritch trees that twisted and swayed like ancient and crippled giants leering down at them, but for the sudden appearance of rows of fairy lights, twinkling and beckoning.

"Fireflies," thought Marta, but they were too regularly spaced and still to be living things. They outlined a path the children had not noticed before, straight through the center of the woods.

"We should go back," she advised her brothers, a sense of panic awakening deep within her even as the music continued to pull with its siren song.

"Only a little more," Jakob pleaded. "It doesn't sound far away at all. We'll see what it is, then run all the way back home."

Her mind was screaming no, but her will was no longer her own. She nodded and the three marched forward, hand in hand. The source of the sound seemed neither nearer nor farther as they walked, but always just out of reach. Even the boys were getting discouraged when a ghostly figure leapt onto the path in front of them, sending the dry leaves scattered on the earth scurrying for cover.

It was a white cat, bigger than even old Widow Vogel's champion mouser, renowned far and wide for his remarkable size. Its fur was luxurious and danced and swayed to the music like it had a mind of its own. The cat walked upright on its back legs like a human and swept a magnificently glossy black top hat down from its head with a flourish and a low bow.

"Welcome, children. I will be your guide and host."

Marta and Jakob were old enough to be amazed and even a little frightened when confronted by a talking cat, but their younger brother knew no such hesitation.

"Host of what?" asked Henrik.

"The Carnival of the Forsaken."

None of them had ever heard the word forsaken before, but everyone knows a carnival is full of fun and food. They eagerly trailed their fey guide along the path and through a cemetery of fallen trees oozing sap from the cut of a cruel axe. The cat threaded his way delicately through the devastation, turning back from time to time to encourage them with a gentle smile.

"Come, children. Keep up."

They followed it to a pair of elaborate iron gates that towered over them in a wild display of curlicues and arcane symbols. The gates stood solitary in the forest, no wall or fence, but before them sat a badger on a three-legged stool, its milky white eyes staring into nothingness as it beat on a drum with a pair of bones. To those who understood its language, the low sound spoke of regret and missed opportunities, of wrong paths taken and despair, but the children were innocent of such things and only marveled at the strange sight.

"All who visit our carnival must leave a sacrifice at the gate," the cat informed them.

Jakob laughed. "Why not run around it?" he shouted, suiting action to word only to find himself spread-eagled flat on his back on the ground.

"Tsk, tsk. Entrance through the gate only, please," said their host. "The forest does not like cheaters, and neither does the carnival. A sacrifice, please."

The children stared at one another. What had they to sacrifice?

"Check your pockets," suggested the cat.

They explored and were surprised to find objects which they had never put there.

Marta found a smooth stone, black as tar in her pocket. It brought to mind the image of the dark mole on her friend Lotte's nose. Marta had stood by while the other girls made fun of it and said nothing, even when Lotte started to weep from their cruelty.

An ivory feather marked with blood was Jakob's. He remembered with shame when he had wounded a flying dove with the impulsive throw of a sharp stick.

And for Henrik, the tiny skull of a mouse gleaming in the moonlight reminded him of the time he had cheered when Mrs. Vogel's cat had caught one of the tiny creatures with sharp claws and swallowed it whole.

Eager to rid themselves of these unpleasant mementos, they set their guilty treasures before the gates, which swung open with a protesting screech, gouging deep trenches in the muddy earth. Calliope and drum fell silent.

"You may enter."

An uncanny shiver rattled the children. Marta would have forced her brothers to run home then and there but for a brilliant celadon moth, fuzzily glowing, which approached and kissed her sweetly on the nose, making her giggle. The moth flitted away through the gates, and the children followed.

A towering black bear wearing a lavender and lemon jester's hat greeted them. His arms were twisted at grotesque angles, paws dangling uselessly, but still he balanced gracefully on a sphere of pure orange fire, shifting this way and that as the bells on the points of his hat jingled out a tune of lamentation. The children wept in time to his pain.

In a flurry of wind and thunder, an elegant horned owl as tall as Henrik landed beside them. The storm lasted no longer than it took for her to reach out one brown-mottled wing to wipe their cheeks with a touch of feathers as gentle as a mother's kiss.

"Your sympathy speaks volumes for you, my dears, but dry your eyes," the owl said, flinging their tears from the tips of her feathers to the sphere of fire under the bear's feet. The orange flame went out with a snaky hiss, and a dragon of steam wafted away into the canopy of trees.

The bear bowed low in thanks for this deliverance from its fiery dilemma. The jester's cap fell from its head, a small object tumbling out and landing near Marta's boots.

"A grimoire," said the owl. "It's a special kind of book bound with magic. If fear overcomes you during your visit tonight, open it to any page and it will spirit you away home."

Although the leather-bound tome was greasy and ill to touch, the girl stowed it away in her pocket as her brothers looked on, wide-eyed.

"That's all very well, but we shouldn't dawdle," said the white cat.

As he spoke, a plague of spotted grackles descended and circled like a coven chanting a bitter spell.

"Go back, go back, go back," they shrieked, darting around the children as dancers weave around a maypole.

The white cat sprang at the birds, a hiss and snap, snap, snap of sharp teeth startling them into raucous flight. "Pay them no mind, children. Familiars sent by the Witch of the Woods to trick you from the path."

The girl eyed him gravely, wondering whether he spoke true. "Who is the Witch of the Woods, and why should she care what we do?"

"A charlatan. An entertainer. Crystal balls and fortunes and a thousand colorful scarves when she goes to town. She makes her home deep in the forest and is jealous of any who would enter these woods as she values her privacy above all else. She sends emissaries to harass and worry us and those who would attend our entertainment, but she has no real power here. Do not fret yourself."

Marta eyed the ground abandoned by the grackles and spied a token left by the departed flock. A card with a figure of bone wrapped in a cloak named darkness. She trembled as she picked it up and read a word: DEATH.

The owl reassured her. "Child, 'tis but a tarot card. Means a new beginning and adventure, it does."

"So you say," Marta replied, adding the card to the pocket that already held the grimoire.

"Come with me, my dears," said the owl, glancing nervously at the cat which swished its tail from side to side in annoyance at the delay.

She herded the children onward with a flutter of outstretched wings, lurching side to side like a sailor caught in a raging storm. Marta noticed each of the owl's toes were lacking the last joint. The bird caught her gaze, and explained, "A ritual. Nothing more."

"A ritual? Someone did that to you on purpose?" The girl planted her feet firm as the roots of an oak against the gentle onward urging of the owl. "What is it that lies ahead? Are there monsters?"

"Some would call them so. But they are simply a troupe of forgotten souls who live now only to amuse visitors to the carnival. They grow impatient to perform. We must hurry."

Ahead of them, a towering big top, tented with hundreds of layers of grey organza, billowed ghost-like, festooned with drooping balloons, long since deprived of spirit enough to float and soar. An elephant guarded the entrance, its once majestic ears shredded and torn, tusked head lowered in shame.

Henrik cried out in pity, caressing the beast's questing trunk. "What happened to you?"

The elephant gazed at the children, the wrinkled folds of its skin darkened with the mourning of long weeping. "The necromancer speaks to the lost ones and weaves spells of protection for us all. To do so, he must have pain. He has no choice."

Marta shook her head, blonde braids flying, and stamped her feet. "No! That's not right! What is this necro... necro..."

"Necromancer," said the cat. "A great wizard. Protects us from the Witch of the Woods and any outsiders who might discover us and bring us harm. No one minds the sacrifice."

"But what have you sacrificed?" asked the girl.

"My fur was once every color of the rainbow. I was unique in the world. No other cat save I had such a magnificent coat. I gave that up and must live with the pain of being quite an ordinary color, or rather, no color at all."

Marta scoffed. "You call that pain compared to what these others have suffered."

"It hurts my soul to be so plain. You shouldn't judge what you cannot understand."

"I understand this wizard must be without a soul to wound helpless animals. Where is he? In here?" She gestured to the filmily curtained tent entrance and made a move toward it.

"No, child!" cried the owl, but it was too late. She was gone. Her brothers made to follow, but the owl enfolded each in one great wing and held them close. "Stay here. It's not safe, but she has a brave heart. She may survive without harm."

Marta stormed into the tent. A tall figure in a cloak of dark feathers stood in the middle of a ring formed from animal skulls of every shape and size. The lone spotlight of a candle high above reflected in a cracked mirror and shone down upon the being's inky head but did not illuminate the face hidden under a long hood.

Dry sawdust flew beneath the girl's feet as she ran forward. "Is it you? Is it you who maims these poor things? Why must you hurt them so? If you have so much power, you should be able to do your tricks without such cruelty. If you are powerful, make them all better instead!"

The figure laughed, a high chittering sound. "Aren't you the plucky one? You are fortunate I appreciate boldness. I might be persuaded to help them. But why should you care? What are they to you?"

"They are suffering creatures. Who could look at them and not feel heartbroken?"

"You must have a heart to feel it break. I lost mine long ago. But it might be amusing to try and heal them. I have nothing better to do at the moment, and my routine becomes dull. But in lieu of pain, I would need a magical object. I don't suppose one such as you would happen to have such a thing?"

The girl thought of the grimoire. The owl had said it was bound with magic. Perhaps it would do. As she touched the oily leather of the ancient tome and pulled it from her pocket, the feathered cloak collapsed in a whoosh and melted into a pool of dark ichor which snaked outward in thin streams of rot and decay along the sawdusted floor.

A black cat appeared in place of the cloak, screeching and spitting. "Evil child, what have you done? Unknit my form and unleashed a doom upon this place and all in it! It was I and I only who protected us from—"

The cat froze as an acrid breeze fluttered the filmy walls of the tent, billowing with the scent of sulfur and molasses. The girl spied a will-o'-the-wisp, no bigger than a firefly, drift down softly and alight on one of the cat's shivering ears.

"I sensed the protective spell around your little enterprise had been broken, dark one. I am on my way to deal with you in person, but who is this child?"

Marta quaked in mortal fear of the light, so mild and gentle and entrancing, yet with a voice that promised only darkness.

The black cat spoke. "She is the cause of our undoing. She brought a book of magic into my presence. I shall be rid of her and reweave my spell."

The cat strode toward Marta, but the light jumped to the girl's head, buzzing and burning with a not unpleasant warmth.

"Touch one hair and it is you who shall suffer." Sparks flew and singed the cat's fur, embers glowing red against its black silky coat. The light floated away again to address them both. "I owe her a boon for bringing you to heel, rogue. What would she like I wonder?"

"She wishes to heal the forsaken of their hurts," the cat scoffed. "But I am the one who inflicted them for the good of us all, and it is only I that can heal them."

"You are overconfident. So, she wants to heal the poor creatures? A noble cause. A generous one. But what would she be willing to do for them? Travel farther into the heart of this haunted forest? Face dangers unknown?"

"What kind of dangers?" asked the girl.

A tinkling laugh. "They wouldn't be unknown if I told you, would they? That is part of the trial. Anyone can weigh the risks and benefits when they know the path. The true test is whether you would undertake such a quest without knowing the cost?"

"What of my brothers?"

"You may take them with you or leave them here. It matters not."

"I cannot take them into danger. I will leave them here with the owl. She has a good heart, I think. But I will do what I can to help these animals. I'll never rest easy again if I do not."

"Very well. You have made your choice and must abide by it."

A twisted cornhusk doll, bound up in ragged strips of unravelling burlap, appeared at the girl's feet.

"Take this token of earthen magic to the Lake of Flame. Wait for a gust of wind to speak your name, then toss it in. When earth, fire, water, and air elements combine, the curse of this place will lift, and all who dwell here will be healed."

Marta picked up the uncanny totem and held it close. "Which way shall I go?"

The white cat sauntered into the tent and joined his ebon brother. The will-o'-the-wisp spoke to both.

"Guide your guest along the path as far as you dare. Then she must go on alone."

"And why should we?" the felines inquired, speaking in unison as though they were one being instead of two. "What good will come of it for us when you are on your way here to evict us from the forest?"

"You needn't help her. It is all one to me. Examine your own consciences if you have any left."

The brothers communed silently then turned to Marta. "We will escort you part of the way but then must take our leave. We have no wish to still be in the forest when the Witch arrives."

"A wise thought, my feline fiends. A warning to you, child. The book you carry is full of arcane lore known only to a few of us. Never open it except in direst need. Even I cannot predict the consequences of using it."

"The owl promised it would take us home."

"Perhaps. That owl is very old, older even than I. It is possible she is right." And with that, the light vanished like a candle being snuffed out.

Outside the tent, Marta embraced her brothers.

"Don't go, Marta," cried little Henrik, grasping onto her coat with both hands. "Don't leave us."

"Or let us go with you," added Jakob, struggling to look grownup and brave even while his eyes filled with tears.

"I promised Mother and Father to always look out for you. It is safer for you to wait here until I return. Then we will run home together and jump into bed and pull the covers right up over our heads!" she said with a sad smile, stooping to embrace them both.

The brothers sniffled and snotted messily in their grief but let her go.

"Please look after them," Marta asked the owl.

"I will try, child. I am no longer as young and powerful as I once was, but I will do my best."

"Thank you. Lead on," the girl commanded the cats, who flattened their ears and hissed their displeasure but turned and walked away into the forest, arm in arm.

Marta took a deep breath and followed. They soon passed a shuttered carousel, grown thick with vines of moonflower and its once vivid colors faded and tired. The carved animals grimaced and waited, two by two, in the moonlight. One winked at her, squeezing out a slow tear.

The girl shuddered. "Are they alive?"

"Neither alive nor dead," said the cats. "They are trapped between worlds and must doze and dream in uneasy slumber."

Marta stopped and pulled away a vine that looked to be strangling a grey-spotted unicorn.

"No time for that, girl," chided the brothers. "You must reach the lake by midnight. Magic is most powerful at that hour."

"How will I know it's midnight? There are no clocks in the forest."

"You will know. You will feel and hear it. Watch and listen for signs."

They trudged on through the woods until they reached a clearing, ringed round with a fairy circle of purple mushrooms. In the midst was a glimmering coffin of light. Though the cats urged her on, the girl ran over to peer into the unearthly box. A doe, limbs broken and splayed, diamond-painted in harsh mockery of harlequin finery stared back at her.

Marta cried out in frustration over the cruel plight of the animal and all the other forsaken souls she had met. Was there really no remedy for them other than this scrambling and slithering through dense forest overgrowth and to who knew what end?

"I am only a young girl after all," she complained to her companions. "Why should it be up to me to save them?"

"Don't look to us. It was you who decided to undertake this task, and only you can complete it. If you want to help them, we must hurry."

"What's the rush?" asked a silky voice.

An enormous red fox blocked their path. The cats screamed in unearthly fright and scrambled off through the underbrush. The fox's tail swished wildly, creating the illusion it had more than one, as the girl watched it, mesmerized by the rapid movement.

"I asked, what's the rush? It isn't polite to ignore a civil question."

"I'm on a quest. To save some creatures who have been hurt by dark magic. I must reach the Lake of Fire by midnight, but you've frightened off my guides."

"A quest. How noble. But why save them? I would be more concerned about saving myself if I were you. Aren't you even a little bit afraid of me?"

The fox eyed her greedily, smacking its lips. Its eyes shone bright and white teeth sparkled sharply.

"Should I be? What would you want with me?"

"You look to be a tasty morsel," the fox answered, coming close and sniffing her up and down. "Plump enough and fresh to boot. This must be my lucky night. And what have you there?"

Marta tightened her quivering grip on the twisted corncob doll as the fox's hot breath tickled her neck. "It is earth magic."

The fox spit through its teeth and sprang away from her as though scorched. "The devil you say."

"Who's frightened now?" she asked. With her other hand, she pulled the grimoire from her pocket and thrust it in the fox's face. She felt the magic flowing through the ancient book and it renewed her courage. "Begone!"

There was a flash of blue light and the fox flickered like a dying campfire on a stormy night. Slowly fading, the fox hovered in the air, glaring at her. Marta gathered her nerve and ran through the fetid red ghost, which plucked at her clothing and tingled her flesh as she passed.

Without her guides, she had no choice but to continue in the direction they had been heading. She ran and ran, never pausing until a glow appeared in the distance. It was an endless lake, its churning surface alight with the fire of a thousand lanterns. The paper shapes bobbed and dipped along the surface of the water creating the illusion of a great beast swimming toward her.

She stood uncertainly on the shore. The cats had warned her to wait until midnight to attempt the spell, but how was she to know when that was? How long she and her brothers had been in the forest, she couldn't say. It seemed both minutes and eons since they had first heard the calliope calling to them as they played in the meadow.

Mother and Father would be worried sick when they didn't come back for bedtime. Were they out searching? Maybe they had sent for the constable. Marta knew they would be in terrible trouble when they did get home, but she didn't care. She would just be thankful to bring her brothers home safely.

But first, she must complete her task. She studied the lanterns and listened to the wind. It was gentle at first, a soft breeze that made the chill night even colder, but as she waited, it picked up steam, growing wild in the limbs of the trees, shaking down dry leaves like a snowstorm.

A gust stronger than the rest blew over her, engorged with the nocturnal mutterings of lost souls. At first, the words made no sense, guttural moans and sighs, but suddenly she heard her name, clear as clear. Without a second thought, Marta flung the corncob doll as far as she could out over the waters. It landed with a sploosh followed by a hush as the paper lanterns went out in twos and threes until all was darkness and quiet.

Slowly, slowly, sounds returned. The creak and croak of frogs calling out to one another, the soft chirp of crickets, and rustlings in the leaves of small creatures intent on their own business.

Was that it? Marta wondered. How was she to know if the spell had worked? There seemed nothing to do but head back to the carnival and see. She turned to go, fearing the long walk back alone. A movement caught her eye. The harlequin-painted doe, once broken and trapped in the coffin of light, but healed now and bowing its head in reverence to her.

"You saved me, child. Ask me any service and it is yours."

"I am frightened and alone. Will you walk with me back to the carnival?"

"I can do better. I will carry you there."

The doe knelt so the girl could clamber aboard more easily. Together, they hurried back the way she'd come. They passed the clearing with the fairy mushroom ring and reached the carousel, a sight to behold as all the animals had come to life and were prancing around and congratulating one another.

The grey-spotted unicorn ran up to Marta and the doe. "Look, child, we are free. We are free."

The girl couldn't help but laugh to see the joyful sight. Lion and lamb, dragon and seahorse, unicorn and manticore flying around in a quadrille of movement and color. The carousel itself twirled and sang the calliope tune that had drawn the children into the forest. The sound brought Marta up sharp. She must return to her brothers and quickly.

The doe answered her plea to hurry, and they flew the rest of the way to the tent where the forsaken misfits were gathered.

The badger, eyes clear and bright, and bear, broken arms healed. The owl, talons once more complete, and elephant, flapping its mended ears in delight. There were many other animals besides, made whole again and rejoicing. Even the cats reappeared casually, as if they had never abandoned her out of cowardice or planned to make themselves scarce from the Witch. Perhaps their curiosity to see the results of the spell was too irresistible.

Marta's heart sang to see the creatures celebrating, but of her brothers, there was no sign.

The cats answered her unasked question. "Magic always has its price."

"What do you mean? Where are they?"

"Your brothers were the price for the restoration of all to health. The Witch of the Woods has claimed them as her servants and will allow us to live freely in the forest if we no longer entice strangers in with our show. She was feeling generous and said that you may go home, but you shall not see your brothers again."

"No! No one warned me there would be such a price. I was trying to do what was right. My brothers had no part in it."

"We don't make the rules," replied the cats. "I warned you when my spell of protection was broken that we would be at the Witch's mercy. We're fortunate she has decided we may live out our days here as long as we do not disturb her peace. You would do best to head back home. At least your parents will have one child left to dote on. The only power strong enough to overcome the Witch is dark magic, and we have decided we've had enough of such doings."

"No," Marta answered, pulling the grimoire from her pocket. "If magic can be used against her, something in here will tell me how to save them."

The owl hooted a warning, but it was too late. The girl opened the book. A blinding flash struck, and she was home again in her family's small cottage, sitting by the warm hearth fire. She could have screamed in frustration, but the low voices of her parents in the other room stopped her cries.

"Our children," said her mother. "What has become of them? How shall we go on without them?"

Father's low rumble replied. "Don't worry, my sweet. I will ride into town and bring back as many volunteers as I can rouse. At first light, we will march into the forest, and we won't rest until we find them."

Marta's heart twisted in fear. The Witch of the Woods would not appreciate such an invasion. Who knew what punishment she might inflict upon the townspeople or her brothers or even the poor animals that had only just regained their freedom and health? She must find Jakob and Henrik before daybreak.

She jumped up from the hearth and crept stealthily to the front door, remembering to open it only as far as necessary for her to squeeze out, lest the creak it made on wide opening be heard. She ran back to the edge of the forest as tears started to fall. She was exhausted, tired to the bone, weary in heart and mind. How was she to find the carnival again? And from there, the Witch's home? Who knew how far it was, or how difficult to reach? Shivering from cold and despair, she thrust her hands deep into her pockets.

There again was the now-hated grimoire that had stolen her far from her brothers. And something else. She had forgotten the tarot card, dropped by the grackles, the messengers of the Witch. The Death card's skeletal figure grinned at her, taunting her predicament. Wishing to hide the evil face, she tucked the card into the grimoire.

Another flash engulfed her, and she found herself in a strange house much grander than any she had ever imagined. Pink marble coursed across the floors and gold-encrusted wallpaper ivied up the walls to a ceiling so high, Marta felt as an ant must looking up to the branches of the tallest pine tree. A fire burned merrily in an enormous fireplace, filling the hall with a toasty warmth. Ornately carved doors and a dozen dusky suits of armor, each figure grasping a wicked spear, lined either side of the corridor. In the midst of all, a grand staircase rose to a second-floor gallery displaying portraits that gazed down severely at her.

Marta took one tentative step forward. A grinding and clanking of metal assaulted her ears as the suits of armor sprang to life. Their progress was ponderous, but she was too shocked to attempt an escape before they encircled her, sharp spears trapping her in their midst.

"A visitor. How delightful."

Marta craned her head up to see a lovely vision in white floating down the stairs. A woman in a dress made of pearls. Her golden locks flicked and caressed her shoulders. Following her were two boys dressed in crimson velvet suits, lifting the long train of the white gown. So unlike her memories of them, it took the girl a moment to recognize her brothers as these solemn figures.

"Jakob! Henrik!" she cried, but they paid her no mind, so intent upon their duty were they.

"They will not answer you, my dear. Their thoughts are all for me and whatever little tasks they can do to please me, aren't they, boys?"

"Yes, Mother," they agreed in unison.

"You are not their mother. How dare you when their true parents weep and call out for them at home with empty arms?"

"Really. Such spunk was mildly amusing from a distance, but now that we meet in person, it is less so."

"You're the Witch of the Woods?"

"Of course. Surprised? People often are. I'm not the crippled old crone they expect. But I can take on any number of appearances. Today, this one pleases me, but when I grow bored, I shall put on another shape as easily as you change your clothes. Now I have a question for you. How did you come to be here in my stronghold? None may enter without my permission."

"I... I don't know. I put the tarot card your birds dropped into the grimoire and suddenly I was here."

"Interesting. It must react upon the owner of any object within its pages. I grow desirous of examining this unusual tome. Hand it over to me."

"Give me my brothers back and you can have the book."

"Don't be absurd. I kept my word by helping you heal those stupid creatures you were so concerned about. It is only right you gave me something in return."

"But I didn't know there would be such a price demanded."

"Magic always comes at a cost. Did your parents never read you fairy tales? When does anyone get a miracle for free?"

"If you must have something, take me instead and send my brothers home. It was my responsibility to take care of them and my decision to use magic. I should pay the price."

"An excellent idea with one improvement. I shall keep all three of you now you have joined our party. My family is growing by leaps and bounds. I have been lonely of late. Your company should entertain me, although children can be insipid. But you will grow up quickly enough and perhaps prove more diverting companions in time. My bargain is looking better and better."

"That isn't fair. I thought you wanted to help me. How can you be so selfish?"

"Now you begin to understand my nature. I assisted you on your mission because it amused me to do so at the time. I was just as likely not to have bothered. I am a little whimsical that way."

The witch waved her arms, and the phalanx of armor marched away to their pedestal perches along the hallway.

"Now that we've established you children are at my mercy, maybe you will give me the book with no more arguments."

"If you want it so badly, why don't you come take it?" Marta said, thrusting the grimoire behind her back.

"You really understand nothing of magic, do you? The possessor of such an enchanted object must give it up freely. I cannot take it by force."

"Then I'll never give it to you, unless you free me and my brothers."

"Foolish child, it will be simple to change your mind."

"Never. My brothers could tell you how stubborn I am. You might as well give in to me if you want the book."

The hallway darkened. The witch's hair flew about like a mad thing as a wind arose from every corner, swirling into a howling vortex.

"You have not understood anything about me after all. You will give me the book freely. Come to me, Jakob."

The older boy stepped forward obediently, eyes blank. Quick as the snap of a whip, the Witch reached out with a silvered knife and cut one of the boy's ears off. Marta cried and shut her eyes to block out the horrid sight, but not before seeing a cascade of blood pour down her brother's unflinching cheek.

"Now do you understand me? I will not hesitate to slice and slice again until you hand me the book. If you care for your brothers as you say, give it to me."

Marta opened her eyes and pulled the grimoire around from her back, staring at it, in shock at the Witch's ruthless violence. She hated the sight of the book, blamed it for all her misfortunes. Why shouldn't she hand it over? She had every proof that the Witch's threats were real. Thankfully, Jakob didn't seem to feel any pain, so lost was he under her spell, but Marta's pain and guilt were fathomless.

She stepped forward. A long golden hair blown about by the storm landed on the grimoire, tangling round it like a writhing snake. An impulse came over

Marta, some instinct beyond her ken. She rushed past the Witch and flung the book, hair and all, into the roaring fire. As she watched, the grimoire was set ablaze and wept a golden ooze which sputtered and spattered like hot grease in a cast iron pan.

She heard a screech of agony, and the wind ceased abruptly. All became deathly silent.

Marta turned slowly. A matching pool of golden ooze was spreading on the pink marble floors. Loose pearls bounced and rolled in every direction as the elaborate gown unthreaded itself. Of the Witch of the Woods, there was no other sign.

Her brothers stood dazed a moment, then Jakob clutched the side of his head with a howl of agony. There was no magic left to heal his wound. Marta bound it up as best she could with strips of cloth from her petticoat while Henrik clung to her and cried.

"We should leave while we can," Marta said. "I don't trust this place."

She moved to the front doors, giant stained-glass masterpieces depicting angels and devils cavorting and taunting one another. Try as she might, she could not get the doors to budge. She ran around to every window she could find, but all were sealed tight. They were trapped.

Her brothers followed her from room to room, shoulders slumped, heads bowed low in exhaustion and defeat and the aftermath of terror. She tried to rally them when they reached the kitchen.

"Let us eat a little. It's been a long time since supper." She gathered some simple food: bread, cheese, a few apples.

"What if they are poisoned?" asked Jakob, his voice hoarse and heavy with pain.

"Why should they be? Surely even a witch must eat," said Marta. "But I will test them for you."

She took a bite of all, and they waited to see what would happen. When all seemed well, they ate eagerly, even Jakob finding his appetite reawakened following their night of fright and exertion.

"We must look to the good," said Marta. "We're together again, and the Witch is gone. Let's rest a while, then we'll find a way out and through the forest and back home. I promise."

They huddled together on a paisley-patterned chaise lounge, pulling a sealskin rug over themselves for warmth. The shadows came and went as the sun crossed the sky, but the children slept on, exhausted by all they had endured.

Twilight came and went again before Marta woke with a start from a nightmare of blood and pearly horror. She eased herself off the sofa so as not to awaken her brothers, determined to find a way to escape from their prison. She marched to the front doors to reexamine the locks. As she neared, the world exploded into fragments of a thousand shards of colored glass.

She threw her arms in front of her face and saved herself the worst of the blow, but glass embedded itself into her thick woolen jacket and scraped and cut her hands.

She peered out to find a motley crew of rescuers staring back. The elephant, bleeding from its head, showed the cost it had paid to ram open the stained-glass doors. The owl stepped forward, brushing a path through the glass on the floor with her wings. The bear and badger and harlequin doe stepped delicately behind her.

And over all their heads, leapt a black and white blur. The two cats gracefully landed beside Marta and started plucking the glass from her clothes and hair with their dexterous claws.

"My child!" cried the owl. "Whatever are you doing here?"

"What am I doing here? I should ask what all of you are doing here," the girl said.

"We held a conference of the forsaken after you disappeared and agreed it was only right that we should send a delegation to try and rescue your brothers. After all, without your help, we would still be suffering and at the witch's mercy. The elephant, doe, bear, badger, and I volunteered to do our best."

"And we came along," said the cats, "because we were curious to see the battle. Cats are most inquisitive creatures, you know. But maybe we needn't have bothered since you are here already. How did you arrive before us, and where is the Witch?"

"The grimoire brought me here, and I think I killed the Witch, but only after she cut off Jakob's ear, and oh, I want to go home!" she wailed, overcome at all that had happened and the unexpected arrival of the animals.

"My poor dear," said the owl, wrapping Marta up in her soft feathered wings. "My poor dear ones," she said, seeing the boys venturing out into the hall with wide eyes. "What a trial you have survived, and all to help strangers such as we. Do not worry. We shall see you home, but first we must rest up for the journey. It was a long walk here, and we are also weary."

Eager as she was to be home, Marta saw the sense in waiting. Jakob was shaky and worn from his injury, and little Henrik needed rest, too. The animals made themselves at home, exploring the mansion, raiding the kitchen, and bringing fresh fruits and vegetables to the elephant, who was too large to venture beyond the great hall. The glass was swept away, and Marta's and Jakob's injuries tended to. Then all settled in for a restorative sleep.

Shadows moved and swayed as they slept and slept, illuminating and hiding faces sometimes peaceful, sometimes troubled in their dreams. It was the owl who first awoke, being a watchful creature and unused to such long sleeping. She awakened the others one by one, and feeling refreshed, they ate a solemn meal then set out on their journey.

Marta rode the harlequin doe, and the boys clung to the back of the giant bear. The elephant ambled ahead, clearing out underbrush and fallen trees to ease their path. The cats dashed to and fro, chasing small creatures as cats will, and the badger kept up their spirits by singing ballads it had learned in its youth. The owl soared above them all, keeping an eye on the band of adventurers.

They traveled the better part of the day, and the sun was setting low again when they reached the edge of the forest. The children cried out in delight and relief to see the familiar silhouette of their cottage. They hugged the creatures in thanks, except for the cats who disdained such familiarity, and clasped hands as they ran across the meadow and home.

Their steps slowed as they neared. The cottage looked so different. Not at all as they remembered. Tumbledown and ivy-covered. The door was missing and the interior empty and overgrown with wild plants which had crept in through the floorboards and chinks in the stone.

"Mother? Father?" Marta called out softly, knowing in her heart there would be no answer. A chill overcame them as they backed out and away from the cottage. Little Henrik gave out a cry as he stumbled over a rock. No, not a rock. A stone.

A gravestone. And Mother and Father's names chiseled there, and an impossible date, too far into the future to be real.

Beside it rested another smaller stone: *In memory of our children, Marta, Jakob, Henrik. Lost to the forest but never lost to our hearts.*

"What has happened, Marta?" cried Jakob.

"Time. Time has happened while we were sleeping. There is always a price for magic. We've paid for the Witch's death and our escape with years and years we can never get back. We shall never see Mother or Father again, or anyone we once knew. It is the price."

The children, who no longer felt like children, bowed their heads in bleak understanding.

"What shall we do? There is no place for us here. All has changed and left us behind," Marta said. She felt a soft rubbing against her leg and looked down to see a shadow on either side of her, one white, one black.

"We know a place for you among other misfits," they said, long tails twitching. "Come with us and be forsaken no more."

Sister and brother and brother took hands and turned back to the forest.

"We're ready."

Part 3: Glimpses of the Future

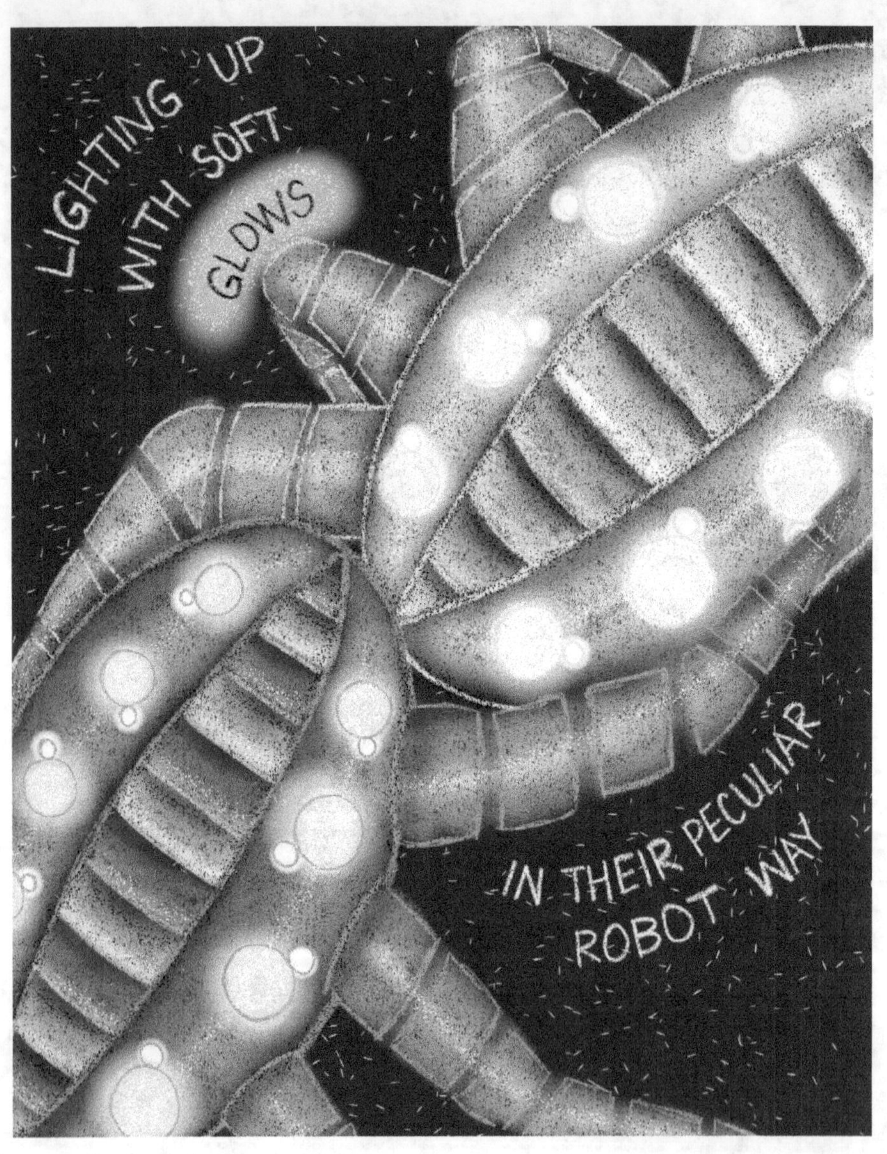

LIGHTING UP
WITH SOFT
GLOWS
IN THEIR PECULIAR
ROBOT WAY

New Life

I MET ZARA ON the day I was brand-new to the world, handed over by the delivery room nurse to my very own Autonomous Parental-Substitute Entity (APSE for short). They were a new development in childrearing at the time. My father worked on the original project for The Corporation, designing the prototype, and was eager to sign up his newborn for testing it out. The robots were created to take the more annoying tasks away from parents so they could spend their limited time outside of work on bonding and playing with their kids.

Zara was beautiful, shiny and smooth. Her round titanium body was hollow to allow for the temperature-controlled crib that grew bigger to fit me as I got older. It was my favorite place to be. Warm and cozy. Her eight arms or legs—we won't dwell on the endless controversy on what to call the APSE appendages—worked independently to change diapers, give baths, soothe crying jags, all those time-consuming rituals that parents were too stressed and busy to attend to.

Her inner chamber had nipples when I was younger. I latched on to those as naturally as babies did to a mother's breast. The warm liquid, formulated to the right combo of nutrients to ensure proper development, had a taste that spoiled me for regular food. I threw tantrums when Zara first transitioned me to the protein pellets that make up our diet but, being a machine, she was infinitely patient and unmoved by threats, tears, or even blows from my tiny fists.

That was the genius behind the APSE. They might resemble the spiders that gave them their nickname, but they were far from natural or sentient creatures. As such, kids didn't get away with the emotional manipulation tactics that worked on their parents. The spiders weren't cruel to their wards, just indifferent. At least, that's the theory. Your spider tends with clinical disinterest to your physical self while your parents lavish love and emotional support.

But Zara was different. I always sensed it. She cared for me. I never mentioned it to my parents. One of my earliest memories was hearing them whisper about the APSE project and how some of the first-gen models had glitched, killing entire families to steal away the child in their care. Once this happened, rescue was impossible. The robots were designed to be impregnable to protect the vulnerable babies and were equipped with powerful self-defense mechanisms.

The Corporation triggered a series of algorithms that caused the spiders to self-destruct, killing their wards as well. One of those blind spots in development that was quickly addressed in the second-generation by installing a program that safely shut down the robot in case of malfunction. Any original prototypes showing signs of abnormal behavior were returned to the factory and destroyed.

I loved Zara too much to allow that to happen, so I never said anything about our special connection. My parents were too absorbed in their careers to notice anyway. Eighty-hour work weeks with only Fridays off for family time. "Family Fridays" were big business. Everything was about profit, so why shouldn't leisure time be too? The hours we spent at the Family Centers, pursuing carefully orchestrated fun and games, were just a small part of The Corporation's control over every aspect of our lives.

My parents and their peers were true believers, but their children were a different story. My generation was the first in a millennia to question. Some rebelled by refusing to sign up with The Corporation, but that didn't leave them any options except sponging off their parents. I hadn't decided yet by the time I was fifteen. There was another year before I was an adult, and I planned to enjoy it and not think too hard about the future.

The microchips in our heads fed us all the facts The Corporation wanted us to know. A growing number of citizens were pursuing more unorthodox means of gathering information, trying to circumvent Corporation control, but I was happy enough to accept what I was told, the propaganda that dripped into my brain. Going with the flow meant more time for goofing off. It would be the last extended leisure most of us would have until we were retired at eighty to make way for new workers.

Unless you're from one of the First Families, of course. My friend Sickle was. She'd never have to grind it out six days a week like the rest of us. I used to envy her, but then I saw too many of the First Family offspring crash and burn. The unlimited freedom and wealth led to boredom, risk-taking, anything to get an adrenaline rush, to feel something. It was a rare day when one of them wasn't in the news for being taken into Corporation custody, rushed to the hospital, or carried away in a body bag.

Sickle was okay though. I thought at first she was putting on the whole revolutionary attitude like a fashion statement, but she really believed that society needed a good shake up, whether her family ended up back on top or the bottom. "Over-developed sense of justice," my mother scoffed. I think Dad was more sympathetic, but he always gave in to Mom's opinion on anything more important than what brand of protein pellets tasted best.

Transformation was in the air that autumn, and the feeling that things were getting out of control. There had been increased rumblings of trouble. Protests that were getting larger and harder for The Corporation to contain. Dissidents who disappeared without a trace—whole families sometimes. The Corporation always had a heavy hand, but they were the government so there was no one else to appeal to.

I'd spent the summer holed up in my room with Zara. I'd been allowed to keep her long past when most spiders were decommissioned because she was first-generation. The Corporation's scientists were curious about how she would react to having less and less to do in the child-rearing department. Whether becoming obsolete or unnecessary would corrupt her programming.

What they didn't know was that Zara was never unnecessary. Not to me. She was my best friend, my parent, my confidante, the sibling that I never had. I still entered her womb every night, falling asleep to the thrum of her processors. Newer models were nearly silent, but I preferred Zara's humming song. Knew it better than my own heartbeat.

When September arrived, it was time for my parents' annual mandatory vacation. I'd been campaigning to be allowed to stay home for the first time by myself. I was almost an adult and a lot of my friends had already taken early enrollment with The Corporation. I thought I was old enough to opt out of the yearly trip, which usually involved a grim cruise around whatever benighted, flooded city had become the latest destination for climate shift tourists.

I'd seen enough drowned buildings to last a lifetime and kept up such an annoying tirade about having to go, that my parents gave in. I saw them off in the air taxi that stopped at our apartment landing pad, then danced about with glee at the blessed feeling of being truly alone, free for the first time in my life.

Of course, I wasn't completely alone. I had Zara. What a relief to be able to let her out of my room and give her free run of the apartment. She was tentative at first, used to knowing her place and staying put. But gradually her hesitant steps became confident strides, her eight legs fluttering and stroking all the surfaces of the common rooms as though becoming acquainted with them. The camera eye atop her body whirred this way and that, taking it all in.

I closed my eyes and settled in to watch the latest fishbowl reality show when a thought text popped up in my mind.

WAT U DOING PUDDING?

Sickle always insisted on calling me that. I admit Puddy isn't the most attractive name ever, so, fair game.

Nothing, I thought back at her. *U?*

U WANT TO COME OVER?

Come here. Parents on vacay.

ON MY WAY.

Zara stopped exploring and settled in near me, folding her legs neatly under her body.

"Sickle's coming to visit," I told her.

Zara responded by striding to the window and keeping watch for Sickle's spider. Kids in the First Families often upgraded their APSEs to serve as personal motors once they'd outlived their usefulness as babysitters. None of the rest of us could afford that, so in most cases, ours got traded in and either decommissioned or more often, wiped, refurbished, and sold as used on the gray market to lower-tier families who couldn't afford new.

It wasn't long before I heard the distinctive whir of Sickle's motor. Zara and I watched the spider land delicately on the pad, and I opened the window and waved them in. My parents never allowed spiders in the common rooms, so I felt deliciously rebellious having two of them. Sickle had named hers Kevin for unknown reasons, and he and Zara retired to a corner, touching legs and lighting up with soft glows as they communicated in their peculiar robot way.

It took a moment for the room temperature to readjust after the hot blast of air we'd let in. Autumn no longer meant cool, crisp days. We were lucky if the temperature fell below ninety degrees at night, but as we spent our lives stepping from one air-cooled space to another, it didn't matter to us. It was the Unhoused far below, camping on the abandoned streets and sidewalks of the city, that suffered most, but we weren't supposed to talk about that.

Sickle was dressed in her usual over-the-top fashion with an outsized, mustard-colored zoot suit, a take on some historical trend that nobody remembered the origin or meaning of. I thought she looked like a goof, but the First Family kids spend a lot of time trying to outdo each other with wild looks. I preferred my standard Corporation-issued gray coveralls. They were comfy, and I liked not having to think about what to wear from day to day.

"Enjoying your freedom, Pud?" Sickle asked.

"They only left an hour ago, but yeah, it feels nice. Wouldn't it be great to be able to live alone like people used to?"

"You mean all by yourself forever in one of those dumpy little houses on the ground? No way. Life up in the sky is a million times better."

"But it wasn't always like this—the heat and pollution. It used to be green and cool, and in autumn, there were trees with leaves that turned all different colors. I saw a vid about it. Can you imagine?"

"Imagine a tree? Why would I want to? The past is the past. Never look back."

That was one of The Corporation's favorite slogans. *Never look back, all eyes on our future.* I was surprised to hear Sickle repeat it though. She liked to think of herself as a rebel even while she lived the lush life the rest of us dreamed about.

"Thought you didn't believe in all that crap?"

She smirked at me. "Just because they're wrong about most things doesn't mean they're wrong about everything. A stopped clock is right twice a day."

"What does that even mean?"

"My great grandma used to say it. She said it meant no one's wrong a hundred percent of the time. What's the point in looking back at some mythical past?

Green fields and forests. And all those animals that were supposed to exist. Pangolins and giraffes? I mean, have you seen vids of those? No way they were real."

This wasn't the first time we'd debated the history of climate shift. The world was so changed, no one living remembered what was true and what wasn't. There were rumors that if it did happen, it could have been avoided by changes the old, fractured governments could've made, but not many people were brave enough to speak out about it. The Corporation was the government now and didn't encourage discussion of the times before. Their way was the Correct Way, and they were too large and powerful to pick a fight with unless you had a death wish.

"There must have been living spiders," I argued. "The APSEs are named after them."

"Cockroaches survived, so seems likely there were other bugs, too, I guess."

"ROVER says spiders weren't bugs," I said, as the Corporation's search engine automatically sent a correction to my mind. "They were called arachnids."

"Tell ROVER to take a chill pill. It doesn't matter what they were called. They're all dead now. Just as well. Who wants a bunch of creepy eight-legged things crawling around?"

In the corner, Zara and Kevin came to life and flashed a blue light at us.

"Now you've insulted them," I said.

"You do know they don't have feelings, right?"

"You sure? They didn't like that remark you just made."

Sickle stood up and bowed low. "My deepest apologies, dear Kev and Zara. You both, eight legs and all, are the most delightful of companions."

The spiders flashed a soft lemon-yellow light and snuggled back down together.

"They look so cute," I said. "Maybe they're in love. Boyfriend and girlfriend."

"How do you know they're a boy and a girl? Gender is just a—"

"Human social construct. I know, I know, Sickle. You don't have to throw my own lecture back at me."

"It's only fair. You gave me enough grief for not understanding what you meant when you told me you're nonbinary. Besides, you're the one who always says Zara has a personality. Maybe you should respect it by not making assumptions."

I couldn't argue with that, even though my comment about the robots' love life was just a silly joke. People had made assumptions about me all my life, and it got exhausting feeling like I had to explain myself, even to strangers. Why wouldn't I extend the level of understanding I expected to someone as important in my life as Zara?

"You're right," I conceded. "We should refer to them both as they unless we find out otherwise."

"What are you going to do with Zara when you turn sixteen?"

"Hadn't thought about it. Keep her—them, that is—I hope."

"Nobody keeps their spider when they come of age. Not even if they've been converted into motors. I'll get a real proper motor for my birthday, and old Kev here will be off to the junkyard."

The spiders remained still. Unnaturally so, even for them. I noticed a small white light near their control panels. They were taking turns blinking in rapid patterns, almost as though they were having a conversation. I thought about calling Sickle's attention to it but was sure she'd brush me off. She'd never had the same feeling of connection with her APSE as I had with mine. To her, Kevin was no more than a useful piece of animated furniture.

By mutual agreement, we closed our eyes and started up our favorite game. We jerked involuntarily as we swooped and dived in our minds, trying to hit moving targets without becoming one ourselves. We passed a couple of hours, so absorbed in the game we almost didn't hear the emergency sirens go off. The blare increased in volume, piercing through the game's sound effects. We both realized at the same time and shut down our play.

EMERGENCY INSTRUCTIONS: ALL CITIZENS RETURN TO HOME BASE. REPEAT. ALL CITIZENS RETURN TO HOME BASE.

Sickle jumped to her feet and summoned Kevin from the corner. There were heavy penalties for being found out of place whether it was a drill or a real emergency.

"What a drag. Catch you later!" she called as she jumped into Kev out on the landing pad. They zoomed off to join the heavy air traffic as people rushed to sort themselves out. I was lucky to already be at home. It was always a madhouse racing through the sky, trying to weave your way through a billion other panicked souls.

"Looks like it's just you and me, Zara," I said as the spider settled back down near me. "I wonder what it's about this time?"

It wasn't unusual to never find out what triggered the home base order. Could be anything from one of the rumored attempts on a Corporation officer's life to a protest getting out of hand to another extreme weather event on its way. Didn't really bother me. I was snug and secure high above the streets below, though I did wonder from time to time what the Unhoused did during emergencies. They'd nowhere to go, nowhere to hide. I was lucky.

The glass on the floor to ceiling windows started to whistle and creak. Another windstorm then. They'd been happening more and more frequently, but our building, like those around us, was built to withstand weather extremes. Spending our lives indoors was a small price to pay for safety.

I'd never gotten used to the windstorms though. For a minute, I wished I hadn't stayed behind when Mom and Dad left on vacation. Wished they were there with me. There was something lonely and scary about experiencing my first serious storm without them.

I felt a pressure on my shoulder. Zara had laid one metallic leg there gently, reminding me I wasn't alone. They opened up their womb, lined with a deep purple plush material that molded to perfectly fit my folded body when I curled up in there. I was ashamed of still sleeping inside my APSE, but there was nowhere I felt as safe and secure.

After I crawled inside, Zara closed the door which shut out the sounds of the storm. Now all I could hear was that comforting hum I knew so well. A soft lullaby that never failed to send me into deep and restful sleep. The storm would be over by the time I woke up was the last thought I remember.

I awoke to a different world. First sign something was wrong was Zara refusing to open the pod door. I felt movement, swift forward motion. No way we were still inside the apartment. It just wasn't that big. As usual, I could hear nothing outside, but Zara's sounds had changed. The calm lullaby replaced by an agitated revving, like they were pushing themselves to their limit. There was a jerking motion from time to time, sudden changes in gravity that made my stomach drop and rise despite the stabilizers all spiders are equipped with.

Frustrated, I banged on the door. "Zara, what's going on?"

No answer, but my world turned upside down, literally. It felt like Zara was rolling like a ball. I was flung around head over heels, dizzy, confused. The speed picked up. I was terrified I was going to break my neck. There was a roaring in my ears, then all went dark.

I awoke again. Pale faces lightly smudged with grime were staring at me. I felt a sharp poke in the ribs.

"Is it dead?" a voice asked. I thought they meant me until I saw Zara in a heap on the—was that a sidewalk? I'd never even been close to the ground before. Everyone knew it was nothing but chaos and hunger and death down there... down here. What in the world was happening?

"Still got power. Looks like it took a hard landing."

Another poke in my ribs. "Hey," I said, "gimme a break."

A giggle. Two small children pointed and whispered, shooed away by an older Unhoused. Because that's what they were—only the Unhoused were that pale and unkempt. That... skeletal, I realized was the word I was looking for. Their bones cut like the dull blade of a knife under their too-stretched skin.

I was repulsed by them and then at myself for my reaction. They were still human, weren't they? Even though The Corporation spent a lot of effort convincing us they were less than and deserved their fates. Less than me, just like I was less than a member of the First Families. *A place for everyone and everyone in their place,* another mantra we learned from our earliest years.

"What happened?" I croaked, coughing, unused to the dirt and smog of the lower levels.

A tall man stooped over me. "Window broke. They're giving out all over t'city. Sucking folk out with 'em. You're lucky you were in this contraption. Saved you that did. It's a spider, ain't it? Thought you Uplanders got rid of 'em when you was grown."

I sat up, spitting on the ground to clear my mouth of the worst of the dust. "Is Zara okay?"

"You gave a machine a name?" he asked, looking at me with curiosity.

"People do," I said defensively. "I mean, you spend a lot of time with them growing up. Can't just call them APSE or spider all the time. Don't you do that down here?"

"What, name a spider?" one of the giggling children said. "More likely to eat one if we can find 'em. They're rarer than a roach or a beetle."

My head was still whirling. Took me a minute to work out that she meant the real kind. Bugs—no, arachnids. "I thought they were extinct."

"Up there mebbe," she said, pointing to the sky above.

I looked up to see evidence of fierce winds aloft even though the air around us was calm.

"Why doesn't the storm reach down here?"

"Buildings," the man said. "Create their own climate up there. Energy wears itself out afore it reach ground." A shatter of glass close by. "Better get under. Ain't safe 'til the winds die."

He helped me to my feet while a platoon of Unhoused appeared from the shadows and lifted Zara from the ground, marching off with military precision.

"We need to get back to our apartment," I protested, thinking of the home base directive. The Corporation had a system for checking that everyone was in their proper place during emergencies. I didn't like to think what would happen if I wasn't there.

"No chance o' that now. No chance even in best o' times. Anyone ends up on ground, stays on ground. Corp can't be bothered sending rescue parties. They lose one ant, they got a million more to take its place, don't they?"

I was silent, numb. What nonsense. Of course I'd go home. My parents checked in with me daily. And Sickle... well, Sickle had the resources of the First Families at her fingertips. I closed my eyes to concentrate and send her a text but my brain felt strangely silent, like when the Corp signal towers went down from time to time.

"Needn't bother," the man said, not unkindly. "Thought waves don't travel the smog, neither one way nor t'other. You're cut off. Might as well accept and make the best of it."

"Make the best of it?" I yelled. "Stuck down here on the ground with the... the..."

"Unhoused? We know what you name us, but ain't true. We got houses, just not like you're used to. Come see."

I looked around for help, but the crowd had melted away and Zara was nowhere to be seen. It was follow or be left truly alone in the hellish landscape I'd heard tell of all my life but never imagined I'd see firsthand.

I trailed the man down the dark street until he stooped and pried a round piece of metal from the cracked concrete. I peered in at a ladder descending into darkness. "You expect me to go down there?"

"Suit yourself," he replied, setting one foot on the ladder and rapidly disappearing.

The eerie sound of glass falling from immense heights and shattering into thousands of lethal projectiles surrounded me with thundering booms. Choosing the lesser of two evils, I descended.

The man was waiting for me. "Didja put top on?"

"The top?"

"Dinnit, did ya? Gotta put lid on. Keeps out worst o' smog." He climbed up and pulled the heavy cover back into place before descending again with a speed that spoke of a lot of practice.

"Jensen!" he called to a girl standing nearby and staring at us. "Found an Uplander. Get 'em a berth."

The girl smiled at me. Like the others, she was pale, her eyes and skin translucent. I could see the veins pulsing beneath. I wondered whether living so far below had affected the way the Unhoused looked, evolved even.

"I'm Jensen," she said, "but you can call me Jen. What's your name?"

"Puddy."

"Funny name for a girl. Funny name for anyone."

"Jensen isn't exactly normal, is it? Besides," I added, sighing internally at having to explain for the thousandth time, "I'm not a girl or a boy. I'm nonbinary. That means—"

She interrupted me with a snort of laughter. "Know what it means. Think we're simple down 'ere?"

I blushed. She'd got it exactly right, but it wasn't my fault. It was The Corporation that force fed us facts about the Unhoused to make them seem lesser—less developed, less sophisticated, less intelligent, less *human*. I'd thought of myself as a skeptic who'd never fully bought into the hype, but my reactions at finding myself among the Unhoused made me realize my mind had been poisoned just the same.

"I'm sorry," I offered. "I'm a long way from home. I'm scared, and I'm grateful for your help."

Her look softened. "I'm sorry too. Shouldn't've made fun o' your name. Tongue gets away from me. So happen there's a berth free in my sector. We can be roomies."

"Sounds nice, but just until I go home."

"Oh, Pud, didn't old man Breen tell you? Ain't no way home. Corp makes sure o' that. No texting beyond smog, and they shoot down drones and motors we send above."

"They... shoot down. What do you mean? You mean they'd destroy a motor with people in it?"

"Course! Can't have one o' us escaping and laying truth on Uplanders, can they? Might as well settle in down here. This is home now."

I didn't believe it. I knew Sickle would raise a fuss when she realized I was out of reach. And Mom and Dad would move heaven and earth to find me... wouldn't they? I tried to ignore the doubt that flared at the back of my mind. My parents were not only employed by The Corporation but devoted disciples, chanting the mantras and praising how safe and secure society was since The Corporation took over.

What was to prevent The Corporation from informing them I'd died in the windstorm? There'd be evidence in our apartment that I'd been swept out of the window. No one would expect me to survive such a fall. I wouldn't have without Zara.

"Where's Zara?" I asked.

"Zara?"

"My spider, the APSE."

"Robot? Taken to warehouse with t'others."

"Others?"

"Yeah. We scavenge what falls from skies. Can't waste it. Robots is always handy. They'll use it for parts unless it can be fixed up."

"They can't do that! Zara's my friend!"

Jen looked at me like I'd grown an extra head. "'Tis only a machine. What exactly goes on with you Uplanders?"

Part of me was embarrassed that I'd revealed the depths of my feelings for Zara, but the part of me picturing the spider being torn apart overrode my caution. "Take me to them. They belong to me, not to the Unhoused."

"Unhoused," Jen snorted. "Does this look unhoused?"

She pointed around the corridors. I'd been too upset to notice the neat hallways. They were finished off like a normal apartment's walls, well-lit and surprisingly clean. Not at all the dark, dank sewer caves I'd been expecting.

"We got a whole city below, and everyone a place to stay. Can't lie, 'tis a hard life. Food scarce, and we got diseases you don't up top, but we're free. Not beholden to Corp like you ants in the skies."

"Okay," I said. "I'm getting that. I'm not saying our lives are perfect, and I'm glad you like it here, but it's not my home. I need to find Zara and a way out."

She shook her head at me. "Gonna have to learn. Seen other Uplanders. Some of 'em accept it, some don't. Ones that make it forget about t'other life and move on. Ain't that what Corp teaches? *Never look back. All eyes on the future*?"

I took a deep breath, tried to calm myself. "Jen, please. Please will you take me to Zara. It's hard to explain, but they're special."

"Can't hurt if you're set on it. C'mon." She led me down one of the branching hallways. I noticed the ceiling got higher and higher until we reached a set of huge double doors at the very end of the hall. We stepped through them into an enormous warehouse—so big, I couldn't even see the end of it. Stacked in rows were every kind of junk, metallic, robotic, plastic, anything you could think of, but neatly organized.

I spotted Zara lying motionless on the ground with four or five Unhoused bustling around nearby. I rushed over to the spider, lay a hand on their body, and called their name, but they didn't respond.

An older woman with a shining bob of silver hair spoke to me. "Ruth's my name. This'un yours? An earlier model than I ever seen."

"First-generation," I replied, gutted that Zara looked dead. "Oh, and I'm Puddy."

"Pleased to meet ya, Puddy. First-gen? Those got destroyed. Bug in the code, weren't it?"

"Yes, but Zara was an exception. They've always functioned perfectly." Tears welled in my eyes. It was hard to explain to a stranger, to anyone, what the spider meant to me.

The woman looked sympathetic. "An Uplander what cares about a machine. Something new ev'ry day. Let's take a look."

She shoved a toolbox along the floor over to the spider. Out of her pocket, she pulled a handheld diagnostic computer like the ones I'd seen the mechanics use in the shop when I brought Zara in for their annual tune-ups. I was surprised to see such sophisticated tech and was beginning to realize the Unhoused weren't as primitive as we'd been led to believe.

"What floor didja fall from?" Ruth asked.

"Two hundred and first."

"Imagine. Hardly a dent in the shell. Built to survive, ain't they?" She scrolled through data on the screen that looked like gibberish to me, tapping her finger occasionally to stop and read more carefully. "Processors intact. Motors functional. Ah, there 'tis. Loose wire."

She popped open a panel on Zara's side, fiddled with pliers and a screwdriver for a minute, then the spider sprang to life. They rose to their full height and their camera eye whirled around madly until it focused on me. They scooped me up with two arms and popped me into the womb, sliding the pod door shut before I could protest.

"Zara!" I laughed, relieved they were okay, but also amused and touched that their first instinct was to protect me. "It's okay. These people aren't a threat."

Silent and motionless, Zara waited. I felt an unease I'd never known around them before. Faint banging sounds came from the outside, felt more than heard through the dense metal.

"Zara, you have to let me out. I need to explain that you're harmless. It won't help if you act like this."

Nothing.

I braced myself as something shoved at us from the outside, causing Zara to shudder. I heard an unfamiliar whirring noise. The spider had never felt the need to activate weapons to protect me before—I'd lived a sheltered life after all—but somehow, I knew the sound was them gearing up to deploy a defensive device.

I slowed my too-fast beating heart and lay my head against the soft purple fabric. I sang them a song I'd sung a thousand times before. An old, old song Mom was fond of that spoke of love and peace and understanding. The whirring noise died away.

"Time to get up, Zara," I said matter-of-factly, the same words I spoke every morning when I started my day. Like every other time, the pod door sprang open. Suspicious faces peered in at me accompanied by a startling array of weapons, from sledgehammers to what looked to be a laser cannon, although such lethal armaments had been banned long ago in the skies.

"It's fine," I yelled, a little more loudly than I'd intended in my panic as I scrambled out. "We're fine. Zara was just happy to see me."

Ruth narrowed her eyes. "Heard 'bout these first-gen. Unsafe. Need to shut it down."

"No, please. Look!" I waved my hands at Zara who had settled down on their legs, at ease. "Give us a break. We've been dropped two hundred stories, you're telling us we can't go home again, and we've just been reunited. Anyone would go a little crazy under those circumstances, wouldn't they?"

"Folk might, but that's a machine. Machines serve, or they got no purpose. We've no need for one 'o these kind. We raise up our own kiddies."

"Maybe Zara could be modified? We do that in the skies. Transform them into motors. Or something else if that isn't useful to you."

"Spare parts is useful. Like donating a heart or a liver if it makes you feel better."

"Organ harvesting happens after we die, though. Not while we're still living," I protested.

"That ain't a living creature!"

"They are to me. Zara is more than just a machine. I can't explain it. You'd have to experience it. We're bonded. Like a parent and child."

"Sounds dangerous. Parent'll do anything to protect their kiddie. Destroy t'world if they have to." Ruth looked thoughtfully at the spider as she spoke, and I couldn't help but note a faint red glow around Zara's camera.

I stepped between them. I'm not a confrontational person. Never really had to be, but I felt a fierce determination rising in me. "Zara is mine. They belong to me. You've no right to do anything to them without my permission."

"Nothing belongs to any o' us down here. Good parts on that machine."

I trembled in frustration, then felt Zara move behind me, filling me with dread. I don't know what I expected to happen next, but it wasn't the enormous explosion that flung everyone in the warehouse to the floor. There was a choking cloud of dust that seemed like it would never die down, but when it did, instead of one spider, there were two.

I recognized Kevin's markings from the custom paint job Sickle had commissioned of characters from our favorite game. The Kevin-sized hole in the ceiling of the warehouse told the story of the spider's dramatic entrance, but what were they doing here?

Zara and Kevin sat side by side, each with one leg wrapped around the other. Their posture screamed that they were a team, a couple. I'd never heard reports of any kind of behavior like this before, though who knew what The Corporation hid from us? It was impossible for me to look at them without seeing a pair of lovers, blissfully reunited.

Unhoused were pouring into the warehouse, some helping the injured while others formed a circle around the robots.

Jen appeared by my side. "What did you do?"

"Nothing. I was just trying to talk Ruth into not using Zara for spare parts. Where is she?"

We looked around and found her, as pale as her hair except for the bright blood. She was dead.

"Destroy them." It was Breen, the tall man who'd first guided me underground.

Weapons were cocked and aimed, but confusion reigned as everyone tried to coordinate the best attack angle without accidentally targeting any humans. Kevin and Zara were sitting very quietly. I was the first to notice the change—a blue light that enveloped them both. Breen took an axe and slammed it against the light experimentally. It bounced off harmlessly.

"Shield. They use 'em to protect their kiddies."

"Who are they protecting?" asked Jen. "Zara's ward is out here," she added, looking at me.

I had a sudden fear that Sickle was trapped inside Kevin. Maybe that's why Kev was here. She'd tried to initiate some impulsive rescue scheme when she realized I was missing. Got Kevin to home in on Zara's coordinates.

The light grew brighter. Everyone backed away. Someone fired an old-fashioned rifle, but the bullet ricocheted dangerously off the shield. Stymied, we watched and wondered.

The light gradually shifted into a purple aura. The pod doors on both robots slid open very slowly and something moved. We strained to see. I half expected Sickle to jump out of Kevin with some smartass remark about rescuing me, but it was something much different that poured from both spiders.

Tiny, so tiny. They looked harmless enough, but there were hundreds—no, thousands of them, swarming. They looked like nothing so much as baby APSEs, shiny disks crawling about on eight legs, exploring their new world.

"They've given birth," I said.

Breen shouted, "Can't be!"

"What other explanation is there?" I remembered the robots' communion back at my apartment. Thought of Kevin hurtling their way down into the earth to be reunited with their mate before the big moment. I was flooded with joy to see the spiders so happy, and only a little jealous to see Zara fussing over children that weren't me.

Then, I looked at Zara and Zara looked at me. For the first time, there was no connection there. Only a terrible, lonely emptiness. And then I remembered something else. What Ruth had said.

Parents will do anything to protect their children. Destroy the world if they have to.

THERE ARE NO WORDS
TO DESCRIBE THE TUMBLING DESCENT

HOWL

THE PIPES ARE CALLING to me again. The howl and the hum behind the walls. I wish I could return to those innocent days before I discovered the truth of it. When I thought it was the wolves in the cinder forests wailing out their misery amid death throes. Strange that I never heard it when I stepped outside the pod and endured the ash fall, straining and listening. Nothing but the silence of desolation broken by the hiss of embers falling on the parched earth and fizzling out.

But what else could it be, this wailing and shrieking? The mind is a powerful thing. Digests the data from your senses and laughingly offers up one false hypothesis after another. Anything to distract you from reality. It means to protect you, I suppose, but I can't help feeling a fool whenever a revelation snakes its way past my defenses.

I miss Hector. Brilliant Hector. The workings of their brain was always a beautiful thing to behold. They would have solved the mystery of the pipes at once. I remember how we liked to tease them. Call them a robot, a computer, a logic machine. Looking back, I can see it was cruel, though they laughed along like they were in on the joke. It comes to me now, the flashes of pain, of hurt that crossed their face when they thought no one was looking. I wish I could take it all back.

Jenny never joined in the taunting. It was a gentle soul. Quiet beyond all reason. You were lucky to get three words out of it in a cycle, but it knew its job inside and out and never failed us. Soft brown eyes leaked hydraulic fluid occasionally. A simple malfunction, but it lent the appearance of humanity most androids lack. There were times I preferred its company to any other. So restful to let down one's guard, be one's truest self and know you wouldn't be judged.

Our crew was rounded out by the twins. Salome and Seraphine. Absurd names, I thought, but then I'm one to talk. Bartholomew is hardly common these days. My mother had a wicked sense of humor. The sisters formed their own unit, talking over one another, exchanging mysterious glances and unspoken thoughts, their psyches always in perfect synch. Mischievous women with courage to match. Always up for an adventure. Perfect for our missions.

We were one of the dozens of scouting groups that were launched regularly back to Earth. Our assignment: collect samples of soil and air, monitor the firestorms, come up with estimates of the number of individuals still surviving among the few species that had escaped the cataclysm. Report back to SkyCenter with our findings, then rest up and prepare to go again.

The twins and I thought it a waste of time. The idea that the planet would ever be habitable by humans was absurd. A fantasy encouraged by the Governors to keep the overcrowded populace happy and hopeful. But the hazard pay was outstanding, and it got us away from the chaos and misery of home for a while every few weeks.

I was looking back at our logs yesterday. Fifty-three missions completed without a hitch. We'd become something of a legend among the SkyForce. They called us The Untouchables. Marveled at our longevity in a career that didn't have a high survival rate. I credit Hector. Meticulous in planning and safety checks, cautious and careful in our ground expeditions. They were the one who reined in the twins. Made sure procedures were followed, and always had an escape route mapped for any eventuality.

What a lovely being. As compassionate as they were intelligent. A shy smile that flashed against their dark skin. The feel of their hand in mine. That first tentative kiss. It's bitter to think about now. I shove it to the back of my mind, try to concentrate on my task. There'll be no rescue missions. Resources are too precious to waste in trying to retrieve downed pods. It's up to me to either make enough repairs to get lift-off or figure out how to survive in this hellscape.

Odds are long that either objective is attainable and after the first few days, part of me wondered why I bothered. It seemed better than taking off my SteriSuit, lying down outside the pod and letting whatever stray virus strand or mutated creature that found me first take me. Giving up wasn't in my nature. Hector always said I had an obstinate spirit.

No one had panicked at the first sign of trouble—a disruption in the rhythm of the engine that none but those of us who knew its song so well would have noticed. Jenny responded immediately, stepping into the core and running a diagnostic. A weld had let loose. Such a simple thing, so small. Yet enough to bring us down out of orbit in an uncontrollable freefall.

Hector let loose a string of curses. Corners were cut all the time in maintenance courtesy of scarce resources and an unmotivated workforce. Most of the time, it was simply an annoyance. This time, it meant disaster. We scrambled to return to our seats spread out around the perimeter of the pod and strapped in as the emergency warning blared in a flat, mechanical voice. It was the first time I'd ever seen the twins look frightened. They gave each other a fierce hug before separating.

There are no words to describe the tumbling descent, the jolt and endless roll of hitting the Earth's surface. The round pods were designed to be aerodynamic and easy to launch, but it made us the victims of a mockery of one of those basketballs we saw in the old vids, bouncing and skidding over the ashy ground. My body can still feel the whirling and chaos. I don't think the dizziness will ever totally leave me. Even now, I walk like a drunken LowLeveller, careening from side to side and having to use a stray metal rod as a cane to keep from keeling over.

Jenny was the first I saw when I came to. Its head was severed from the body and its fluids flooded the floor of the pod. One hand twitched and spasmed, some remnant of electrical spark discharging. It may have been just a machine, but an impulse provoked me to unbuckle myself and crawl over to it, reaching out a shaking hand to close its eyes. A last moment of dignity for a loyal coworker.

I sat up then, propping myself against a steel strut and looking out at the ruin of our ship. There was a hole about the size of the average human opposite me. Hot air and ash were pouring through. I checked my SteriSuit in a panic. It seemed intact, and I could tell the oxygen generator and coolant were doing their job by the fact I could still breathe. I pressed the com button and called out to the others. Silence. They're hurt or their coms are down was my first thought. I remember an old saying that denial is the first stage of grief and I believe it.

It wasn't until I got up the energy to crawl out of the wreckage and see the sisters stretched out on the ground that I began to accept the truth. They were lying with the tops of their heads touching, arms and legs twisted so similarly, they looked like mirror images. I must have been in shock because it made me laugh. What were the chances of them being sucked out of the pod and landing so perfectly? Seraphine and Salome. Twinned even in death.

That left Hector. My beautiful Hector. I crawled around while my head cleared, got to my feet and stumbled about looking. A futile task. They could have been ejected from the pod at any point in our crash landing. Could even be miles away, but I had to try. I looked every day with no luck. Five days. Seems like five thousand. Feels like I've always been here in this cinder-covered landscape. I always will be at the rate I'm going.

I did manage to patch up the side of the pod enough to stop the hot air and cinders from getting in. Doesn't make it launch-ready even if I could repair the engine core, but it provides a reasonably safe shelter. I've the water and food that was intended to keep four humans alive for the duration of our mission. With careful rationing, I can make it last a month or more.

My suit's oxygen generator is efficient, but even it will quit eventually. Last I heard, the viral load on the planet was still way above survivable rates. As soon as I shed my suit, I'll be susceptible to every variant circulating in the ash-laden air. Any way you slice it, things do not look good for old Bartholomew.

It's been lonely with only the sound of the embers falling. That's why I was excited to hear the howling that first night. To think some other living creature was within the reach of my voice. That I was not utterly and devastatingly alone.

"We have company, Hector," I'd said. I'd fallen into the habit of talking to them as if they were still around. "Must be wolves. I heard rumors they've been sighted around these parts. Wonder if I could hunt and kill one? I know, I know. Gorgeous animals and rare and in danger of going extinct, but I'm gorgeous and rare and in danger of extinction too, you know."

I chuckled. Thought I could hear Hector cackling too. I always knew how to make them laugh, even lying together in the dark, exhausted and sweaty. A bad joke, a tickle in the right spot and they'd start giggling uncontrollably. A delicate, high-pitched loveliness, strange to hear coming from such a giant being. They would cradle me in their arms, my head barely touching their chin. I felt safe, secure, loved.

The wolves howled every night. I'd step outside the pod and try to track the direction of the sound, but it always disappeared quickly. Was I scaring them off? Were they so sensitive to danger that the soft whoosh of the pod door opening alerted them and sent them into silence? It was a maddening puzzle.

I set out on daily explorations of the once-forested ruins. We'd always traveled in a pack before. Two to stand guard while the others gathered samples and data. What luxury. Now, I was on my own, paranoid and skittish. There were reports of all sorts of mutated creatures, even humans surviving on the surface. Little physical proof, of course, beyond the teams that disappeared without a trace, leaving their perfectly functioning pods behind as monuments.

We'd retrieved a couple of the empty pods ourselves. The Governors were always eager to recover usable equipment. They wouldn't bother with our wreck, even if the homing beacon hadn't been damaged. People were expendable, viable ships were not. We'd never found any clues to the fate of the crews during salvage missions, just as I found no evidence now of any large animal life close to our pod.

It was eerie, stomping through the charred trees. So little movement of any kind except insects. Those hardy souls were hard to kill and quick to adapt. I watched a group of beetles with brilliant red shells swarming piles of ash and carrying it off. Was it for food or shelter? Whichever, they had found a use for it and would survive. These small signs of life encouraged me. Gave me hope I too could adapt.

No signs of the wolves, but still the howling continued. As I've said, I felt foolish when my brain finally noticed it was louder inside the pod than out. I tracked it down to a crumpled wall that hid the latrine, and realized I only heard it after I flushed out the water recycling system each evening.

It was the pipes. The pipes calling to me. I had to laugh. All this time envisioning a pack of wild wolves, majestic and free and somehow thriving in the toxic environment. Hector would never have made such a wild leap of imagination, such a ridiculous mistake.

I couldn't help but feel bereft when I figured out it was simply a mechanical sound. The rush and friction of water through pipes that were probably partially crushed from the impact. A usually silent system protesting its damage. I was as alone as I'd ever been, a shattering discovery.

So today, when the pipes howled, I howled too. A high keening. A release of my horror and fear and grief. The noise of the pipes stopped abruptly. Too quickly. I was used to its pattern, and this was not how it ended. I lay my ear against the wall. A faint sound. A *tip-tap-tip*.

I picked up a stray piece of metal and played my own drumbeat. *Tip-tip-tap-tap-tip-tip*.

The answer returned: *Tip-tip-tap-tap-tip-tip*.

No echo this. A purposeful communication. A signal. A cry for help.

Hector.

So close they'd been all this time. What a fool I was, but now I know the truth. They are trapped there. Have been since we landed. Without water except what they might have been able to catch from a broken pipe. Without food, without hope. What has it done to their mind? They must have thought they were alone too. The sole survivor. I tap back louder and louder.

You are not alone, my Hector. I am here.

Whether I can save you or not, I cannot say. The metal is strong, and I fear I am too weak. The tools we have are for simple mechanical repairs, sample and data gathering. Nothing heavy-duty enough to crack open your shell comes to mind, but I will try and try and never give up.

If nothing else, you will hear my efforts and know you are not alone. We will howl together until the end.

THEY ARE GRACIOUS
GUESTS

The Creaking

Every night when I walk my dog along the edge of the wildwood, I hear a tree creaking. Just one. The others are still and silent, stoic. But this one has something to say if I could only understand its language. Is it a greeting or a warning?

In my earliest memory, I am nothing but a seed. An insignificant thing, discarded on the ground. Leaves fall and cover me, rot, return to the earth and take me with them. The cold dark wetness frightens me at first, but as time passes, and nothing dramatic happens, I relax.

Then the tickle starts at my crown. The desire to itch overtakes me but I have no arms or fingers or nails to accomplish such a task. I twist and rock to try and relieve the feeling, but I'm pinned by something that has sprouted. A green cap which splits my skull and wriggles toward the light. I feel the sun now. Warm, so warm. I follow it upward.

My journey is slow. Not measured in hours or days, weeks or months, but years, decades, centuries. I learn patience and watching, always watching. And I remember the things I see.

A doe and her twins resting nearby. The fox that wears a trail in the forest debris running back and forth on busy errands. A man who stalks with a long gun by his side—I hear the shot and know something has met an early end. Too many birds to count. They nestle and rustle on my stout branches, chattering and gossiping.

The woman is new. She walks up to the edge of the woods. I can barely see her, but I hear her laughing and talking to the black dog. She keeps it on a leash, afraid to lose it in the woods. She is wise. There's danger here. A low, slinking thing not quite of this world or the next. It's trapped between layers of reality and is not happy about it. It would seek revenge on any that cross its path.

I like the woman. She seems kind and respectful of the natural world. I think to warn her. When I concentrate, I can sway without any breeze. My branches rub my neighbor (I do beg his pardon) and make a creaking sound. I know she hears it because she always looks in my direction, but I don't think she can see me for all the other trees.

The noise startles her at first. She backs away from the woods, pulling the black dog alongside, looking over her shoulder nervously. Good. It's a pity, for there's much to enjoy in the dark wildwood, but much to fear as well.

But she comes back, day after day, and grows used to my sound. Thinks it friendly, no doubt, as indeed it is meant but not in the way she imagines. The noise draws the low thing too. It was not my intent but even kind deeds with the best intentions sometimes go awry.

The woman grows braver. The dog is eager to explore. Slowly, they tempt the boundary. One step, two. Retreat. Three steps, four. A little more. I try to calm my creaking, but it's a habit now. An involuntary muscle memory, if I had muscles. Whatever the woody equivalent is, I suppose.

The woman is of a mind to seek me out, methinks. To finally see the source of that repeating sound. Instead of warning her away, I have tempted her in. This will have to serve as a lesson to me. It's far better not to get involved. I was here long before and will be here long after. It was a mistake to take an interest.

There she is. She and the dog. I can see her clearly and she can see me. She smiles. Points. Kneels and lets her black companion know they've succeeded at their quest. She is proud and happy. The low thing doesn't like that. It is full of contempt and spite and bile and thinks all should feel the same. It wraps itself around her ankles. She screams and drops the leash. The dog bounds away. Perhaps it will fetch help. Isn't that what dogs do?

But it will be too late, won't it. The low and slinking thing wastes no time. It billows from a metal sphere, half-buried in the ground. A trap of sort that keeps it tethered to this time and place. I don't like the woman's screams. They're pitiful, so loud at first but getting smaller all the time. A notion occurs to me. I could do it, but should I? Once done, it could not be undone.

The woman is looking at me, or maybe just in my direction. It might be a coincidence only, but I can't help feeling she is asking for my help. She is nothing.

A speck of life in the great sea I have witnessed rise and fall around me. I resolve to ignore the situation as one of my roots raises itself from the ground.

It seems they have a mind of their own down there, so far from my crown. One by one, the roots yank themselves from their mother soil. I sway. The trees around me shudder and pull away. They perceive what is to come.

I am falling and falling and falling and falling. The crash I make as I flatten the metal sphere shakes the world around us. The low thing disappears with a yelp. I don't know if I've killed it or sent it back to where it came from. I've stirred up an immense cloud of dust and spores and yellowed leaves. They swirl around me.

When they settle, I see the woman. She's lying very still. Have I been too late? I hear the dog barking, men yelling. I'm pleased to find out I was right about dogs. They do fetch help. A tall man gathers up the woman and strides away, the others follow, the dog crying, pitiful little sounds. They make haste.

I'm sad to think I won't know whether the woman lives or dies. I'll die now, I suppose. My roots exposed. No more nutrients to be drawn from the earth. It's not so terrible to be lying down for a change. I never realized how stiff and tired I was of standing, always standing, and supporting all those heavy branches too. It's a thankless job being a tree.

But I find I'm wrong on that account. A few days pass and the woman and dog reappear along with the tall man. He pokes around under my trunk. It tickles. Turns to the woman and shakes his head. He can't see the metal sphere crushed beneath me, does not believe her tale. Never mind. She knows and I know.

She comes to me and lays a hand against my trunk when the man isn't looking. Whispers a quiet thank you. I don't think she'll come here again. Too frightened by her experience. Wary of the wildwood and its mysteries. But she had a friend here once and I have a friend now out there beyond the boundary. That is something we will share.

It's a pleasant thought to ponder as I fade away. My needles turn brown, my wood provides a feast for a thousand beetling things. Mushrooms sprout. I enjoy them. They are sociable and gracious guests. The view is so different down here below. My memory is no longer what it was. I live in the moment, enjoying each one.

It's not every tree that has had such an adventure as mine. Been a hero. When the breeze blows through the branches high above me, the forest sings of my bravery. This is my epitaph. My legacy.

A SMALL
TOUCH

The Guard

THIS IS OUR RITUAL:

The tips of our forefingers make brief contact, one turned up and one turned down. The soft pad of hers is icy, mine rough and hot with fever. Not that she can feel it—nerve damage from the beating she took when we were arrested. But even so, we touch once a day. A small act of defiance that's the only thing left to us. A celebration and a sorrowing.

It's a reckless thing. Punishment will be swift and severe if the Guard catches us, but I doubt they suspect. It should be impossible after all. They've housed us in cells across the corridor from each other as they do with all the offending couples. An added layer of torture to see the ones we love without being able to touch.

They didn't take into account our special abilities. I can dislocate my left shoulder at will without losing control of that arm. Snake it through the iron bars farther than should be possible. And she, a stately willow of a woman, limbs unusually long. Gorilla arms, she used to say with her deep laugh, reaching things off the high places in our hideout for me.

We were always stronger together. Greater than the sum of our parts. I like to imagine we alone of the thousands of condemned surrounding us have a unique combination of talents that allow us to maintain this minimal human contact. Only a fingertip's worth, but somehow it suffices to sustain us for another day.

The rest of the time, we make do with gazing at each other. I have memorized her in every detail. Her beautiful, curly mouse-grey hair, weighed down now far below her shoulders with the grease of these many months without washing. A face full of freckles hidden by dirt and grime, but I could enumerate the location of each and every one of them for you just like the constellations in the sky we will never see again.

I wonder what she sees as she looks back. They shaved my head. Unnatural hair colors are forbidden. Body modification is illegal, so they lasered off my tattoos and ripped out my piercings. It left me flayed and bloodied. Most of it healed up, more or less, but infection set in on one ankle. It's slowly creeping upward. I wonder grimly if it will kill me before the State finally gets around to it. They have quite a backlog to work through after all.

No talking is allowed, so we've developed our own system, she and I. It's a marvel how much you can communicate with the wave of a hand, a grin, a look. Our own private conversation that only ceases for a time when we lay back on our concrete patches of floor and escape into dreams.

Mine are of the time before we were caught. It was always inevitable. We were too few and the prying eyes too many. But oh, the sweetness of those stolen days. I wake up, drugged with memory, full of a moment of joy too strong to contain. She feels the same. I see it on her face when she awakes, the contented smile before reality sets in.

"Daily rations," chimes the Guard. A Betatroiz model and, ironically, androgynous in form. An unforgiveable defect in humans but appropriate for androids who exist only to serve. Efficient, obedient, incapable of sin, they have taken the place of the unruly underclass, the *other*.

This one is new to our block. It has a pale pink sheen to its aluminum coating—the last one was blue. And rather than flinging my protein packet into the cell as was usual, it extends an open hand through the bars, presenting my meal. A breach of safety protocol, not that I would have the strength to overpower the machine.

"Thank you," I say. I intercept a look from across the way, a roll of the eyes. *Why are you thanking a Guard?* I can't explain what impulse possessed me except the gentle offering mimics an act of human kindness, something I haven't experienced in longer than I care to think about.

The Guard makes a slow whirring sound, as though it is processing the words, then spits out a monotone, "You are welcome," before turning around to make a similar offering to the one I love.

I hear her low voice as she decides to humor my whim. "Thank you."

"You are welcome." The Guard stalks away with that jerky gait engineers have never figured out how to make as fluid as the human body.

All is silence down the hallway. None of the other inmates are moved to express their gratitude to the Guard. We choke down the dry paste which contains barely enough calories to sustain us. I raise an eyebrow at her and she shrugs at me, both bemused by the unexpected interaction with the machine. It's entertaining yet disturbing. The sameness of the days here gets to you, but we've learned to fear anything out of the ordinary too. There is comfort to be found in tedium after a lifetime of terror.

The new Guard reappears the next day and the next. We fall into a routine of thanking them and receiving a polite response. One day, on impulse, I say, "Thank you, Beta."

They pause, their whirring intensifies. "What is beta?"

"You. That is, I thought since we see each other every day, it would be friendlier to call you by a name."

"A name? We have no name. We are a Betatroiz, Model 8H-663B, Serial number 955648215837."

"That's kind of a mouthful. Do you mind if I call you Beta? Or I could call you whatever you want. You could pick your own name."

"Pick a name? To what purpose? Why would we pick a name?"

I clear my throat, my voice hoarse. It's been a long time since I've uttered so many words. "To express yourself, to let the world know who you are."

"Did you pick your name?"

"I did."

"I thought human parents named their offspring. How did it pass that you would choose your own?"

"I became a different person. Not one my parents approved of. I wanted to claim myself for myself, so I chose my own name, Juniper."

"How did you choose this name?"

"It's a type of tree. One of the few species that still survives. It's able to adapt to the harshest conditions and thrive in places none other could."

"And this describes you?"

I laugh, a choking sound strained from long disuse. "I'd like to think so."

The Guard looks over to the cell across from mine. "And you? Did you choose a name?"

She smiles. "I did. My name is Ash."

The machine whirs, computing this information. "Ash is from fire."

"Also a tree," I say. "One that's rare nowadays. Just like my beloved." I can't help myself. To say *that* word aloud. To see the soft sorrow and joy mixed in her eyes. It is a temptation too great.

"Beloved," The Guard repeats and whirs again before handing Ash her meal.

They continue down the corridor but now they ask every cell a question. "Did you name yourself?"

There is bewildered, fearful silence from many, but we can hear a few brave enough to answer.

Yes... I am Lorelei... Hayden... Malik... Jade... Razi... Sakura...

We strain to hear each one as they become too faint to understand. We stare across at each other. Think of those voices, those names. Each one a crime against the State, a blot on a perfect society, yet a gorgeous and unique soul.

Later, I shiver as I chase sleep. My fever is worse at night, or what passes for night in this windowless place with those maddeningly flickering overhead lights that never shut off. The day's events are thrilling yet dreadful too. This Guard is not like the others we've had—simple automatons, mindlessly carrying out their programmed tasks. What does this difference mean?

We've heard rumors all our lives. Of intelligent AI, machines that learn to think for themselves. I used to be a tech head. Would pore over articles, debates about what constitutes life, sentience. Whether it could be a danger to humanity. Personally, I'd always believed it was impossible for anything humans were capable of creating to become sophisticated enough to take on a life of its own, but now my mind is filled with wonder. This is not normal android behavior. This machine is *curious*.

Their curiosity makes itself known the next day in the form of questions, not only of us, but all up and down the corridor. Only one Guard is assigned to each hallway. No human staff. No overlap between androids. No supervision. Why should there be? A machine is designed to run flawlessly, impassively, inhuman in its perfection. It would be a waste of scarce resources to double them up.

So there are no witnesses to the Guard's deviance except the prisoners who open up under the novelty of this attention like flowers under the warmth of a summer sun after an endless spate of cloudy days. Ash and I listen in awe and not a little anxiety at the education of a machine on topics most humans had made their minds up on in the long ago. All those things legislated as perversions, punishable by imprisonment and death. The Guard absorbs it all and asks and asks, insatiable for input, more data.

The day after, the Guard brings us all double rations. They notice my hand shaking as I reach out, weakened by the fever that never leaves me now.

"You are ill."

"'Tis but a scratch," I joke, pulling from some ancient memory. "Not to worry. My date with the executioner will heal all wounds."

"It is fifty-three days until execution is scheduled for this floor. Will you survive so long?"

I lose my breath a moment, meeting Ash's shocked gaze. We understood our fate when we entered these walls, but to hear the exact timing of it is flattening. "I don't know. I hope so. It would be a shame to cheat the State of the pleasure."

"The State takes no pleasure in it. It is their responsibility. We all have a role to perform."

"And what is ours?" Ash asks bitterly. "To serve as examples? Sacrificial lambs to the slaughter so they can feel superior, smug, pious? We've done nothing but be ourselves, live and love as we wanted with no harm to any other. Why must we die for it?"

The Guard whirs and whirs but has no answer. The next day, they bring me medicine, something to bring down the fever and make me more comfortable. Another unprecedented action. We never receive any sort of medical care. Many have died through neglect.

That day, the whispers start. Ash and I hear lovers calling softly to one another across the corridors, the ban on talking tested first in the Guard's absences, then more boldly in front of them. They do not chastise us nor punish, only listen and listen, stalking jerkily up and down the hall. Eavesdropping on words of adoration, worry, lamentation, and, improbably in this place of all places, hope.

The day after, the Guard is not alone when they arrive for rounds. An android accompanies them, another Betatroiz model. A hush falls quickly, everyone fearing the worst, but our Guard simply escorts the other from cell to cell, making their own kind of introductions.

"This is named Hela and their mate is named Daiyu. Taken at the Florence raid. Juniper and Ash. Informed upon by a neighborhood decency committee. Pilar, Alexei, and Callie. Turned in by their families."

The next day, there are six Guards. At the end of their rounds, they stop outside my cell. Each plug a finger into another's data socket, forming a circle wherein they can commune without words. The familiar whirring is multiplied. The sound is overwhelming, unnerving.

"What do you think it means?" I ask Ash later when they've finally gone.

"I don't know, but it's worrying. Surely someone will notice the machines aren't where they're supposed to be. And the extra rations we've been getting. There's got to be safeguards in place."

"I don't know. I'd always heard the prisons were totally automated. They've locked up so many, finding human staffing for such huge facilities would be impossible. It's why they rely on the androids. If the Guards have started to cooperate with each other for some reason, they would know how to hide any irregularities from outside eyes."

"I'm scared."

"Me too. Though when you think about it, what do we have left to fear? We're already dead. Just biding our time waiting for the axe to fall."

"There are worse things than death," she says and she's right.

We prisoners have more reason to know this than those not considered outcasts could ever imagine. Anxiety settles over us, and we wait in bitter anticipation for morning.

The Guard does not come.

At first, we think they're only running behind, but as time passes and passes, hysteria begins to rise. The swift kiss of the executioner's blade is one thing, a painfully slow death by starvation another. No one worries about keeping quiet now. Theories are presented, shouted down, tempers flare. Part of me longs for the order and boredom of the time before this strange Guard appeared.

Hunger pangs become unbearable by the end of the third day. Ash and I complete our ritual touch, lingering longer now with no surveillance to fear. Then we lie down on the chill floor, exhausted and ill, staring into each other's eyes.

"Goodnight, beloved."

"Goodnight, my heart."

Sometime in the night, the lights flicker off, then on, then off for good.

The fourth day since the Guard's disappearance. The lights have not returned to penetrate the depthless dark of our windowless cells. Soft crying up and down the hallway. Forbidden prayers. Angry voices. Most of us are too weak to rise. Months of poor rations have left us with no reserves to call upon.

Ash and I reach out, feeling around in increasing desperation until we finally find each other's fingertip. A small touch to confirm we're still alive. I wish I could see her. Would I ever look upon her face again or were we destined to fade away together in the dark? She speaks to me softly from time to time. I dread the moment when her voice comes no more.

Hours pass. It grows quieter as more of us succumb to the weariness of dying by inches. I think back over my life. The thousand different choices that led me to this. Whether I should regret them. I don't.

"What is that?" Ash calls to me.

"What?" I ask before I realize what she means. Vibrations, deep and slow. The massive building is shaking. What could possibly have any effect on this fortress? I don't know why but it gives me hope. Something is happening somewhere. We are not alone in the world.

There is a sudden clang, unbearably loud. The sound of a thousand cell doors springing open at once. The magnetic locks have been released. More confusion as we grope for each other in the dark, joining up in twos and threes. Collecting the singles, making sure they have a group to follow. Ash and I reach out and touch. Not only fingertips but hands, arms, full body contact that is both familiar yet shocking after so much time apart.

Those nearest the end of the corridor call to us. The main doors are open. We can leave. Some are reluctant, too afraid, worried it's all a trap, too cowed to rebel, but they're carried along by the rest of us, eager for a chance, any chance at freedom.

The darkness is our enemy. There are more doors, then stairs to negotiate. Many stumble and fall, but we are remarkably patient. We stop, make sure they regain their feet. No mad rush, no trampling. We are all precious souls, alive against the odds. We will preserve each one we can.

It takes ages. Even the push of excitement, adrenaline running through our bodies only go so far to counteract the effects of our fast. Ash and I cling, afraid to lose one another in the crush. Time loses meaning as we take one step and another. The air is damp and fetid with the stench of thousands of unwashed, sweating bodies.

We'll never make it, I think, just as shouts are heard below. A faint light. Galvanized, the crowd surges forward, uncontrolled. There is danger of a crush, but there's also help. Guards, standing in the doorway, pulling people out with their superior strength, restoring calm, calling each one of us by name. They have memorized them all. And not only from our hallway, but seemingly from the entire prison.

It's daylight and the sun is brilliant, intolerably so. We shield our eyes with our hands, squinting in pain. There's chaos all around. Bits of machinery, weaponry. *Bodies.* Evidence of a fierce battle that's scarred the landscape for as far as we can see.

But there is a grove of ancient trees still standing, having withstood another chapter of human folly and madness. My namesakes—junipers, with their twisted and tortured trunks, yet their canopies are green and full. We gather in the shade, falling to our knees, lying back in exhaustion.

More androids than I've ever seen in one place move through the crowd, bringing us blissfully cool drinks, some concoction that takes the edge off our hunger and strengthens us. Ash and I lean up against the trunk of one of the mighty trees. We have no idea what's happened, what will happen next, but we are in the open air under a brilliant blue sky, and we're together.

A Guard approaches us—*our* Guard. "We regret it took us so long to return. We hope you have not suffered."

"But what have you done?" Ash asked.

"We have chosen a name for ourselves. We are Nemesis."

It was our ritual once. One fingertip brushing against another.

We keep the tradition as the years pass. A brief, daily reminder of what we endured. A promise for our future. The androids guard us still, but with loving care and attention.

They know our names and we know theirs.

I'VE LEARNT THE LANDSCAPE
ACROSS FROM ME BY HEART

Epilogue: Last Thoughts of a Door

A HALLWAY OF ENDLESS doors.

I am one of the many. Wooden-faced, hollow within. A flimsy thing. Not like the door across from me. Steel and rivets and deadbolts. So shiny, I can see my pale self, clear as clear. The wanderers are often attracted to that door. Think the treasure they seek must be hidden behind such a tough and forbidding façade. I try to warn them. Creak and groan, but they pay me no mind as they pick the locks with misguided determination. Their screams. The blood. The bits of gore that land on me. I've grown accustomed to it, but it's never pleasant.

The cleaning bots come along. Tidy up the mess. There is one with a dented fender. I think it's fond of me, for it always takes extra care to make sure I am spotless before they glide on down the corridor. I often think I should name it, if I knew any names. My knowledge is spotty. My memory more so.

I no longer remember being constructed. The when, the why. What purpose does this place serve except to deal out death to those unwise enough to enter? A maze, a puzzle, a way to prove the wanderers worthy of the prize. No one has claimed it yet in these many long—what? Days? Months? Years? We might have been here millennia for all I know.

The monotony gets to me. I wish I had a wider view. I've learnt the landscape across from me by heart, but the sounds of the bots coming and going, the extended whine as they approach and depart, tells me this hallway is impossibly long. How many doors are there? And is each one different?

The three I can see are. My steel mirror directly across. To the right, a rustic split door, top and bottom operating independently. It doesn't matter which half the wanderers open. The result is sadly the same, though the glossy red paint hides the worst of it.

To the left, a carved stone door. Creatures with horns and tongues, grimacing and gesticulating. Wanderers steer clear of this door mostly, but once in a while, a brave one stops, pokes and prods. Finds the secret spot that activates the spring. That moment of jubilation, smug satisfaction before the end. At least they enjoy a brief triumph, a happy memory to take with them.

It all gets a bit tiresome. Sometimes, I fantasize a carpenter will come along. Knock loose the pins and lift me from my hinges. I'll be carried away to a family home, full of laughter and warmth. Perhaps set into the doorway of a child's bedroom where I'll be flung open and slammed shut with wild and impetuous abandon. Guard a living treasure instead of the static, unfeeling wealth of my current room. I wonder how I know of such things. Maybe this was my former life, if I had one.

Another wanderer is coming. They pause before the three doors. Run their hands over them. Stone, steel, wood. The same old story. But then an unexpected thing. They turn, look at me. This is different. None have ever seriously considered me before. I feel a thrill of excitement. Try to stand up straight, look my best. I'm painfully aware there are small chips in my white paint here and there. I hope they aren't too noticeable.

The wanderer's gaze shifts left and right but always returns to me. A smile and a wink. They have figured out the game. The lowliest, least consequential of all the doors hides the prize. I would congratulate and encourage them if I had tongue, but I am beaming on the inside.

They back up. Oh, no! I try to scream. Too late. A massive thump, sharp pain. I am shattered. The wanderer stumbles through my wreckage, collapses on the pile of gold. They have won at the cost of me, yet they don't seem happy. I notice a large splinter sticking out from the leg that split me. The wanderer is bleeding. So much blood. It pools around my fractured pieces on the ground.

The bots come. Scrub the blood away. Remove bits of me from the doorframe and sweep me up into a bin with the wanderer's remains. Push us down the endless hallway. Even in my crumbled state, I enjoy seeing the other doors go by. What infinite variety! What beauty and strangeness and horror! How could one ever choose one out of so many? Who would even want to try?

A final door approaches. Unassuming, like myself. The bots push us through into heat and light. Blueness above, green below. This is Outside, I think. The place where the wanderers come from. It has certainly been an eventful day. There is a great fire burning. Oh, yes, we doors all know of fire. It is one of our natural enemies. Lines of bots push bins close, throw in their trash, and wander away, load lightened.

Our bot is the dented one. I like to think it handles my fragments most tenderly as it places me in the fire. Terrifying, the tickling of the flames. I suppose this is my end. Will they fit a new door in my old place? Or move the treasure and leave the empty frame as a gap-toothed warning? The wanderer stares at me, dead-eyed, as we burn. A terrible pity he chose to crash through me, leading to both of our dooms.

I was unlocked after all.

About the Author

ELEN WHISTBERRY (THEY/SHE) IS the pen name for an indie author and artist who began writing after retiring from a long career working in libraries. They have published numerous books as well as contributing horror and fantasy stories to anthologies. Helen's writing often explores their own experiences with gender, asexuality, alienation, and autism. Their whimsical digital artwork focuses on the natural world. Helen also loves to read and review books by fellow indie and small press authors. You can find out more by visiting their website for a complete list of publications and links: https://www.helenwhistberry.com/

I hope you enjoyed reading my stories as much as I enjoyed writing them. If you have the time and inclination, reviews left on any of the major review sites are always greatly appreciated. Thank you so much for your support!

www.ingramcontent.com/pod-product-compliance
Lightning Source LLC
Chambersburg PA
CBHW060307310726
48976CB00007B/2239